TROUBLE AT FISHERS WHARF

TRACY BAINES

Boldwood

First published in Great Britain in 2023 by Boldwood Books Ltd.

Cover Design by Colin Thomas

Cover Photography: Colin Thomas and Alamy

A CIP catalogue record for this book is available from the British Library.

Paperback ISBN 978-1-80426-539-0

Large Print ISBN 978-1-80426-538-3

Hardback ISBN 978-1-80426-540-6

Ebook ISBN 978-1-80426-536-9

Kindle ISBN 978-1-80426-537-6

Audio CD ISBN 978-1-80426-545-1

MP3 CD ISBN 978-1-80426-544-4

Digital audio download ISBN 978-1-80426-543-7

Boldwood Books Ltd
23 Bowerdean Street
London SW6 3TN
www.boldwoodbooks.com

To the memory of
Raymond Evans – 'Evans the tenth' – 1945–2022
Skipper and gentleman

GREAT GRIMSBY, AUGUST 1914

1

Ruth Evans had never stood on Fishers Wharf with these women before, waiting for the tide to turn and the lock gates to open. Wives and mothers of the close-knit fishing community huddled close in the cool of the August morning, and as the crowd swelled, she moved a little nearer to them, only for her father to guide her back with a gentle hand. Ruth could get close, but not too close, and Richard Evans's touch was a reminder that though she might think she was one of them, she was not. A few weeks ago, she might have agreed with him, but not today. Today he was wrong; war had made them equal, and as they waited for the trawlers to enter, her thoughts were only of her brother Henry's safe return.

The kaiser had ignored Belgium's neutrality in its quest to conquer France, just as the women in front of her had ignored the notices printed in the local newspapers. On 4 August, Great Britain had declared war against Germany and the Royal Dock and Fish Docks had been closed to the public, allowing entry only to those on business between the hours of nine and five. But this was *their* men, and this was *their* business – and woe betide any jumped-up official who had tried to turn them back. These women were an army. Ruth had always admired their grit, their fortitude, and the manner in which they stood together. Waiting. Always waiting. She wondered how they could bear it.

Grimsby was home to the largest fishing fleet in the world and the people of the town prided themselves on its success, working hard to keep it so. Families had travelled from Suffolk, Norfolk and elsewhere to make their fortunes. It was a town of innovation and of industry – and fishing was at the forefront, one job on ship giving work to five more on shore.

Many of the Grimsby trawlers had been in the far reaches of the White Sea, off the Russian coast, and had hauled their nets and headed for home when word of war had finally reached them. Not all had been so fortunate. News had already come that trawlers were missing, the whereabouts of ship and crew unknown. The German ship *Königin Luise* had been seen laying mines in the North Sea and HMS *Amphion* had given chase, successfully sinking the ship and rescuing any survivors. But it too had fallen foul of a mine and sank within fifteen minutes, with the loss of over 130 men. It could only be assumed that the trawlers had met the same fate. Ruth tried not to think of the reports she had read in the *Herald* and the *Telegraph*. The town had been prepared to receive casualties from a great naval battle these past weeks, but nothing had happened. So far. It was rumour. There were too many rumours.

'The *Northern Queen* is third in line.' Her father pointed to the ships.

She saw the white marking on the funnel, knew the rake of the bow. It would only be minutes now.

As river and dock reached its equilibrium to allow them entry, the lock gates parted, and as the ships began to ease forward, the women craned their necks in search of a beloved face among the men who stood against the ship's rail, though it was difficult to make out who was who with any certainty from such a distance.

Seagulls soared above, screeching and crying out, their voices mingling with those of the men who shouted instructions as they threw ropes and secured them. Row upon row of ships, steam and sail, were as tightly packed in the dock as the women were on the wharf, and shawls and jackets were adjusted as the sun rose higher, warming the air and dispersing the early-morning mist.

The trawlers were still a fair distance from the wharf, there being no room for more. Latecomers would have to wait it out in the river or try Hull or Immingham further down the Humber. The fishing fleet had been recalled by the government, ships confined to dock, while trawler owners and insurance companies thrashed out the finer details of who would be responsible for the insurance premiums if the admiralty requisitioned a trawler. One hundred and fifty-six trawlers from ports around the British Isles had been converted to minesweepers and as ships were lost, more would be taken. Would there be anyone left to fish – men or ships? Today, her father had set his concerns to one side as they waited for Henry – for he and his older brother Charles were the future of the Excel Trawler Company.

Each ship was lashed alongside its neighbour, and presently there began a parade of men, jumping like fleas, quick and nimble, kitbags slung over their backs, vessels moving up and down in the water as they leaped from one to another to reach the wharfside.

The women pressed a little closer. It wasn't as if they weren't used to waiting –wives and daughters, mothers and sisters, had spent a lifetime of it, praying for a safe return more than they prayed for a good catch. Of this ritual, Ruth was a stranger.

'Can you see him?' her father said, without moving his position, the tremor in his voice barely disguising his concern.

'Not yet, Father.' The boats were too distant, the men indistinct, recognised only by difference in weight and height as they came forward, and as foot met with land, those gathered on the dockside moved like water, an ebb and flow, creating spaces for bags to be dropped and arms flung wide, for children to be lifted from their feet and swung in the air, for wives to be held, the softness of their skin a cushion from the harshness of life aboard a trawler. Somewhere among them was Henry.

Ruth recognised the skipper of the Hammond trawler *Black Prince*, Alec Hardy, in his cream sweater, his cap low against his brow, and she searched the crowd for his wife Letty, caught sight of her red headscarf. At twenty-two, Letty was a mere six months older than Ruth, and even though they were set apart in class, they were of the same mind in so many things.

As if sensing her gaze, Letty turned and caught Ruth's eye. The woman nodded her head in greeting and Richard Evans tipped his hat to her. It was the briefest of exchanges but signified the standing in which Letty was held in the community. The Hardys had arrived in Grimsby as newlyweds two years since, but Letty had not settled for a life as a fisherman's wife, staying at home to braid as so many did. She'd found work at Parkers Chandlery in Henderson Street and had transformed the ailing business in a matter of months. It had been the talk of Fish Dock Road and, ever on the lookout for recruiting women with spirit, Ruth's aunt, Helen Frampton, had commandeered her to help with the Ladies Guild and the Fishermen's Mission.

Letty's life was not easy, but it was a full one, and despite its hardship, Ruth envied her. She had more freedom than Ruth would ever know. The Hardys were well-suited, like her older brother Charles and his fiancée Daphne Willoughby, and watching them only made her realise she did not feel that way about Arthur Marshall.

Ruth turned again to the boats, to the last of the men coming forward, and recognised Henry by the familiar tilt of his head, the shock of fair hair, the heavy fringe that went its own way, much as her brother himself.

'The second row deep, a Branston ship, the *Saturn*,' she said to her father. 'He's stepping onto the stern of the *Sovereign* now. Do you see him?'

He tipped his head slightly and she knew exactly the moment he caught sight of him. Her father, always so tall and impressive, seemed to swell and take up greater space on the dockside as his boy came close to the rail of the *Sovereign*. 'I do.'

Henry looked across to the offices of Excel Trawlers on the wharfside, then drew his focus forward. Seeing her, he grinned, nodded to his father and turned to come down the ladder that had been propped on the bow, the boat high in the water, quickly followed by the skipper. Henry, all of nineteen, had not been out on the *Northern Queen* to haul nets and gut fish but as an observer, to understand the workings of the ship and the crew. Knowledge that would help greatly when he took his position on the Excel board.

'Ruthie.' Henry was in front of her, the skipper at his side.

Richard gripped his son's hand and shook it in welcome, then the skipper's.

Henry kissed her cheek, pressed a hand to her shoulder. She longed to throw her arms about him as the other women had done to their beloveds, but her father would not appreciate her outward show of joy. Henry's face was red and peeling from too much sun and salt, but there was a way to go before his skin was as leathery as the skipper's beside him. She had never seen Henry unshaven before and the small fine stubble about his chin made him look older.

'Thank the good Lord you're home.'

'Thank the skipper for that. He was the one steered us right.'

He slapped the older man on the shoulder. 'We put our faith in God, but the skipper's at the wheel.'

Richard nodded in agreement and was about to speak when, among the crowd, a woman let out a shrill and anguished cry, taking their attention. Ruth felt the very pain of it and shuddered as if suddenly cold.

'A Hammond man was lost overboard,' the skipper explained. 'Lenny Owen. Deckie.'

The men turned away and continued their conversation, the loss of a man's life no more than an interruption. Ruth could hear them talking, the sound muffled, as she watched the goings-on further along the dockside. The crowd had thinned to give the woman space, a crate had been found for her to sit on. She was holding a baby, a toddler at her skirts, and a girl of about six or seven was taking hold of the toddler's hand. Letty was in the thick of them, giving instruction; Ruth could not hear the words but knew that that was what was happening.

The widow began to wail again, the baby too, and Letty took it in her arms, passed it to Alec, who jiggled it up and down and crooned to it. Boiled sweets were produced from a pocket for the children, a handkerchief for their mother. Letty spoke to a boy, who immediately left and hurried down towards the dock road, probably to fetch the port missioner, Mr Wilson. Ordinarily, Ruth would have loitered, hoping for a chance to be in his company, but not in these circumstances.

It was said that many of the fisherfolk respected only two people – the King, and the port missioner. In charge of the Grimsby Mission to Deep Sea Fishermen, he was the person the men and women turned to in times of trouble. He was strong and he was kind – and many a time, she had tried to summon the courage to distance herself from Arthur, and failed, knowing her family would never agree to it. A port missioner had status, but he did not have the power the trawler owners possessed – and, more importantly, did not have wealth.

Instinct made Ruth move towards the crowd, but once again she felt her father's restraining hand. 'Mrs Hardy is more than capable. Leave the women to care for her in the manner they know best. It is our duty to assist in other ways.'

Ruth turned back to her brother, and his eyes her held hers, understanding her fear as she knew he would. Their lives had always been connected to the sea, to the fishing, but at a distance. Their father owned a trawler company, along with many of the attending businesses – a fish merchants, a repair yard, a chandlery. She knew men were lost, that ships were lost, that was fact – but waiting here this morning, witnessing the reality of it, had left her cold. A man had gone to sea and he hadn't returned.

'What catch did you make before you turned for home?' It was her father speaking and if she didn't know him better, she would think that money was more important than the life of the man. She knew it did not. The lives of those gathered on the docks that morning were entwined, along with their livelihoods.

She tried to pay attention, but her mind was on what was going on around them. Skipper Blaney's face was mottled, beaten by the intensity of the elements, the salt of the sea, but his eyes were sharp and bright, his weariness, if he suffered from it, not evident in the way he held himself. Yet Ruth well knew the journey home would have been fraught with danger. The summer trips were more calm, the trips north less hazardous weatherwise – but rather the weather as an enemy than unexploded mines and U-boats. They did not speak of it here, talked only of fish, of the catch. It was what they always did.

'A fair one, but when we got word, we hauled and turned for home. We were doing well, though we avoided going too far north.'

'Easier than avoiding the Hun,' Henry said.

'You caught sight?' Ruth was aghast.

'Aye, in the distance,' the skipper replied. 'They were after the *Lysander*.' He turned his attention to her father. 'We tried to draw them away, but with no weapons and only tactics at our disposal, we could but watch. Through the binoculars, I saw the crew get into the small craft and board the German ship. They fired at the *Lysander* with heavy guns. She went down in minutes.'

The *Lysander* was not an Evans trawler. Ruth knew each one by name, each skipper, the tonnage and the catch, when it was in for repair and refit. It was all they talked of at home and war had brought a different conversation – but not a better one. Would it have been the same had her mother lived? She was sure it would not. The *Lysander* was out of Hull. Knowing of its demise, no one would wait for its return.

Her father replaced his hat and glanced to the crowds that had begun to disperse, men moving closer, any scrap of news gathered to be bloated and distorted from one man to another – but her father would want hard facts. 'Shall we, gentlemen?' Richard stretched out his hand to his son and the skipper and indicated for them to join him in the short walk to the offices. Ruth took one last look over to where Letty and the other women were gathered and followed him inside.

2

For a time, Ruth was blinded and waited in the doorway for her eyes to adjust to the light, or what little there was of it inside the Excel offices. The walls were simply panelled with timber, the oak countertop of the reception desk running along the length of the entrance room. Behind it were eight desks; two of which were occupied.

Old Mr Tate came over to greet them and Mr Swift got up awkwardly, nodded to the men, and to Ruth, then sat down again and attended to his work. Neither of them would be called to fight, Tate too old and Swift because of his disability.

'Young Master Henry. Good to see you safely ashore.'

'It's good to be back, Mr Tate, although rather not in the present circumstances.'

'Quite right, quite right,' Tate agreed, his head nodding like a small dog. The old man had been with her father for over thirty years, moving with him from the small office he had started out with on Maclure Street to the premises that held prime position on Wharncliffe Road at the north end of the dock peninsula. He'd known each of the Evans siblings from birth and was as much a part of the fabric of Excel as her father. It would seem strange to not find him there, so familiar, with his white tufts of hair either side of his wrinkled bald head and his round wire spectacles perched on his small nose.

Mr Swift kept his head down, the scratch of his pen and the ticking of the large brown clocks above him marking the time zones of Moscow, Oslo and London the background to their conversation.

Henry looked about him. 'Where are the other men?'

'Gone,' her father answered before Tate could reply. 'Most to the army, Wilkes and Stafford for Royal Naval Reserve duties. They had been off training each year for the last two.' Preparations for war had been ongoing. War was expected, but no one wanted it. Six years ago, after discussions with many trawler owners, the admiralty had taken two Grimsby trawlers for minesweeping trials and met with success. Thereafter, trawlers had been requisitioned and men trained in the work, slowly at first, but then more suddenly in the days preceding the declaration of war. Her father had discussed it endlessly with his sons. Ruth had merely listened, in the background, much as Mr Swift was now, there but not there. 'We've got through worse haven't we, Tate?'

'We have indeed, Mr Evans. And we shall survive this.'

Her father did not reply.

Over the last few years, there had been numerous disputes, a fair few strikes and general unrest, the fishermen forming a union. Nothing as bad as the lockout when she had been a small child, but enough to have her father working long hours to keep the company stable. It had been discussed over breakfast, dinner, tea, and all the hours in between, her father informing his sons of the challenges of running a trawler company; that she had been present changed nothing. Her opinion was never required. The sons were the future, not her. Ruth's only duty was to marry well.

She had not been aware of it when she was younger, still grieving the loss of her mother. Kathleen Evans had died of cancer when Ruth was only eleven. Their father had not remarried and, in the absence of a wife, his sister, Helen Frampton, had taken over the guidance of his children, choosing their schools, and latterly steering Ruth towards Arthur Marshall, son and heir to the Marshall Trawler Company. Their marriage would consolidate her father's position and unite two of the three largest trawlers firms, the third being that of Framptons, owned by her aunt and uncle. One of their many investments, and Ruth had slowly become aware that she was yet another. Arthur had called to see her father only yesterday and she knew it was to ask for her hand – only she didn't want to give it. Yet she had no idea how to extricate herself from such a well-meshed net.

Her father indicated for Henry and Skipper Blaney to join him in his office upstairs.

Mr Tate came to her. 'Can I get you anything, Miss Evans. While you wait?' He was kindly, his eyes small berries behind his round spectacles. She noticed that his stoop was more severe, years spent over a desk taking its toll.

'That's very kind of you, Mr Tate. I think I will remain with them awhile. I have not seen my brother in over two weeks. I shouldn't think they will be long.'

She joined the men in her father's oak-panelled office, the room thick with the rich smell of musk and leather. Gilded framed oil paintings of some of his cherished trawlers decorated the walls about him, and leather-bound ledgers containing the details of his acquisitions were kept locked in the glass bookcase to his right.

Henry looked up as she entered but her father remained seated, deep in conversation with the skipper. Her appearance did not warrant a pause – not that she had thought it would – and she took a seat by the window, still mesmerised by the state of the docks. She had never witnessed things so full, nor so still. Entry and exit of vessels loaded with fish or with cargo and heading for the Royal and Alexandra Docks were ruled by the tide, but the work ashore was constant. The ships that arrived today would have their catch landed in the early hours, but until then they would be kept iced over in the hold until the markets started at six. She had come here once, and once only, at that hour to see row upon row of cod, haddock and plaice laid one upon another, eyes bulging and mouths open. Each ship had a number marked on the basket and the merchants walked along, the auctioneer taking bids. It was fast work, boxes swiftly loaded onto wagon and train, taking it to London and elsewhere.

Outside, a cart stopped below the window and what was left of the crowd moved towards it. The young woman, now widowed, and her children were helped up onto it and Letty climbed beside her, leant forward and said something to Alec. The little child was soothing the toddler, and an older woman, her face wrought in sympathy, handed the baby up to Letty. Other women grabbed her hand in turn and shook it, hoping to pass on some of their strength. It was clear to Ruth that they were giving words of encouragement, for it could have been any one of them in that cart, but for the grace of God. The widow did not respond, her face immobile with grief. Letty took hold of the woman's right hand as the cart began to move along Wharncliffe Road and some of the women followed along behind. It was a town used to loss; the fishermen took a chance every time they headed out to the North Sea, but now there would be more men at risk.

Ruth twisted, suddenly afraid, and looked to Henry. Her brother raised his eyebrows at her. Father needed a nudge. The men usually came to him the day after they landed, settling day, when the fish had been sold at market and the monies paid over – or not. Many a time, a ship came in dock and owed money. If a net had to be cut away and the ship lost its gear, if the catch was small, or they were late to market and prices were low, they might have spent three miserable weeks at sea for nothing. Skipper Blaney would be wanting to be home. She smiled at him. 'You'll be away to your family, Mr Blaney?'

'Aye. The lass will have been worried. She'll be relieved,' he paused, 'but then others are not so lucky.'

'No, it will be difficult for many...'

'And more yet,' her father interrupted. He was about to say something, then thought the better of it. 'You'd best get off, Blaney. I'll see you tomorrow as usual. I should think the catch will fetch a good price. There is little competition, and it looks like yours might be the last for some time. For Excel certainly. Do you have an idea of what Hammond's catches were?'

'Not full, Mr Evans. They arrived at the fishing grounds after I did.'

Her father clasped his hands together and stared into the gap between the two men's shoulders. 'It's all a bad business.' He got to his feet, Blaney followed suit and the men shook hands over the desk. The skipper doffed his cap at Ruth, and Richard Evans showed him to the door and closed it behind him, then went back to his seat. He did not speak and the three of them sat there in the quiet room, listening to movement downstairs, the heavy drag of a foot as Swift moved about the room below. Henry looked to her, shrugged his shoulders.

'Shall we go?' Ruth ventured. 'Henry will want to bathe – and shave.'

It was some time before their father answered, and she didn't want to press him. These past few weeks had been difficult, losing men as well as losing ships.

'Yes, yes, of course.' He smiled wearily at them and forced himself from his chair. 'Let's go home.'

Their father's Wolseley was waiting for them and the driver, Hawkins, stood away from the car as he saw them and opened the door. Ruth slid inside, followed by her father, Henry taking the passenger seat. He twisted to talk to them as they drove down the dock road and halted before the railway junction at the Dock's Crossing, then again on Cleethorpe Road. Despite the early hour, men gathered outside, smoking, leaning on walls, their faces tilted to the warmth of the morning sun as it began to rise above the rooftops.

'Looks like the mission is busy,' Henry observed.

'They are overwhelmed,' Ruth replied. 'Many of the men are not from this port and have arrived with only what they stood up in.'

'It is only temporary,' their father insisted. 'Things will move again. Once the government get their damn finger out. It's about time they agreed something with the insurance companies.'

'How long has it been like this?'

'Since the fourth, when war was declared. Whatever was in the docks stayed there and more have come to join them. Not all Grimsby ships, I might add.'

'Any port in a storm.'

'Something like that.' Her father settled back in his seat.

'Skipper Blaney did well to get us all back in one piece,' Henry said, turning to face forward.

Her father looked out of the window and Ruth closed her eyes, hearing again the woman's cry and the bewilderment on the faces of her children etched on her brain. No matter that her father thought they were set apart from the ordinary fisher folk, he was wrong. Privilege and wealth would not protect them from the ravages of war, and each would be called to play their part for king and country. They were, indeed, all equal now.

3

The heavy blue curtains were wide, the sash pushed up and a warm breeze circulated the air about the breakfast room of Meadowvale House. Ruth's father was already at the table reading the *Grimsby Herald*, the housekeeper, Mrs Murray, hovering back and forth with tea and toast.

The past weeks had been a dreadful time, worry for his sons of more concern than that of his business. Charles was in the territorial army and had been at annual camp in Bridlington with the 5th Lincolnshire's. On 4 August, the battalion had been recalled to Grimsby and mobilised the following day. Men had been billeted at the Doughty Road Drill Hall, the docks, two schools and at Waltham, a small village on the outskirts of the town, where they awaited their orders. Many of his trawlers had been requisitioned and his crews diminished. Those men that were not idle, like his ships, had already enlisted, so that if, and when, the fishing fleet was allowed back to work, there would not be sufficient men to sail them. His concern for his youngest son's safe return added to an already heavy burden, but Henry was home now, and Ruth noticed her father appeared a little brighter than he had been of late.

Ruth took a seat to his left and Henry joined them a few moments later. They had barely settled themselves when they heard the front door open and Mrs Murray hurry from the kitchen, her shoes clicking briskly on the tiled floor. A moment later, Charles came to join them, so dashing in his uniform, his cap under his arm. Ruth thought it made him look older than his twenty-three years – but old enough to be in charge of a battalion? They were all so young. Henry got up and the brothers shook hands. He went over to Ruth and kissed her cheek.

'Will you be wanting breakfast, Mr Charles?' Mrs Murray asked.

'No, thank you. I have already eaten at the officers' mess. Tea will suffice. I can only stay a half-hour. I'm on my way to the recruitment office and took a brief detour to see how things were, with the company – and of course to see my charming little brother.' He slapped Henry on the shoulder, then took a seat beside Ruth.

Their father folded his newspaper and placed it in front of him.

Henry glanced at the headline. 'How long do you think this will go on for?' He blew gently over his cup to cool the tea, then sipped. 'I don't mean the war; I mean keeping the ships in port.'

'I have no idea. It's gone on long enough as it stands. Ships in docks are costing us dearly. The knock-on effect is beginning to bare its teeth on the town. Many of the factories are on short time.' He tapped the paper. 'If men can't work, they can't earn. Those applying for poor relief are gaining in number. It's a poor show.'

'How many ships have they taken for minesweeping?' Henry asked.

'Eight of ours – so far.' It was already accepted they would take more as needed. 'It's the same in Hull, Lowestoft, Boston, Fleetwood, Aberdeen… They've taken the biggest and the best.'

'And left us with the older, less able boats for fishing.' Henry looked to his father. 'Can we survive it?'

Richard Evans shrugged, pushing his lips forward before speaking. 'We're not as heavily into the bank as some. Our borrowings on the ships are low... we've been prudent.' He reached across and indicated for Ruth to pour more tea, which she did. 'A fixed rate has been agreed with the admiralty for some time, an amount per tonnage, another for power. It's a fair price but does not take into account the profit that successful companies such as ours would have made. The small companies might struggle. And then there's the mines of course, and the wanton destruction of our trawlers. They will need to be replaced and that takes time. The shipyards and boatwrights are already working full pelt converting the trawlers to minesweepers. We will be at the back of the queue. As for fishing? Who knows what will happen?'

'But where can men fish?' Ruth asked. 'If the mines are scattered along the coast?'

'These men face danger each time they leave the shore, Ruthie,' Henry replied. 'The mines won't hold them back, it's not in their nature.'

She knew his words were said to calm her, but they did not. 'Please God that it will all be over soon.'

'By Christmas, Ruthie. They say it will all be over by then.' She caught the look exchanged between the brothers. 'Once the Germans invaded Belgium, we had to act, whether we wanted to or not.' Henry put his hand to hers, smiled. It didn't make her feel any better.

'There's always some who want a fight,' Charles said. 'Like the chaps at school. The only way they got it into their thick heads was to bloody their nose.'

'But if someone won't move on their stance, won't negotiate, how can it be resolved?' It had puzzled her from the beginning. 'If both think they are right?'

'And that is why we are at war,' her father explained. 'All sides think they are right.'

'Well, aren't they?' Kaiser Wilhelm was the King's cousin – surely they could have come to some sort of agreement?

The three men turned to her.

'Of course not,' her father barked. 'We're right. We're going to the aid of the Belgians. The Germans think they can march right in and take what they want on their way to conquer France.' He thumped the table. 'We'll be next if we stand by and do nothing.'

She jumped at the harshness of his reply. He rarely raised his voice, not in the home.

Mrs Murray came rushing in. 'Is everything all right, Mr Evans?'

'What?' he softened immediately, confused at his own outburst.

'Shall I bring a fresh pot of coffee?' She looked to Ruth, who nodded in reply.

'It's timely that you're home,' their father said to Henry when the housekeeper left the room. 'Your Aunt Helen has a gathering at Saxon Hall this afternoon. There will be the usual crowd to welcome the admiralty. Charles is coming along with one or two of his fellow officers to rally support for the regiment.'

Henry pulled a face at Ruth. 'Such a shame I came back yesterday.'

Ruth bit back a smile. It would be dull as ditch water but unavoidable. Aunt Helen threw frequent gatherings, garden parties and fundraisers for numerous worthy causes, and the Evans siblings had attended more than their fair share once they were of age. Ruth could hardly bear to think of the years that stretched ahead of her, making polite conversation with the great and good of the town.

'Now, now. I'll not have you take that flippant attitude, Henry. Your aunt might be demanding of you all but nothing as to what she demands of herself. She could quite easily spend her life doing nothing more than needlework and drink tea. That she chooses to use her immense influence to the good of the town is to be admired.'

Henry rolled his eyes at Ruth. They had heard it all a hundred times before.

Charles glared at his brother. 'Duty first, last and always.'

'Quite,' his father agreed. He took his fob watch from his pocket. 'I have to meet with Blaney at the office to go over the trip and see what the catch yielded at this morning's auction, then we three will travel together. Charles is being accompanied by other fellows from his regiment. We shall meet him there.'

Henry cleared his throat. 'I rather thought—'

His father stopped him. 'Don't think, Henry. You *will* be there. There are connections to be made. Admiral Frost, the man who has overall command in Grimsby and Immingham, will be attending, along with other officers from the admiralty. It will be in your favour to present yourself.'

Henry finished buttering his toast and carefully rested his knife, wiped his hands on his napkin and looked to Charles. Ruth tensed, knowing his avoidance meant it was something her father would disapprove of. 'I'm joining the trawler section of the Royal Naval Reserve.'

His father narrowed his eyes. 'Now look here, Henry. The Royal Naval Reserve is all well and good, but that's for the fishermen and retired navy personnel. You'd get a commission with the army, like your brother. I know you're young, but—'

'I don't care for a commission, Father. I want to be with the men. Evans men. Grimsby men.'

Richard Evans sat back in his chair and gave a small laugh. 'Do you think a few weeks each summer makes you a fisherman? You won't last five minutes. You've been playing at it, boy.'

The remark cut Henry as her father knew it would. But Henry was no longer a child. He had changed these past months and when he showed his hands, calloused and blistered, she realised why.

'Do these hands look they have been playing, Father?'

Ruth saw her father's jaw tighten and he threw down his napkin in disgust.

'You blithering fool! You were there as an observer, not to haul ropes and gut fish—'

'You wanted me to know all parts of the work—'

His father got to his feet, placed his hands on the table. 'What the blazes were you... When I see Blaney, I'll—'

'It wasn't his doing. I insisted – and he hardly dare disagree.' Henry remained seated, kept his voice steady, and for that Ruth was grateful. Many times, Henry had pushed their father to his limits, but lately he had been quick to anger. If only Henry would give a little under the present circumstances, wait for a better time to discuss his plans.

'You put the man in a damn awkward position.'

'For my own ends. I did.' Henry was contrite about that, but he wasn't to be quietened. 'I don't want to be given respect because of who I am, I want to earn it. The men see me do the work and know that I understand. That they're not empty words.'

'And mine are?' her father looked ready to explode.

Ruth reached across, pressed Henry's arm, warning him to stop. Her father didn't need this, not with all the difficulties he faced at the moment, but then Henry had always been the one to challenge, unlike Charles, who had readily accepted his position as heir to the family business. He and Henry were as different as the sea and the land: Charles the constant, Henry the unruly. It was ever thus.

'I didn't mean to imply that at all.' Henry remained calm, in spite of their father's anger. 'I don't want to take the easy route. You of all men should understand that.'

Their father looked down at the table, and for a moment or two all were quiet, until Charles said, 'You must be insane.'

Their father sat down.

'Why so?' Henry squared his shoulders. They were broader now and Ruth suddenly understood that it wasn't due to his age, his growing into manhood, but the hard physical work that had made him so. No wonder her father had been lost for words.

Charles shrugged. 'It's not expected; none of it is. We're on board to observe, as Father says, that's our part in it.' He pressed his fingers to the edge of the table. 'I spent most of my one and only trip with my head in a bucket. I didn't observe a blessed thing from the moment we went out into the open seas.' He paled at the memory. It broke the tension a little, but their father was still silent.

Ruth looked to Henry, willing him to stop talking, but he had no intention of being quiet.

'I loved the adventure of it,' Henry explained.

'*Adventure!* Good Lord, you sound like your Uncle Joe, and look where it got him!'

Their father's brother was rarely spoken of, the errant youngest son, the black sheep. Over the years, Ruth had been able piece together little snippets here and there. It was said he'd got a girl in the family way, and when her body had been found in the Royal Dock, he had left for Liverpool. A postcard had arrived from America and nothing more.

'Well, it was... *is* an adventure. Standing at the bow with the third hand as we sailed out, the wildness of the seas, the sight and beauty of huge waves as the *Queen* cut through them.' Ruth watched as he became more animated. 'The sea is magnificent. The hunt for the fish, hauling the nets, the fish caught, heads and tails thrusting to escape, the cascade when they fall onto the deck.'

'But you'll not be catching fish in the RNR, little brother, you'll be dodging mines.'

'You'll be dodging bullets,' Henry countered.

'Don't joke about such things, you two.' Ruth came between them as she always did, not wanting things to escalate.

Henry touched her hand to calm her, and she could feel what she had only seen, surprised by the roughness of it. 'My fault,' he readily admitted. He had always been quick to make a joke of the most difficult things. That was his way. Charles was more like their father, more measured in thought and response. She wondered what her father was thinking now. 'I've got to get in yet. But I will. I've talked to the other men. The training is short, nothing like what you'll have to undergo, Charles. Two weeks, perhaps less.'

So soon? She remembered again the woman on the wharf, that haunting sound, and her heart began beating hard in her chest.

'But you can't. You must wait,' Ruth urged him. 'Talk it over with Father.' She could see that he would not change his mind, but if he could at least be quiet, not spoil the morning.

He nodded, smiled at her, then looked to his father. 'Of course. Ruth is right. She always is.' He let go of her hand and fiddled with his napkin.

Their father got to his feet. 'I need to be at the office. We will *all* be at Saxon Hall. Two o'clock sharp.' He spoke directly to Henry: 'You might well be set on joining the Reserve, my boy, but you might think differently when you talk to those in command of the sea. Your aunt has worked hard to bring this all together so quickly.'

'Aunt Helen is a magician,' Henry said, cheerfully, but his father was not amused by his comment.

'Your aunt knows what's important.'

Had his father meant it as a slight to his son? It was obvious Henry acknowledged it as such.

'You underestimate me, Father. I know full well what is important.' Henry got up. 'I have to be out myself. I have to meet with someone on the docks.'

'Then you can come with me in the car.'

'I'd rather walk. If that's all right with you?'

Ruth could hear the challenge in his voice again. He was only nineteen, not yet a man. Surely, he would need their father's permission to enlist.

Her father sighed heavily as Henry left the room and Ruth got up. 'I'll go with him.' She leaned forward and kissed her father's cheek, touched her hand to his shoulder. 'I'm sure Henry will come around, see that he's being unreasonable.' She spoke as much to reassure herself. 'I'll talk to him.'

He patted her hand in thanks. 'You seem to be the only one who can.'

4

Letty wrapped the warm bread in a cloth and put it on top of the jars of honey and jam. Beneath them were carrots and apples, a paper bag filled with plums. Her movements about the kitchen were punctuated by the clicking tongue of her mother-in-law, Dorcas, who, although she pretended otherwise, watched each item go into the willow basket. Letty lifted it from the pine table to test its weight. It would be as much as she could carry.

'We'll have nowt left if you keep giving it away to all and sundry,' Dorcas carped as she bustled her way to the sink, flicking her head towards the table as if Letty didn't understand the source of her irritation.

'We can spare it. Mary Owen will be in need of it more than we are.' Yesterday, she had taken the woman home, waited for the port missioner to call. People would help, they always did, no matter how little they had themselves. But with the docks at a standstill, so many would be going short.

Sun streamed through the back door, which had been opened to dispel some of the heat from the oven and let in much-needed fresh air. At the table, six-year-old Alfie was sitting beside Stella, whose high chair had been pushed next to him. Letty's eighteen-month-old daughter was eating fingers of bread and jam and Alfie slipped down and picked up a piece that had fallen on the floor, blew on it and popped it in front of her. Stella grinned, showing her four teeth, and Alfie reached up and rubbed a hand over her head. 'That's a good girl.' Anyone who didn't know otherwise would think they were sister and brother.

'Good lad, Alfie. Now help nanny Dorcas while I'm gone.'

Dorcas picked up a damp cloth from the draining board and rubbed it about Stella's face, wiped over her hands. 'I thought you'd be taking the boy with you.'

Letty looked up from her basket. Dorcas could still be brusque when it came to Alfie. Letty had taken the boy in almost two years ago when his mother, Anita, had died. A widow who had fallen on hard times and had nothing left to offer but her body. Letty wondered now how many women might fall prey to the same future. She had never had cause to venture into a workhouse, and she counted her many blessings for that, but it must be a vile place, if women would rather do such things than go there.

Her thoughts flitted again to Mary Owen. She had three young children to care for and although she had family close by, they too were at the sharp end of poverty. Letty gave Alfie a reassuring smile before answering, but catching her expression, Dorcas cut across her.

'I wasn't being funny, lass. I thought he might want to see some of his old friends. Sally Penny's boys will be about.'

Alfie looked to Letty, waiting for his future to be decided for him. He had barely spoken when Letty had first taken him in, and no wonder at that, with all he had seen in his short life. Letty had discovered him sitting with his dying mother, ravaged by butchery, trying to rid herself of an unwanted child. Dorcas had not wanted him to stay and there had been numerous rows about it, but over time, Dorcas had grown fond of the boy, even if she didn't want to show it, for to do so would be to admit she had a soft heart after all.

'Would you like that, Alfie?' Letty asked. 'To see Stanley and Sam?'

Before he could answer, a call came from the neighbour over the wall. 'Are ya there? Letty?'

Dorcas rolled her eyes and Letty bit back a smile. 'Yon door's not been open five minutes and she's at it.'

Letty went outside and walked towards the part where the wall dropped down a foot or two, away from the back door and the windows, the higher part of it offering a semblance of privacy downstairs, if not from above. They had moved to the larger house in Park Street at the dawn of the new year, leaving the grimness of the two-up two-down dwelling in Mariners Row behind them, the future full of promise. Business had been going well and her shares in Parkers Chandlery had made a handsome profit, not that she would draw on them. It was an investment, but hers, like that of so many others, was now at risk. The prosperity of the entire town was connected to the fishing in one way or another, and everyone was beginning to get twitchy.

Her neighbour, Thelma Kirman, was waiting at the wall, a couple of woollen jumpers in her hands that she raised up when she saw Letty. 'For the mission. Would you drop them in when you're passing? I wouldn't ask, but my lumbago's giving me a bit of gyp and I fancy I couldn't get that far today.'

She was the same age as Dorcas but did not have her disposition, for where life had made Dorcas bitter, Thelma Kirman weathered life's storms with equanimity. She'd given birth to seven children, three had survived, one of them a daughter, Ethel, who still lived at home and worked in the clothing factory. Letty liked her enormously. Despite her hardships, she was not given to melancholy and, as such, deprived Dorcas of a good gossip, unlike their old neighbour at Mariners Row, Bet Chapman.

'It's not much, but perhaps some young lad far from home can make use of them. I know it's not the weather for sweaters, but by and by, it'll change. It always does.'

The sun had warmed the curved tiles on top of the wall and as Letty reached over she brushed at the rosemary bush, releasing the calming scent.

Thelma reached in her apron pocket and passed over a twist of paper. 'I got Ethel to pick up a couple of liquorice sticks for the bains. Babby might like it for her teeth.'

Letty took them with her free hand. 'That's so kind of you.' If only Dorcas understood that a little kindness went a long way.

They chatted for a few minutes before her neighbour waddled back inside, one hand at her back.

Letty walked down to the coop at bottom of the yard and checked on the hens. It had been a scratch of useless grass when they had moved in, but it had not taken her long to dig it over and create her little bit of Lowestoft, a reminder of the small farm she had left behind, along with her family. She couldn't wait for Alec to do it, for he would not be returning home at the end of the day like men who worked ashore, and things would get out of hand if not seen to. Her father had often said that a minute's job could turn into a week's if left too long. She would like a small shed in time, to store the tools and suchlike, but that would have to wait. All the small plans had been set to one side for the foreseeable future. The war had given them greater things to worry about.

She had erected a trellis, and sweet peas and green beans scampered up it, below them were the leaves of the small crop of potatoes and carrots she had sown from the seeds her mother had sent from their farm. Her mother had written of her fears for her sons. They would stay until the harvest was gathered, but the army had already taken their horses for the war effort – as they had from so many farms about the country. How long before they would take her sons? Letty pushed the thoughts away, not wanting fear to take hold. It served no good purpose to think too far ahead.

Her old home was a world away from the backstreets of Grimsby, the air constantly heavy with the smell of smoke, from trains and ships, as well as factory chimneys. And always the smell of fish. She had got used to it now, had found the green spaces, the park a few streets away. One day, she would have land of her own, hens, pigs, a goat for milk and cheese, but for the time being this small patch of yard would suffice.

Alec was in the kitchen when she returned and she placed the sweaters on the table, next to the basket. Alec picked up a plum.

'That's for Mary Owen,' she told him.

He polished it on his sleeve and put it back in the basket.

'Poor lass. I don't think she took anything in when the missioner talked to her.'

'It's a poor do,' Alec agreed.

'Aye,' Dorcas said quietly. 'I had lads at least when your father was lost. She's left with three lasses. They'll not be of help.'

Letty bit down her irritation. She knew what Dorcas meant, but it was always about the boys. And yet hadn't she, Letty, forged a life for them all?

Alec pulled his cap from his trouser pocket. 'There'll be a bit o' settlin' money. The markets have little fish to sell so what we caught will bring a good price. But it weren't a full haul. We had to turn back.' He pulled on his cap, tugging at the peak. 'What a bugger it all is.'

'You'll come straight back?' Letty didn't want to nag, but what money he did get needed to be spent wisely. So many men drank what they earned, and Alec had taken time to adjust to being a married man. The pubs had been busy, not just with men who had nothing better to do, but with soldiers and sailors who had swarmed into the town since the beginning of August. There had been calls from the Temperance Society to close the pubs completely, but that would never happen, for there was a pub on almost every corner and each one of them had to make a living.

'Leave the lad to think for hisself,' Dorcas sniped. 'He deserves a break.'

Alec bent forward and kissed Letty's cheek, winked at her. If she didn't love him so much, she doubted she could put up with Dorcas at all.

'What I get I'll not put over the bar of the Albion, you can be sure of that.'

She nodded. He had not always been so wise.

'I'll call in at Parkers when I've seen Mary,' Letty told him. 'We could meet?'

'Aye. That'll be grand.' He ruffled Stella's hair, grabbed at Alfie's nose and stuck his own thumb between his fingers to show Alfie he had stolen it. The boy grinned and Alec pinched his cheek, smiled at him. 'After I'm done with Hammond's, I'll call in at Solly's for a brew, and see what's what.'

When he left, Letty changed Stella's nappy and put the soiled one to soak in a bucket outside the back door, finished the remainder of her chores and removed her apron, hung it on the pantry door, checked herself in the small square of mirror beside it, smoothing her dark hair into place.

'Well, Alfie, get your boots on, lad, and we'll go see Mr and Mrs Parker at the shop. How about that?'

The lad got up and went to fetch his boots from the cupboard under the stairs, and seeing him pull them on, Stella began to wail.

Dorcas picked her up. Letty gave her a liquorice stick and, suitably distracted, she ushered Alfie out of the room and into the hall.

Dorcas called after her, 'If you see Bet Chapman, give her my regards.'

'If I see her,' Letty answered, praying that she would not.

5

Alfie skipped a little way ahead of Letty. It was good to see him so joyful, for his start in life had not been favourable, though his mother had done her best. He was like her, with his sandy hair and freckles, his serious blue eyes, but he was as quiet as his mother had been brash. Letty wondered if she had started out that way, defensive lest someone attack her first. She would never know, and she hoped that, unlike Anita, Mary Owen would have people around her to help now that she was widowed.

Letty adjusted the basket on her arm as it was beginning to pinch and, as she did so, Alfie caught an uneven part of the pavement and went flying, letting out a cry as he hit the ground. A man coming towards them dashed forward and helped him to his feet, checked his scuffed and bleeding knees and brushed the dirt away. Alfie's lip trembled, tears pooling.

'There's a brave lad, no tears for your mother now.'

Alfie nodded, rubbed at his eyes with the back of his sleeve, then looked at her, his lips pushed forward in misery. The man tipped his hat to Letty before going on his way.

'It's all right, Alfie. The man made a mistake, that's all.' It had become more difficult as time passed. He had called her Mrs Letty when his mother was alive, but these awkward moments had to be addressed once and for all. She had meant to talk to Alec about it this morning, but there had been no time. There was never any time, all their living packed into the few hours he was ashore.

She turned onto Victor Street, and as they passed St Anthony's orphanage, Alfie slowed, staring up at the high windows.

'What is it, Alfie?' The basket was heavy, and she had too much to do for Alfie to dawdle.

'Is that where the bad boys go?' he said, his voice almost a whisper.

'Whatever makes you say that?'

He looked at her from under his long lashes. 'Nanny Dorcas said it was for bad boys and girls, and if I don't be good, she'll send me there.'

Letty felt her anger rise like a flame. She'd half a mind to turn right back and give Dorcas a piece of her mind. She put down her basket, squatted down to his height, tugged at his jacket, brushed her hand gently over the lapels and looked directly into his serious little face. 'It's where children go who have no one to care for them. But you have me, Alfie, and Mr Alec, and' – heavens, it made her spit to say it – 'Nanny Dorcas. You'll never have to go there. Do you understand?'

He nodded and she got up, picked up her basket, and took hold of his hand, gripping it more tightly this time. They walked a little quicker, Letty mulling over exactly what she'd say to her mother-in-law when they got back.

They soon came upon the courtyards that ran to the rear of King Edward Street, with the tiny back-to-back houses, one of which had been their home when they'd first arrived in Grimsby. It was a dirty hovel they'd come to, and Alec had been full of apologies, but to give Dorcas her due, she had worked alongside Letty to make it habitable. That was more than two years ago and she and Alec had been wed only a week. Alec had promised her that they wouldn't be there long, and he had kept his word. Now she wondered whether they should have stayed; they would have had more savings behind them for times like this. They had money put by from the sale of the *Stella Maris*, the sail drifter that Alec had half-share in with his uncle. It had been passed to him and his brother, Robbie, when their father died. But when Robbie had met with an accident and been washed overboard, Alec had wanted a fresh start. The *Stella* had been sold and the money saved. One day, Alec Hardy would own his own steam trawler, that was his dream. But not hers.

Letty left Alfie with Sally Penny and her boys and made her way to Mary Owen's house. The entrance to Victoria Buildings was similar to that of Mariners Row, an entryway that led to a courtyard, four poorly built dwellings either side of it. The day she had arrived there was burned on her brain. How grim and disappointing it had been, the shock she had felt when they had pitched up, the three of them, she not really aware of the life of a deep-sea fisherman. A longshoreman out of Lowestoft might be away a few nights, but Alec and his crew could be away three weeks or more – and she was left alone with a mother-in-law who didn't care for her. Letty was of the land, and Dorcas was of the sea and Alec's choice of a wife had irked her. They had got along as time passed, more so since Stella had been born, but she still found Dorcas difficult to live with.

The air was filled with the stench of horse manure and urine from the yards the other side of the wall and flies hovered, thick in the stale air. She wafted away a bluebottle with her hand and made her way to number 3, knocked on the door. When no one came to answer it, she knocked again and opened the door, calling out as she entered. Inside, she found the eldest girl, seven-year-old Emily, seated in a chair, the sleeping baby on her lap, the toddler, Kitty, playing with a rag doll at her side.

'Where's your mother, Emily?'

The child raised her eyes at Letty's question.

'Is she upstairs?'

The girl nodded. 'She's in bed. Nan will be back soon.'

There had been little in the way of food when Letty had called the day before. She had made hot tea, borrowed milk from a neighbour. The elderly woman next door had brought bread and a scrape of dripping for the kiddies. Everyone was holding on to what little they had, not knowing when work would start again, but they had shared what they could. The neighbour had said she would keep an eye on Mary and the kiddies and had been as good as her word.

Letty walked through to the small room at the back and placed her basket on the table. Someone had cleaned the kitchen since she had left them yesterday afternoon, for there was the end of a loaf and a jar of jam and the pitcher was full of fresh water. Letty took out the bread and sliced it, then covered it with her own honey and took it through to the children, telling them, 'I'm just going to see your mother; I'll not be long.'

Upstairs, Mary Owen lay on the bed, sacking curtains pulled across the window, shutting out the morning sunshine. The woman's face was puffy, her eyes sore and vacant. She looked beyond Letty as she came to her and covered her hand with her own.

'Mary, I'm going to make you a hot drink and while you drink it, I'll boil some water for a wash.'

The woman gave the smallest shake of her head.

Below them, Letty heard the front door open, someone speaking to Emily, then slow and heavy footsteps on the stairs. Mary's mother, Edna, appeared in the doorway, stood a moment to catch her breath. She was a tiny, shrivelled woman, with grey hair and few teeth and she pressed her hand to her chest until she had breath enough to speak.

'I brought a few bits and pieces of food,' Letty told her as the woman coughed and wheezed. 'I thought it might help.'

'That's kindly of ya,' Edna managed to reply. 'I've been... with her sister. Her husband was on the *Coventry*.' It had been one of the ships reported late, presumed missing. 'Dear God, how we'll all manage now, I don't know. That's two of my lasses, and my lads with no work.'

Letty felt sickened. At least she'd had the opportunity to put money aside for times like this, and Alec was doing well as a skipper. But many of the deckhands earned little enough to live on.

'Was there any insurance?' Letty asked. There was a scheme whereby the men contributed to see them through difficult times.

Edna shook her head. 'If he paid it. He drank most of what he earned, and that was when he had a ship. If she complained, he beat her black and blue.' She pushed her bottom lip forward. 'And three littl' 'uns to care for. A bloody wastrel, he was. She's well shut of him.'

'Mam,' Mary said, her voice thin. 'Not now.'

Edna went to her daughter and patted her hand. 'You need to get up out of this bed and see to the kiddies, they need you.'

Mary turned her head away, and Edna looked to Letty, sighed heavily. The poor woman looked worn out herself, and no wonder with her troubles.

Letty sat on the edge of the bed. 'There's help, you know that. The mission and the Salvation Army. The mayor's fund is there for such times as this.'

'Aye, we'll have to get in the queue, won't we?' Edna chimed. 'It'll be a long one, no doubt about that. A lot o' men have no work, others are on short time. That's not counting ones that's lost...' She glanced to her daughter. 'I'll get her sorted when she's feeling up to it. At least she's got us.'

Letty squeezed Mary's hand and got up from the bed. 'Yes, and that's everything isn't it, Edna. Family.' It made her long for her own mother. She didn't want to think what she would do if anything happened to Alec, for Dorcas would be no comfort. No comfort at all.

Edna made her way downstairs, huffing and puffing as she descended, and Letty followed. Emily had placed the baby in a bundle of blankets and was sitting on the floor playing pat-a-cake with the toddler. The two women went into the back way and Letty removed the remainder of the contents of her basket, found an empty jar to which she added a little water. The girls came through as Letty put the flowers into it. Emily's eyes lit up.

'Sweet peas,' Letty explained.

'Can we eat them?'

'Oh, no, they just look pretty. I thought they might cheer your mother a little.' It seemed silly to her now. For what could a bunch of flowers do when you had lost your man? They would probably be past their best when Mary came downstairs, but at least it had made the children smile.

Letty left soon after. Mary Owen would not be alone in her sorrows, many more women were set to join her, there was no hiding from that. At least Mary could braid nets, and once things were moving again, she might yet be able to care for her family.

Alfie was running around the courtyard with his pals Sam and Stanley when she came to collect him. Their mother, Sally, was on her hands and knees, cleaning her doorstep, her generous backside in the air, swaying from side to side as she scrubbed. As Letty's shadow fell over her, she sat back on her heels, drew her hand across her brow, and got up, holding on to the doorframe to support herself.

'How was she?' Sally asked with no preamble.

Letty shrugged. 'She'd taken to her bed yesterday and she's still there. I doubt she got up from it.'

'It's the tip of the iceberg for what's to come. We can help folk as best we can, but in the end they've got to learn to help themselves.' She squeezed Letty's shoulder. 'Come in, lovey. You've got time for a cuppa, I know.'

'Time for everything these days. More's the pity,' Letty said as she went into the house.

'Make the most of it, lass. Nothing lasts for ever, good or bad. You'll not have time to wash yer face when it all gets going again.'

They settled themselves in the chairs facing the grate and Sally updated her on the comings and goings of Mariners Row. The young couple that had taken the Hardys old house were expecting their first baby and the ones at Anita's had taken delivery of their third only last week.

'What a world to bring a child into,' Letty said as she got up to leave.

'It's the only one we've got,' Sally answered. 'We make of it what we will.'

Letty called to Alfie, who was playing tag with the little gang of kids that hung about together, and he hurried over, his face red and damp with sweat, his hair sticking to his forehead. She put out her hand and he took hold of it, his palms hot and clammy.

'Let it not be too long before we see you again, young Alfie,' Sally said, smiling kindly at the boy. 'You too, Letty. I've missed you living hereabouts.'

Letty missed her too. Sally had been an ally when she had gone through her worst times with Dorcas. It was mostly because of her kindness that she'd got through those first days in Grimsby, always there with a kindly word and a cup of sugar when needed.

The kids called out to Alfie as they walked away, and he turned to wave at them as Bet Chapman came out of her front door, looking Letty up and down.

'Yer still 'ave the lad then? Thought he'd a gone by now.'

She felt Alfie's hand grip more tightly to hers.

'Of course, he's not going anywhere, *Mrs* Chapman. What a ridiculous thing to say. Alfie's part of our family.'

Bet sniffed in derision, and sneered at Alfie as if he was a piece of dirt. 'Dorcas must be going soft in her old age. That's all I can say,' she carped as she folded her arms across her chest.

'She sends her regards,' Letty said, giving the woman the most charming smile she could summon. How she loathed that nasty piece of work and her thieving husband. For every kind, sweet person, there was always one bad apple, and Bet Chapman was a sour one at that. No amount of sugar would sweeten her.

6

In the hallway, Henry waited for Ruth to fix her hat, staring up at the portrait of their mother, which hung on the wall by the entrance door, the last thing they saw before they left the house and the first thing they saw when they arrived home. Kathleen Evans would be forever young, her face unlined, and still very much in her prime. It had been painted three years before illness took her from them.

'Were Mother's eyes really that blue?' Henry leaned forward, then stepped back to take a better view. He had been but nine when their mother had passed away. As the years passed, things became vague – the sound of her voice, the touch of her hand.

Ruth touched his hand now. 'As blue as yours, so yes, they really were that blue.' Was it truth or memory? Or their mother as the artist had seen her? Perhaps it was both.

'You don't have to come with me,' Henry said, stepping back to allow her to go before him, closing the door behind them. 'Did Father tell you to?'

'Of course not.' Not in so many words, he hadn't, but Ruth knew it had been expected of her. 'You've been away. I've missed you.'

She slipped her arm in his. 'I want you to tell me all about the sea.' She leaned close to him. 'When you talked about it just now, I could see how much it meant to you.'

'Could you?'

He didn't believe her, but it was the truth. She had never seen him so passionate about anything before – and she had never heard him stand up against their father so vehemently. That he was determined to go to sea was not in doubt, it was the way in which he chose to do it.

'Yes, truly.'

It was not a lie and her answer seemed to satisfy him, for he nodded quietly and led her down the wide pathway. At the gate, he stopped, released her arm.

'Look, Ruthie, if you're coming along to try to persuade me to think again, then you might as well stay here.'

He wasn't going to let it go, so she might as well say her piece, then at least they could enjoy the walk. 'Father was rather upset that you didn't want the army.'

'I knew he would be.' Henry considered for a moment, looking up at the house, the trees reflected in the glass of the upper windows. 'But it's my life and if I'm to do my bit, then for once I would rather choose that "bit" for myself than be shoehorned into what Father wants.' He opened the gate. 'It's probably the only chance I'll get before I'm set up in the office for the rest of my life.'

She understood completely, for didn't she feel the same way, that she could do so much more than was expected of her, so much more than simply marrying the most suitable man?

Henry closed the gate, and she took his hand in hers, felt the hardness of his skin and turned it over. It was cracked and weeping, an angry red in parts, blisters on the pads beneath his fingers. 'Are they very sore?'

He rubbed at one blister with the fingers of the other. 'Better than they were.' He put out his arm for her to link into his and they walked the remainder of Welholme Road, then turned onto Hainton Avenue, down towards the docks. 'It's my little chance to live another life, Ruthie. Don't you long for that too, a little adventure?'

She didn't know how to reply. Didn't everyone want to escape the confines of their life now and again – heaven knows she had dreamed enough of it these last couple of years. Never had the restrictions of her life felt more binding.

'Arthur Marshall asked Father for my hand while you were away.'

Henry stopped, dropped her arm, turned to her. 'And Father said yes?'

She nodded.

'Of course he did. It would suit him to have his daughter married to one of the Marshalls and the eldest one at that. Why, Aunt Helen must be rubbing her hands in glee at the thought of having a spy in the Marshall camp.'

'Don't, Henry. It's not like that—'

'Isn't it? Ruthie, it's *just* like that.' He shook his head, took her arm again, this time a little tighter. 'You're not in love with him.'

'Does it matter? I like him. Surely that's enough? He's very...' How to describe him? Nothing sprang readily to mind. 'In command.'

'Controlling.' Henry let go of her, leant against the wall, took out a packet of Navy Cut and tapped out a cigarette, struck a match and lit up. He took a long draw and blew out the smoke, wafted it away from her face. 'Has he proposed?'

'Not yet. I am thinking he is waiting for my birthday tomorrow.'

'The day Charles leaves with his regiment?'

'Yes.'

Henry gave a small laugh. 'How crass of him.' He drew again on his cigarette. 'Perhaps he will delay it.'

'Or bring it forward...'

'What about Colin Wilson?'

Ruth looked about her, embarrassed, and pulled at his arm, made him walk again. 'How did you know I cared for him?'

'Because you talk of him the way I talk of the sea.' He drew again on his cigarette, flicked the ash to one side as they went along. 'I've always known – since the first time you came back from the mission service. You'd been there many times with Aunt Helen before Colin Wilson arrived as the port missioner's replacement. But then everything changed – what you said, how you looked.' He shrugged. 'It was obvious – well, to me it was.'

She felt suddenly weak, that her legs would not hold her, the relief of being able to speak of him. 'He's never said anything. Never given me the slightest inkling that he feels anything other about me than being grateful I help at the mission.' She had searched his face, dissected every word he had spoken for the slightest hint that he might think of her that way, but she had found none.

'He wouldn't. A man like him would think you were out of his reach.'

'Then it's hopeless.' She'd always known it was – a girlish dream and no more than that. She had been attracted to him from the moment he was first introduced to the congregation at the Bethel Mission Hall, and had felt something that she hadn't felt for anyone else, certainly not Arthur Marshall.

'Nothing is hopeless, not if you want it enough.'

'That's easy for you to say. A man is more free in his choices than a woman will ever be. It doesn't matter how we try to change things, we will never have the same rights as a man. A right to choose for ourselves.'

'Have you been attending more of those suffragist meetings with Aunt Alice?'

'Not recently, no.' She sighed. 'Everything moves so slowly, and although I disagree with the suffragettes' methods I have sympathy with their frustration.'

Henry stood to one side to allow a woman with a pram to pass.

'Did you know they had released all the suffragettes from prison last Monday – unconditionally?'

He took one last draw on his cigarette, pinched the ends with his fingers and threw the butt into the gutter and shook his head. 'They'll probably need the women when the men are gone to fight.'

'But women won't be called to fight, Henry.'

'They'll be called to do other things, though.'

She caught him arm. 'We will. And I intend to make the most of the opportunity – just as you have done.'

They walked the full length of Freeman Street, the red-bricked Italianate dock tower rising high above the town, leading them forward, a beacon to the fishermen and those on land. It could be seen for miles, in distant villages that had no connection to the sea.

Henry talked of his time on the *Northern Queen*, how he loved the freedom of leaving the land behind and everything else with it. 'There isn't time to think, nor to daydream. It's hard work, and I know I'm lucky, that I can choose, and it doesn't matter if the catch is good or bad, for I have the comfort of not depending on it. But those men depend on us, as Evanses, to run our business effectively. I want to know every part of it for myself. Father is a businessman, not a fisherman. I want to be both.'

They weaved through the crowds of men clustered about the entrance to the docks, and he stopped on the corner of Orwell Street.

'What if you can't have both?' Ruth asked.

He looked up at the building behind her, released her arm from his. 'I have some business to attend to, and you can't come with me. Go inside. You'll be safe there.'

She twisted, saw that they were outside the entrance to the Fisherman's Mission.

'But you can't just leave me,' she called as he began to walk away.

'That's why you wanted to come with me, isn't it? On the chance you might see him?'

'Not at all,' she called after him, drawing unwanted attention to herself. 'Henry!' She wouldn't have dared come here alone, had never been without her aunt or Letty. It was not proper, and she was suddenly panicked. The hostel was for fishermen, it was no place for an unaccompanied woman.

Henry turned, walking backwards, facing her, his grin wide. 'Have a little adventure. I won't be long.' He thrust his hands into his trouser pockets and turned away, blended in with other men heading towards the docks.

Ruth stared at the mission windows that faced the road on two sides, the entrance door at the corner, looked again for Henry, but he was gone, long gone, and taking a deep breath, she went inside the building.

The lobby of the Fishermen's Mission was noisy and crowded and, unable to move her hands up to her ears to muffle it, she squinted her eyes, her only defence. There was not a square inch of space between the door and the desk as men queued for a bed, or bath, a bite of hot food. A mission was a refuge, but it could only take care of so many.

Ruth pushed forward, was jostled from behind, and the man in front turned briskly to object, then, seeing it was a woman, checked himself, stood back as much as he could to allow her to pass. She was wedged deeper into the crowd but no nearer the desk, her hat incongruous against the tweed and linen caps. She began to panic.

It was such a stupid thing to do, whatever was she thinking of? What was Henry thinking of?

She twisted to free herself, to turn about and leave, when she was grabbed firmly by the elbow, and someone leaned close to her ear. Her heart began to thump so loudly that she feared it might break her ribs until she recognised the familiar voice.

'Miss Evans.' Colin Wilson pushed out his arm and the men moved aside in what cramped space there was as he led her to the safety of his office at the rear of the front desk, leaving the door ajar. The strain was visible on his face, and she regretted causing him more concern. The chaos of his office matched the chaos outside of it.

He gestured for her to take a seat and she did so, removing her gloves and placing them on her lap. Behind him was a portrait of the King and to one side a painting of a mission ship, another a portrait of the founder of the mission, Ebenezer Mather. She had been in here many times with her aunt, when they had discussed the needs of the mission and contributions required. The mission had been founded for the benefit of sailors, many who lived a hard life and were treated harshly, easy prey for the grog boats who filled the men with liquor and set them on a downward path. Its first headquarters had been an old sailing ship and as it grew, more were purchased, the crews going out to meet the men at sea, providing warm clothing, boots and reading materials, including, of course, the Bible. But their religion was of no consequence, where there was a need, the mission tried to meet it, and many a man was grateful of its help. Their womenfolk and children were also cared for, and many were kept from the workhouse because of its intervention. Ruth thought of Mary Owen. Had she been here for help?

'Are you here alone?' He could not hide his concern and guilt flared.

'I am.' She felt the heat rise about her neck. 'My brother, Henry...' How stupid it seemed now, how reckless of him to leave her. What on earth could she say in explanation? Her thoughts raced, but she could think of nothing, and being alone with him at last, words escaped her.

'Is something wrong?' He was agitated, and she took it as irritation, that she had come at the most inconvenient time.

'I was with my brother... I lost sight of him.' To be so close, and alone, was exhilarating.

Outside the door, a man shouted and there were raised voices, one of the attendants telling someone to calm down. Mr Wilson glanced at the door. It would be better closed, but that would indicate impropriety, a young, unmarried woman on her own with a man, no matter that there were a hundred outside. If she were braver, she would close the door. If she were braver, she would tell him of her feelings.

'Would you like me to get a message to your father?'

'No.' The thought terrified her. There would be too many questions and Henry would get a dressing-down for leaving her. There was already too much friction between father and son. 'Could I wait?'

'For Henry?'

She felt the heat rise again, her neck hot. 'I... I think he will know I have come here. For safety.'

He nodded, and she clenched her fists, wanting to speak, not knowing what to say, where to start.

'I'll get someone to bring you a drink. Tea?'

'Water, would be lovely.'

He looked at her, just a moment too long, but enough to let her think that he too might...

Outside something broke. A glass? A window? And he dashed to the door, urged her to stay inside and left.

She waited, then got up, went to his desk. On it was a photograph in a plain wooden frame and she picked it up. He was in his uniform, navy jacket with gold buttons, not the black of the attendants, standing behind an elderly woman, his mother she supposed, one hand on her shoulder. They had the same dark hair, the same thin face. Ruth imagined it been taken when he first became a port missioner. It would have been a proud day, indeed, for it was a position of much respect and responsibility in fishing communities.

The noise outside the door grew louder, and hard words became threats. She replaced the frame and hurried to the door, peering around it. A burly man with ginger hair and a full beard to match lifted a man off his feet and barged his way out of the building with him, the other men following, and the room cleared. He stumbled down the steps and Mr Wilson hurried after him. Norman, one of the older attendants, saw her.

'Stay in the office, Miss Evans. You'll be quite all right. A minor altercation, that's all it is. A man came in too full of ale. He didn't take kindly to being told to sober up outside, but rules is rules.'

She nodded, went back into the office and waited. The entrance doors opened and closed many times, and she heard the men chewing over what had happened, Norman telling them to form an orderly queue. When Colin Wilson came back, she was studying the painting of Mather, his long white beard and hair to his collar. He had a benevolent look about him, befitting a man who had done so much good.

'I was sorry to leave you. But you were quite safe.' He smiled, she thought to reassure her, but it was not necessary, she had always known she would be. 'Now, that glass of water.' He disappeared and returned moments later with a small tray, a jug and two glasses, still leaving the door wide, and poured her a water.

As she took it, their fingers met, and it was like a spark of electricity passed through her. He looked away, as if she had burnt him and she sank to the chair, deflated. How stupid of her to think that a man so vigorous, and yet so gentle, could think anything of her. He was more in need of a woman such as Letty Hardy, a woman with spirit – and she had none. She sipped at the water, cursing Henry for leaving her in such a predicament.

Mr Wilson took a seat behind his desk. 'Did your brother state how long he would be?'

'No.' Her anger at her brother supplanted her awkwardness. How could he have ever thought something good would come of this. How could she?

'Then you must wait here until he returns.' He got up. 'I'll get one of the men to look out for him.'

He took his leave of her and there was nothing to do but wait and watch the clock. The minutes ticked by, each one of them laboured, and as they passed, she grew more angered at Henry's behaviour. They would never get back in time to go to Saxon Hall in Father's car. He would be furious and so would their aunt.

When Henry swaggered in, grinning like a fool, she wanted to slap him. He apologised to her, and to Mr Wilson, glib and nonchalant, and Mr Wilson looked at her with pity as he walked with them to the entrance door.

* * *

Colin watched Ruth from the window. Her brother tried to take her arm, but she cast it off. A hansom cab was hailed, and it stopped in front of them. Henry Evans helped his sister climb up into it, the horses' heads shaking up and down impatiently as they waited, then moved off.

He stayed there, noise and men all about him, but for once they could wait. How delighted he had been when she had arrived. He had stood in the doorway, admiring the curve of her neck, the sweep of her hair, the darkness of it at the nape. It had been difficult not to reach out and touch her. If it hadn't been for the disturbance in the lobby, he might well have done.

It had been the same since that first Sunday at the Bethel Mission Hall. How distracted he had been by her, looking so intently at him. But then so had her aunt – who missed nothing.

Helen Frampton was the link to everything and everyone in the town. Her fundraising events were attended by the wealthiest business owners, trying to outdo each other with their donations, and her rallying columns in her husband's newspaper, the *Daily Herald*, swayed opinion. As Ruth's interest in him became more noticeable Helen Frampton had taken him to one side. He had been left in no doubt as to what removal of her support would mean to the mission. They had been raising funds for a new building, this present one no longer fit for purpose. It was far too small for the needs of so successful a fishing industry. The architects had drawn up the plans and they had been close to getting the building started. But with the outbreak of war, it had been put to one side, as had his feelings for Ruth. He was not so stupid as to risk the good work of the mission for a relationship that could never hope to succeed – no matter how much he might have wanted it to. But try as he might, he could not get Ruth Evans out of his mind.

7

After visiting Mary Owen, Letty and Alfie made their way to Parkers Chandlery on Henderson Street. Letty had found work at the single-fronted shop when the Hardys had first arrived in Grimsby. The dwelling at Mariners Row had been the first of many disappointments, and she'd been adamant that she would not sit at home and braid nets with her mother-in-law, in keeping with the traditional ways of doing things. It had probably caused her more grief with Dorcas than she needed, but she knew she had to grasp the opportunity to live life on her own terms. The chandlers was situated at the Fish Dock Road end of Henderson Street, a street, like so many others, that was dotted with shops and smokehouses, offices and small warehouses. To one side was Websters, carpenter and cabinet maker, and the other Gilbert Crowe, tobacconist. His very name set Letty's teeth on edge. He had wanted to buy the Parkers out and would have done for a song until Letty Hardy had come along and made the struggling chandlers a profitable business. He had reason not to like her. That hadn't been the sum of his predatory behaviour, for he missed no opportunity to leer over her.

He was a loathsome man, but she was damned if she'd let him intimidate her.

The bell rang out over the door as she entered Parkers, pushing Alfie gently before her. The shop was busy, but no one was buying – there was nothing to buy for. Ships were still held in the dock and the men who hadn't enlisted to serve king and country were restless. It was mostly the older men, men too old to go to fight. Not that that stopped them talking about what they would do when they were let loose. But mostly they wanted to be back at work, to be earning. They were used to hard graft, long days and even longer nights when they were at sea. Two days ashore and all their living crammed into forty-eight hours that most men had weeks for.

Percy Parker was in his usual place, in the space were the flap lifted to allow passage between counter and shop floor, reading the newspaper, and Wolfie Turner was yarning to their mutual pal, Dennis, who had settled himself on an upturned bucket. At the other side of the shop, five old sea dogs were chewing over a bit of gossip. All looked up when she walked in, and Percy beamed his lopsided smile when he saw Alfie. With his good arm, he pushed his newspaper away in readiness and Wolfie bent forward, swept the boy up and sat him on the counter as was their habit.

Percy had improved since his stroke two summers ago. He still dragged his foot when walking and his right hand was more or less useless, but he could still take his turn behind the counter of the chandlery shop that bore his name. His speech had been badly affected, but with a mixture of bullying and cajoling from his wife, Norah, he could communicate more readily – and although sometimes he lost words and became frustrated, he soon found them, with a great deal of mime and palaver from his friends.

The couple were family to Letty now, and even though she had earned her share in the shop and improved the takings, she was careful that no one could ever say she took advantage. She loved them both dearly and they adored Alfie.

'Nah then, boy Alfie, what have you got to tell us today?'

Alfie pulled down his lip to expose a gap where yesterday a baby tooth had been.

'Ah, has the old tooth fairy been and visited yer in the night?' Dennis winked at Letty. 'Left yer a bright penny, did she?'

Alfie pulled it from his pocket and showed it to them. Percy admired it.

'Wolfie sold all his,' Dennis told the boy. 'Didn't yer, Wolfie? Show the lad.'

Wolfie bared his lips, showing more gaps than teeth, and Alfie's eyes grew wide.

'Well, Alfie will be hanging on to his a while yet.' Letty laughed and, leaving the boy where he was on the counter, she went through to the living space at the back of the shop.

Norah was sitting at the table, her head bent over a ledger, a pencil in her hand, invoices in a neat pile to one side of her. 'Put the kettle on, lass,' she said without looking up. 'I'm ready for a brew.'

Letty was as familiar with the kitchen as she was her own home, and more relaxed, away from the disapproving eye of Dorcas, who, even though things had improved, didn't miss an opportunity to carp at the way Letty did things.

She placed a mug in front of Norah and took a seat beside her, sipping quietly until Norah laid down her pencil, removed her spectacles and rubbed at her eyes.

'Alfie with you?'

'With the boys.'

It made Norah smile. 'They think the world of that little lad.'

'He thinks the world of them. They've been kindness itself and he's not had much of that in his short life.'

Norah moved the ledger for Letty to check the figures. 'There's not much to tally, lass. Nothing coming in, to speak of, and still things going out.'

Letty scanned the columns of figures, looked at the balance. 'We shall have to give Milly her cards. She's young, she'll find something soon enough.'

Norah reluctantly nodded her agreement.

The girl was a good little worker and Letty was loathe to lose her.

'Perhaps we could put her on short time. Mornings only,' Norah suggested. 'Until things pick up again.'

The woman had a kind heart and Letty knew she would rather go without herself than deliver the blow to Milly. 'We'll give it to the end of next week,' Letty agreed.

'Did you hear anything on your way in?'

'Mostly hearsay, but something's happening.' Letty had noticed the change in movement, the comings and goings around the buildings the admiralty had taken over. 'Alec was in Hammond's offices yesterday and the guvnor thinks we'll have news maybe today or tomorrow.'

Norah rolled her hand over the pencil. 'Whatever they decide, it's going to hit us all hard. What's left of the fishing fleet will have the choice of all the chandlers on the docks.'

Letty rested her hand on the older woman's. 'We stuck it through the strikes, and you've survived the lockouts and worse. We'll get through this.'

Norah pressed her free hand to Letty's. 'I'm not thinking of us. Me and Percy have little need of anything. I'm worried about you.'

'Whatever for?'

'You've lately taken on that house.'

Letty made to interrupt, but Norah lifted her hand to stop her.

'I know Alec wanted you out of Mariners Row, and with

good reason, but your rent will be a burden to you.' Letty had been thinking the same herself, but how could they have known that the long gossip of war would finally become a reality. 'If your man could have kept at the fishing, it wouldn't have mattered so much, but with the shop as well...' Her voice tailed off and she looked Letty in the eye. 'You must keep drawing your money.'

Letty shook her head in protest. 'Not if we can't afford it.'

Norah got up. 'I insist.'

'And so do I,' Letty countered, getting to her feet and resting her hand on Norah's thin shoulder. The woman had never been robust, but these last two years with Percy had taken their toll, and Letty worried for the pair of them. It had been on her mind when she'd settled for the house in Park Street, a house big enough for them to have a home there too, not that she'd mentioned it to Alec, but she had half a mind Alec knew her thinking, even if he hadn't said anything.

Norah picked up the ledger and held it to her. 'You're a stubborn lass, and no mistake.'

'It takes one to know one.' Letty pecked her on the cheek. It was odd how affectionate she could be with Norah when she couldn't get close to Dorcas. 'Is it all right if I leave Alfie with you for a while? I wanted to call in on Alice Wiltshire.'

Norah smiled wryly. 'I think you'd have a job taking him away now Percy's got him.'

* * *

Wiltshire's Chandlery was on the corner of Fish Dock Road and Hutton Road. A huge double-fronted shop that faced the Coal, Salt and Tanning Company – the largest of them all. The end wall was sign-written with all they had to offer and could be seen for a good distance. It was an eye-catching shop in every way and Parkers down the side street was no competition.

The shop was empty, Alice's youngest son, fifteen-year-old Matthew, behind the counter when Letty entered. He smiled in greeting, placing his hands flat on the counter as has father, Edward, was wont to do. No doubt the boy had hoped it would give a little of his father's gravitas, whereas it only ignited her endearment.

'Is your mother in?' Edward Wiltshire ran the shop with his four sons, but Alice played a huge part in keeping the wheels of enterprise running smoothly.

He drew his hands together, again so like his father, and, gently slapping the counter, said, 'I'll get her for you.'

Letty waited, admiring the quiet order of the shop, so unlike Parkers, although she liked to think it had improved since her arrival. Then it had been in complete chaos and there would always be a little of that while Percy was around, that was his nature. But there was a warmth and a welcome at Parkers that the other shops could never emulate, and that drew people there. It was evident that business was more than just having the right stock.

When Alice came out, it was clear she had been crying, for her eyes were red-rimmed, her face pinched and drawn. She pushed a handkerchief into her sleeve and offered Letty her best smile. Her eyes, usually so bright, were now dull and lacklustre. 'Letty. Good to see you. What can I do for you?'

For the briefest of moments, Letty regretted coming to ask her anything at all, but then wondered if Alice didn't need the distraction as much as any of them did.

Alice must have noticed her hesitancy. 'It's all right, Letty. I suppose you've heard the boys had signed up?'

She nodded. 'I saw Laurie outside the recruitment office this morning.' She looked to Matthew.

'He's too young. Thank the good Lord.' Her words didn't elicit a smile. 'I couldn't bear to stay home, so I came here to keep busy.' Alice spread out her hands. 'But there's nothing to do. Not yet.'

Not yet. Letty hung on to her words. Alice had connections. Helen Frampton was her sister-in-law, and if there was any news to tell, anything official, Helen would know of it before many of them did.

'I was hoping you might have more news than gossip – about the ships going out to fish again. Anything I should be doing to help Parkers keep going over the next few months?' She didn't want to sound desperate but knew Alice would understand. And, as she had hoped, be eager to help.

'Edward has been in contact with someone at the admiralty.' Alice paused. 'Forgive me, the name slips my mind. I'll go ask him.'

Letty wandered back to the window and peered out. It was odd to see so little activity, with men standing idle along with the trawlers. There had been a strike a few months ago, but it hadn't lasted, they never did, for few had savings to see them through. There was a fund, but its coffers were not as much as that of the trawler owners and a man could only let his family suffer for so long. If the fishermen didn't put to sea, there was no need for net braiders, and the women got by on braiding. Piecework it was too. The faster you worked, the more you got paid. Dorcas had got through the darkest of times with braiding. Now, the owners were suffering alongside the men, for idle ships made no profit. For once, they were all on the same side.

Alice returned, her head tilted forward, fastening her hat in place with a pin. When she looked up, she smiled at Letty, this time with a little warmth. 'You need to register to be on the admiralty approved retailer list,' Alice informed her. 'It might be enough to keep us all going until such times as things return to normal.'

The two of them exchanged glances. There was no knowing when that would be, and Letty sensed that Alice was trying to appear positive for her son's benefit. Although Letty knew that Matthew Wiltshire would be well aware of his mother's distress, no matter how hard she fought to hide it. You could outwardly appear brave, but those who loved you most would see through the pretence.

'I'll walk down to the dock offices with you. I feel the need for a little air and good company and Edward will be glad to get me out from under his feet.'

Matthew rushed forward and opened the door for his mother, and the two women stepped out into the sunshine.

Along the wharf, men stood in groups, and as they passed, they looked their way, more for something to do than because they were women. Crates and fish boxes had been turned on end, and here and there men sat about them, playing cards and flipping coins. As they neared the railway offices, they heard a commotion and turned to see a crate upturned and cards fluttering to the floor, pennies and ha'pennies rolling about their feet. Kids scrambled for the coppers, and a burly man lifted one by the collar and clipped him around the ear for his trouble.

'If something doesn't happen soon, they'll all be fighting each other,' Letty commented.

'Rather they fight with fists than with guns.' Alice was solemn again. 'My boys know nothing of fighting. They can dress them in their fine uniforms, but it doesn't make them fighting men. Does it?'

'As needs must.' Letty was careful in her reply. 'We all want to defend what we hold dear.' It was the kindest words she could offer. She didn't want Alec to fight, or her brothers, but she would defend the right to live as they pleased to the last. For wasn't that what she had done her entire life. Fought for the right to live her life in the manner she wanted. These last years she had followed news of the suffragettes; not that she agreed with the violence of their attacks, of breaking windows and defacing property – but there would come a time when they would all be called to make a stand. 'Something will have to happen soon. More ships will be lost and men too. They can't sit it out, and the men don't want to.'

They walked over the railway line, quieter now that the fish was not being transported to London and elsewhere in any great number.

Alice stopped outside the dock offices. A portion of the building had been given over to the navy while they searched for alternative accommodation in which to house their administration. 'It's Admiral Frost who you need to talk with, Letty. He has overall command of the area. Edward has secured a contract for the supply of provisions. Perhaps you could do the same. It doesn't matter if the trawlers are chasing fish or mines, the men still need to be fed and the ships kept in good order. We might not do as well as we have been doing, but we will keep afloat, and that's what counts.' Alice adjusted her hat and blinked up at the sun. 'I'll take my leave of you here. I have an errand to run for Edward. Best of luck.'

'Will I be in need of it?'

It made the older woman smile and she was instantly the Alice Letty had encountered the first day she had walked down the docks, looking for work. 'Not at all, but it does no harm to wish you well.'

The clock tower atop the dock offices showed after twelve as Letty made her way up the steps. At the top of them, a man pulled back the entrance door, stood back to let her pass, then left, letting the door close behind him.

It was stuffy and airless inside, and light shone through the windows, casting beams of gold on the black and white tiled floor.

Men filled the wooden chairs and benches that were positioned either side of the wide hallway, others standing, shoulders to the wall. There was little conversation, just a general air of stillness borne of long waits. A man sat back, eyes closed, head titled against the wall, and he opened one eye as she passed and walked towards the counter, where two long queues had formed. Letty picked the shortest of the two and got in line, admiring the paintings on the wall, and watching the comings and goings, up and down the grand staircase, and in the wide corridor behind the counter as men in uniform marched briskly about, straight-backed, many with buff folders under stiff arms. She looked up at the high ceiling and felt small amongst the space, doubtless the architect's intention. Small but not insignificant.

The line she was in moved more quickly and she was glad she had chosen correctly as men peeled off, and either left or joined the others waiting. When her turn came, she waited while the clerk picked up a pencil and began turning the pages of a book, wrote something down, turned a few more pages. She cleared her throat to get his attention, and when that didn't work, she leaned forward. 'Excuse me?'

He did not look up immediately and when he did, it was not with any sense of helpfulness. He closed his book, annoyed. 'Yes?'

He looked at her as if she was some small irritation, like a fly to be swatted away. She didn't take it personally, realising why that particular queue had been dispensed with so speedily.

She pulled her shoulders back. 'I'm here to see Admiral Frost.'

He peered down his long nose at her. 'And is Admiral Frost expecting you, Miss...?'

'Mrs. Mrs Hardy.' She moved her hands so that her wedding ring was visible, then, irritated with herself, covered it over. She didn't need to prove anything. 'And no, he isn't.'

'Then I'm afraid you won't be seeing him.' He opened his book again, looked down at it.

'*Then* I'd like to make an appointment.'

He sighed heavily, looked about her to the men either side. It was blatantly obvious that he didn't like dealing with a woman. Well, that didn't bother her, it was nothing she hadn't met with before. 'Admiral Frost is a busy man.' His words were spoken to the room, not directly to her. How it rankled.

'And I'm a busy woman. I have a business to run.'

A smirk played upon the man's face. 'And he has the entire bloody docks to run. You'll not get an appointment this side of Christmas.' He opened a diary and began running his finger down the page.

Letty was aware of the queue shifting as men got into the other line. The man behind her stood a little closer, but she would not leave until she had an appointment.

Presently, the clerk looked up. 'Are you still here?'

'Evidently.'

She kept smiling, knowing that it was annoying him.

He nodded his head towards the men seated along either side of the desk. 'These have been waiting since early this morning. They might wait all day and not get to see anyone. Come back tomorrow.'

'Will I get an appointment?'

He shook his head. 'I doubt it, but if you've time to waste, then by all means.'

'Admiral Frost has a diary? A secretary?'

He placed his large hands on the desk.

She smiled again. 'I'd like to speak with his secretary.'

'Would you now.' He leaned forward into her face, but she didn't lean away from him. She could smell his stale breath as he spoke. 'Then I suggest you get your husband to come and make an appointment.'

'My husband has nothing to do with Parkers.'

The man gave a small hard laugh. 'That'll be nosey parkers then, will it?' He smiled at his own joke, and if she were a man, she might have wanted to drag him over the counter as she had seen a man once do. She looked about the men waiting. How long would they sit there.

'I was recommended by Mr Edward Wilshire. I am part owner of Percy Parkers Chandlery.'

'Then best get Percy Parker here, and we'll deal with it man to man.' He glanced down again.

'Mr Parker is unwell.'

'Then tell him to come along when he's well and I'll see what I can do.'

So, it was like that, was it? Well, there was more than one way to get past this small gatekeeper and she knew exactly how to do it.

'What is your name?'

'Gibbons,' he said, showing his yellowed teeth. 'Make sure you don't forget it.'

She gave him her best smile. 'Oh, no, Mr Gibbon. I won't, you can be sure of that.' Turning away from him, she said to the man behind her, 'Good luck' – words that Alice had said to her only minutes before. Well, he would need it more than her.

She felt smaller still as she made her way to the double doors at the front, the glass and brass gleaming.

A man opened it for her, removed his hat. 'He'll perhaps not be here tomorrow.'

Letty smiled at him. 'Neither will I.' She might not be able to get past some jumped-up little official, but there was more than one way of overcoming obstacles certain men liked to put in her way. Thank heavens she had connections. Alice would help, she was sure of it, and if not, a few words with Mrs Frampton at the Ladies Guild would be enough to start that particular ball rolling.

8

Propelled by anger and frustration, Letty walked quickly around to Riby Square and onto the docks, this time keeping to the left-hand side of Fish Dock Road in an effort to work off her indignation. She might have known nothing about fishing when she had first arrived as a newlywed in Grimsby, but she had made certain to learn – and the men had respected her for it. She knew the tides and the sailings, the trawler companies and the fish merchants, and all the comings and goings of the warehouses and shops on the streets that made Grimsby docks what it was. A town within a town. How dare that man dismiss her so readily. She had not felt so patronised in years.

She walked streets she had trod with Alec the day they'd arrived, getting a feel for the place, all of it so strange to her, a farmer's lass. It was as familiar to her now as anything she had known in Lowestoft, and she took pride in how far she had come in such a short time.

Wagons moved down the road, lads with barrows filled high with scrap and rags, and she was taken aback by how busy it was, the trains still bringing in coal, to fill ships that were going off to be fitted as minesweepers elsewhere. Doig's shipyard was taking on extra men, working around the clock to refit the trawlers. The paint yards were the same, lorries arriving laden with grey paint, admiralty order. The admiralty had swept in and taken charge, quickly and efficiently.

It was only the fishing that had paused, and looking about her, Letty saw that there was still work to be had if you were skilled enough to do it. Many a man would have money in his pocket when perhaps he hadn't before, but it did not comfort her that anything good could come from something so terrible as war.

Here and there, warehouse windows were open wide, and through them came the sound of heavy machinery. Letty walked down to the graving dock, the dry dock where the ships were repaired and fitted out and given a new coat of paint, obliterating the name of each one. There would be no spotting a ship by the colour of its funnel or its markings. All would be grey, all would be identified by a number, the remains of their former life eradicated for the duration of the hostilities.

She sat on a hawser, tilting her face to the sun and closed her eyes, calmer now, her thoughts beginning to settle, the breeze off the water cooling at the same time as the sun warmed her. There was still opportunity when things were bad. She had not been looking in the right place for it.

* * *

As Letty returned to collect Alfie, she saw Gilbert Crowe outside his shop, smoking a cigarette. Oily Gilbert, the men called him in Parkers, and it couldn't fit a man more, with his sallow skin and greasy hair, to say nothing of his demeanour.

Good manners made her acknowledge him with a brief nod.

He tilted his head at Parkers' shopfront. 'Perhaps I'll get next door cheaply after all. You'll not be providing ships if they can't go to sea.'

'Neither will you.' She smiled broadly, hoping to irritate him.

'I beg to differ. Men will always want their cigarettes and tobacco.' He leered, stepping aside for two men to enter. They touched their caps to Letty.

'They won't be able to afford them if they're not working, Gilbert. Think on that.'

At Websters, the shop the other side of Parkers, the blinds were pulled down, the closed sign showing at the door. It had been like that for days.

She knocked on the glass, but no one came.

Gilbert called out to her. 'The old man's already given up. You'll be next.' He tossed his butt on the pavement, grinding it under his boot, gave her another smarmy look and went to serve his customers.

Parkers was empty and the bell rang out over the door as she entered, bringing Norah scurrying from the door marked private. 'Anything to report?'

Letty shook her head, removed her hat and placed it on the counter opposite Norah. 'Alice told me the admiralty were making contracts with local businesses to supply provisions and equipment. If we could secure something, it would tide us over and keep the bank happy.'

'Could we do that?'

'I went to speak to someone, but it was busy, and I need to make an appointment.' There was no point in telling Norah of her encounter with a toady little man at the desk. 'I'll try again in a couple of days. Things might be moving a little more quickly then. It was all a bit chaotic.'

Norah put her hands either side of her neck and pulled them back and forth. 'And if we don't?'

'We will. The engineers are working, the yards are busy, even if we're not. When ships get damaged, they'll need repairing. And replacing.' She thought of the ships already sunk. 'Things won't stay still, they'll change, they always do. We only need to keep Parkers ticking along, we're not in for debt and we can last a good while longer than most business.'

'Thanks to you, lass.'

'It's nothing of the sort. You just needed a little helping hand here and there, and I was glad to provide it.' She picked up her hat. 'Alfie behaved himself?'

'He always does. It's Percy I have to keep an eye on.' The two women shared a smile.

Norah lifted the flap of the counter and Letty followed her into the private quarters. Percy was in one of the fireside chairs, Alfie in the one opposite, the chairs facing the empty grate. Percy's chin had fallen onto his chest, and he was letting out rasping snores, while Alfie curled in the other, his legs dangling over the arm of it. A small amount of light came through the window that faced out onto the back wall of Gilbert Crowe's shop. Parkers had none of the grandeur of the dock offices, and she doubted any architect had found satisfaction in designing it, but the warmth that seeped from every brick and tile filled every corner. This small but cosy room had many times been a haven to her, and to Alfie.

Norah came to stand beside her. 'I fed the boy a little bread and dripping, so he'll be all right when you take him home.'

'This is his home,' Letty whispered, not wanting to disturb either of them. 'His second home. Mine too.'

Norah looked down at her hands. The Parkers had not been blessed with children, it was heart-breaking when some had been blessed with too many. Letty thought then of Mary Owen. How would she manage if the braiding didn't start again. How would any of them keep going?

9

Saxon Hall was on the edge of the town, built on land in a direct line to the docks, the source of Jack Frampton's wealth. He had started out as a builder's labourer when he was thirteen, and before the age of twenty had set up on his own, taking on men he had been at school with, along with many more. In time, he had branched out into trawling, using his profits to take over an ailing firm and make it his own. Over the years, it had become one of the most successful firms in the town, but that was not enough for Jack Frampton, and he had latterly bought the *Grimsby Herald*. In that way, he not only made the news – he owned it.

It was rumoured that Helen Evans had married him not for love, but as part of her mother's strategy. Judith Evans had been ambitious, some would say ruthless, in her pursuit for success, driving her three children to make the best of the opportunities she had worked so hard for. She had started out with a humble market stall on Freeman Street, selling clothing and dealing in rags. Then rags became salvage. With some of the profits, she had bought cheap properties that ran to the back of King Edward Street, renting them out to the hordes of families who had travelled to the east coast port in search of their fortune. In doing so, they had made hers. The other portion of her profits she had invested in her children, in their schooling, and in influencing their social standing.

When Richard was eighteen, he had bought his first trawler and slowly amassed a fleet. Though he knew little of fishing, he knew plenty about profit and loss, and no one was surprised when his sister, Helen, had married the competition, effectively uniting two of the largest trawler firms in Grimsby. Their mother had not lived to see the full extent of their success, but she had died knowing that her children would not suffer the indignities of her own poor start in life.

As the two men amassed their fortunes, they had vied for positions of prominence, taking seats on the boards of the workhouse and the orphanage, and latterly standing for the council as liberal candidates. Jack Frampton had become mayor in 1902 and Richard had been set to campaign the following year. But the death of Richards's wife had been a bitter blow and, in his grief, he had curtailed his public service. He had not been inclined to socialise without his beloved wife at his side and had been reluctant to remarry, for, unlike his sister, Richard had chosen to marry for love. More recently, Ruth had accompanied him, and he'd begun to accept more invitations to the boards of worthy causes, and to the socialising that went with it. Would that all change again when his daughter accepted Arthur Marshall's proposal?

When the cab pulled up outside the grand entrance, Ruth was already distressed. She checked her wristwatch. Twenty-five minutes late. Her father would be furious, let alone her aunt.

The driver opened the door and Henry took her hand as she stepped down. 'We'll go in like two naughty children,' he grinned as they made their way up the three steps to the front entrance.

'It's not funny, Henry.' She spat the words out, not knowing whether she was more infuriated with him for making her late, or the cavalier manner in which he'd responded.

He wouldn't care, but she did. Very much. They should have been there before the other guests arrived, a united front. Having no children of their own, the three Evans siblings were expected to support their aunt and uncle at every turn.

The Framptons' butler, Kingston, welcomed them at the great door, which opened into the wide entrance hall, an elaborate sweeping staircase facing them. At the top of it hung a huge painting of their aunt at the age of twenty-three – the year she had wed Jack Frampton. The windows either side of the vestibule were stained glass, adorned with a compass and a ship's wheel, and red and yellow roses about the family crest. Rich silks hung at the windows, heavy with fringing, and pedestals bearing huge and exotic floral displays were set at various points about the room.

The butler took her hat and shoulder cape. 'You're looking quite lovely today, Miss Ruth.'

'Thank you, Kingston.'

His delight at seeing her calmed her a little, taking away some of the anger she felt for her brother.

Henry took her arm. 'Don't look so worried. I'll take the blame.'

'You will,' she said through gritted teeth, 'but it won't make much difference – not to you anyway.'

As Kingston led the way, she heard her aunt's voice, then a burst of laughter ring out. The drawing room was light and airy, the walls papered with lemon damask, light reflecting from the two enormous chandeliers that bounced patches of rainbow about those gathered. Heavy drapes made from Indian silks were pulled back from the windows and various sculptures and pieces of fine art were set about the dark furniture. Here, there were more flowers, which had been gathered from the extensive greenhouses and the walled garden. Paintings large and small filled the walls, there more to boast of wealth than of taste. Fortunately, her aunt had both.

Ruth caught her aunt's expression through the tilted mirror that hung above the Italian marble fireplace. The flash of her eyes was only fleeting but enough to let Ruth register her displeasure. She excused herself from her guests with a disarming smile and went over to her niece and nephew. 'There you are, darling girl,' she said brightly, raising her voice a little, so that people turned. Lowering her voice as she leaned in to kiss her cheek, she murmured, 'I was beginning to think you weren't coming.'

Henry swooped, kissing her cheek before his aunt had chance to proffer it to him. 'Aunt Helen, how wonderful you look, as always.'

'And how smooth-tongued you are, as always.' It was a quiet reprimand in the circumstances and Ruth was grateful that so many people were in close quarters. 'You're late. I rather expect it of you, Henry, but not of your sister.'

Ruth was about to apologise when Henry cut across her.

'It was my fault, Aunt Helen, but then you knew it would be. I wanted to reacquaint myself with home and dragged Ruth along with me. If you must blame anyone, blame me.'

'Was it ever so. Come, now you're here, you must do your bit and mingle.'

Henry looked about the room. His method of breezing over his misdemeanours, however slight, was to ignore them completely. 'Where's Father? Has Charles arrived?'

'Best to avoid your father for the time being, young man. Let Ruth smooth the way for you – as she so often does.' She gave him a tight smile. 'You'll find Charles out on the lawn with Daphne and her sister, entertaining our guests. I suggest you join them. You have some catching up to do.'

Her words did nothing to dull Henry's exuberance and he wove his way through the room, smiling here and there, saying a quick hello as he passed, and disappeared out of the French window to join his brother, leaving Ruth feeling more dismal than she had when she had left Colin Wilson at the mission.

'I am disappointed, Ruth. Still, this is not the place to speak of it.' Helen Frampton flashed a smile as two young naval officers walked past them, then pressed her hand to Ruth's forearm and leaned close. 'Arthur is here. I hear things are going well between the two of you. That an announcement is imminent?'

Her obvious delight did nothing to improve Ruth's anxiety. Her father would have informed his sister of Arthur's visit. In the absence of a wife, Richard Evans conferred with her on anything and everything relating to his children, though Ruth wished he would keep some things between the two of them, father and daughter. Once Aunt Helen was involved, there would be no question of taking her time over her answer.

She followed her aunt through the open door that led to the dining room and then out onto the terrace. A marquee was set up on the lawn, the side facing the house exposed, and a long table, dressed with pristine white cloths, was at the far side and decorated with ropes of flowers, ivy and other greenery from the garden. To the left, it was set with glasses, bottles of champagne and wine, and at the opposite end was a large tea urn, and fine china cups and saucers.

Some of the guests had settled themselves on the rattan furniture to listen to the string quartet, while others had wandered out onto the lawn and gathered under the shade of a great oak. Wide yew hedges screened pathways that led to seated areas and, beyond that, woodland. All about them were beds filled with roses and surrounded by salvias and lavender. On the terrace, her father was in conversation with Arthur Marshall and his father and a mature man in naval uniform, high ranking by the amount of braiding on his cuffs and at his shoulders. Her father's irritation was well concealed, but Arthur's was not. Plainly the day could only get worse.

Ruth took a deep breath and walked over to them.

'Admiral Frost, allow me to introduce my daughter, Ruth.'

Admiral Frost bowed his head a little as he clasped her hand. 'Delighted to meet you, my dear.' Though his bearing was commanding, he had the kindest of eyes and she relaxed a little knowing Arthur would not make a fuss while this man was in their company.

'Can I get you a drink?' Arthur asked. He indicated with a slight movement of his head that he wanted her to go with him, but she had no intention of leaving her father.

'That would be lovely. A cordial will suffice. The afternoon is only just begun.'

He opened his mouth to say something, and checked himself, looked at the glasses. 'Gentlemen, any top-ups?'

The two men held up a hand to decline, their glasses adequately filled, and with an air of irritation, Arthur walked over to the marquee.

Ruth smiled at Arthur's father, Cyril. 'Is Mrs Marshall not here with you?'

'In the marquee,' he replied. 'Enjoying the music and quite possibly putting the world to rights with her friends.'

Ruth looked over to the marquee, saw Arthur getting her drink, her aunt go over to him and get quite close. Ruth tensed. They might have been having a simple conversation, but she felt like she was being plotted against. Please God, she was right and this party was not some elaborate ruse for Arthur to propose. Her stomach tightened. She smiled at the admiral.

Frost had grey at his temples like her father, and a pale complexion, not the ruddiness of the men who spent time out on the ships. He was perhaps of the same age, mid-fifties, and her father obviously liked him as the conversation was easy, and Ruth found herself disappointed when Arthur returned. He handed her a glass, holding on to it to gaze into her eyes, and she could only think of when Colin Wilson had done the same thing an hour ago. There, she had felt the world shrink and expand. Here, she felt as if she had been placed in a straitjacket. Marriage to Arthur would be seen as a powerful union, bringing together the three largest trawler owners in the town. She had been almost resigned to such a union until the new port missioner arrived. Henry was not the only one forced into a life that didn't fit.

Edwina Latimer joined them and tried to flirt with her father. Ruth knew it annoyed him that the middle-aged widow would not get the hint, that he wasn't interested. She turned to Ruth. 'I didn't see you earlier. You didn't arrive with your dear father.'

'No, I was with Henry, he is not long arrived home and he...' She glanced to her father. 'Had a little business to attend to.'

'Your father will be relieved he has another ship safely to port.' She gave Richard Evans a simpering smile and Ruth gritted her teeth.

'I think this time he was more concerned for his son, Mrs Latimer.'

Her father frowned, gave a small shake of his head to stop her, but she was not in the mood for Mrs Latimer, or her silly conversation.

'Of course, of course. I didn't mean... Silly me.'

Ruth felt her jaw ache with tension.

'Why don't you and Arthur go with the other young people,' her father suggested. 'You don't want to be here with the old fuddy-duddies.'

Arthur needed no encouragement, and led her over to a small cluster of trees, where Charles, Daphne, and her sister, Millicent, were chatting to a group of ratings. They looked dashing in their uniforms, and Ruth could understand why her father had been disappointed with Henry's choice of service. He would rather have the kudos of his son being an officer. But Henry had never wanted to take the easy way, unlike her and Charles, who followed the flattened path before them. Still, there was time to sway Henry – and this was the place to do it. She looked about but couldn't spot him.

'You survived Aunt Helen's wrath then.' Charles grinned as the two of them came to join them. He and Daphne were so close that a penny piece would not fit between them, and even though the atmosphere was light and gay, Daphne could not disguise her sadness at his imminent departure when the Lincolnshires left for camp. Ruth tried to think of Arthur leaving, if she would feel the same – and decided she would not.

'Only for the time being.' She grinned. 'I'll not escape a dressing-down at some point.'

'Why *were* you late, Ruth?' Arthur asked, his voice accusing.

Charles raised his eyebrows.

'You should never ask a lady such questions, Arthur,' Daphne interrupted, smiling broadly at Arthur, then to Ruth.

Ruth had never been certain how Daphne felt about the eldest of the Marshall boys, she was polite to all of them, but Ruth got the feeling that they were tolerated rather than welcomed in their circles. Things were all so finely balanced, everything connected in business and in pleasure. Daphne's father was chairman of Willoughby's Marine Insurance and her mother was a society beauty – as were Daphne and Millicent. Their mother had steered their passage into adult society in a way that Ruth's aunt Helen had not. Mrs Willoughby had guided her daughters with love, and the most Ruth could expect was affection. It wasn't the same.

Arthur took no notice of Daphne and waited for Ruth to answer.

'Henry wanted to walk. I went with him. After all, I've not seen him for almost three weeks.' His questioning irritated her. It was none of his business if she wanted to be with her brother.

'I hear he wanted to sign with the trawler section of the Royal Naval Reserves.'

Ruth glanced to Charles, who shook his head. He was not the source of the revelation. Had Father said something to the Marshalls before she arrived? No, he wouldn't. It must have been her aunt, or Uncle Jack.

'The trawler section! Surely it's all a bit of a lark on his part.' Arthur gave a short laugh and Ruth wanted to slap his arm.

'Have you decided yet, Arthur?' Daphne challenged. 'Army or Navy?'

Ruth cast her eyes to the ground and bit at her lip to stifle her smile.

Arthur shifted uncomfortably. 'Neither. I would have joined immediately, of course, but Father needs me at the office. We are busier than ever, what with some of our trawlers being requisitioned, new ones needed to replace them. As you can imagine, things have been rather hectic with men leaving. Some of us have to stay and hold the fort.'

Daphne was just about to reply when Charles dug her in the ribs. No doubt he thought, as Ruth did, that Mr Marshall would have to cope, just as their father was having to do. Charles and Daphne exchanged looks, all that was needed to share their understanding. Ruth had been thrilled when the two of them had become engaged three years ago. Their union had delighted both families. They were well suited, Daphne the perfect wife for a captain of industry, and their ease with each other only made her question her relationship with Arthur – such as it was.

Millicent smiled at something over Ruth's shoulder, and when she turned, she saw Henry striding towards them, a man at his side in naval uniform.

'Arthur,' Henry said cheerfully, making a beeline for him. 'Good to see you, old chap. I'd like you to meet Lieutenant Proctor.'

'Philip. Philip Proctor,' he said, holding out his hand to them all. He was in his mid-thirties, his dark hair swept back from his forehead, and brown eyes that were full of warmth. He shook hands with Ruth. 'A pleasure to meet you, Miss Evans.'

Henry slipped his arm about Arthur's shoulder. 'Now then, old chap, I've been talking to this *marvellous* bloke. I've told him all about you. You simply *must* come and say hello.'

Before he could protest, Henry led Arthur away, looking over his shoulder and winking at Ruth. She wanted to laugh with the relief of it.

'Sometimes that man can be so rude,' Daphne said as they watched them walk towards the house.

'Henry?' Ruth was uncertain.

'Of course not. He's an absolute darling, always has been.' Daphne linked her arm with Charles. 'Lieutenant Proctor, please excuse us. I need to have a word with Mother. Millicent?'

Her sister came beside her and the three of them walked to the marquee, the ratings keeping a respectable pace behind them.

There was a stilted silence until Proctor said, 'Your brother told me he came in on the last of your father's trawlers.'

'He did.' She smiled at him, glad to be in pleasant company. If Henry had brought him over, then he must have met with his approval. 'We were glad to have him safely home.'

'A tricky business. And he'll soon be away again.'

She tilted her head in question.

'He told me that he'd signed up for the Naval Reserve this morning.'

Ruth briefly closed her eyes, suddenly sickened. So that was what his bit of business had been when he'd left her at the mission, to get what he wanted before anyone prevented him from doing so. For a moment or two, she couldn't speak, couldn't make the small talk required of a good hostess, and that in turn annoyed her. Proctor must think her a fool, and he'd be right. No matter what Henry had done, the fault would lie with her.

'I'm sorry, I thought you knew.' He was awkward.

'I didn't, but that's not your fault.'

A maid came round with champagne and Proctor took her empty glass and replaced it with a full one, took one for himself. She sipped, enjoying the dryness of it on her tongue.

'Would you like to walk?' He indicated to the path that led around the gardens of Saxon Hall and she was glad to be moving instead of searching the guests for sight of her brother, and for Arthur. It stopped her thinking of what would happen when her father discovered that Henry had pre-empted anything he and Aunt Helen might have had in store for him.

'I was the bearer of bad news?' Proctor said as they walked between the yew hedges that led down to the lake.

'No. Not really. Henry had already spoken of what he intended to do.' She sighed. 'My father had other plans.'

'Ah, I see.' He drank a little of the champagne. 'I understand only too well. I thought I'd managed to escape the navy, but here I am again.'

'Escape?'

'The navy is the family business, so to speak. It was expected of me. I was schooled at Dartmouth, so it's been a huge part of my life. But not the life I would have chosen. I retired three years ago.'

'Aren't you a little young for retirement?'

He smiled, such a warm smile it was too. 'I was thirty-five at the time. Young to some, old by others' standards. Of course I only retired from the navy. I wanted to strike out on my own.'

'Doing?'

'Painting. I'm a marine artist. And I sculpt.'

She looked immediately to his hands, and he raised them a little. She coloured and he smiled.

'Don't worry, everyone has the same response.'

'And your family was supportive?'

'Good Lord, no, they were horrified.'

'Your wife?'

'I don't have one.'

She was surprised, and imagined that he had turned down any number of advances. Perhaps he was like Father, looking for the right one. The ideal that didn't exist.

'But your parents, extended family… they must have been…' She hesitated, wanting to choose the appropriate word.

'Disappointed?' he offered.

She smiled. She was thinking that devastation was more in keeping. It was what her father would feel if she turned down Arthur Marshall.

She nodded and he continued.

'They were to begin with, but when they saw how changed I was – for the better, I might add. More at peace with myself.' He was thoughtful. 'It wasn't easy, Miss Evans, these things never are, but I couldn't go on the way I was.'

How she agreed with him. A few weeks ago, she might have been accepting of a loveless marriage to Arthur, for no better reason than making her father happy. But what about her own happiness? Wasn't that important too?

They meandered through the pathways and sat down on an iron bench in the rose garden. 'So, do you earn a living at it. Your painting?'

'A living, yes; a good living…' He made a face. 'It depends on what your measure of a good life is. But I am happier – by and large.'

She appreciated his honesty. What indeed was a good life? 'You're very brave,' she told him. 'For taking a different path.'

'Foolhardy is the word I'm greeted with most often. I've always maintained my position with the reserve. It's a few weeks out of the year – and that I do enjoy. Besides which, it's only right to defend what is dear to us. I answered the call – England expects every man.'

'And woman?'

'Quite,' he agreed. 'Maybe more so than ever before as men are called in greater numbers. Which seems likely. Their positions will be vacant, and only the very old and young to replace them – and there are not enough. The Empire's navy is strong, but its army is nothing as compared to those of the kaiser, and I fear this war will not be over before Christmas as many people want to believe.'

She admired his frankness, and her anger towards Henry was softened by the fact that he had dragged Arthur off, she knew not where, and left her with someone interesting; no doubt his small attempt at an apology.

They made their way back onto the lawn.

'You're rather good at this, you know,' Proctor remarked.

'Good at what?'

'Being here when you'd rather be elsewhere.'

She felt the colour rush to her cheeks. 'I can assure you I'm—'

'Please, don't apologise. I'd rather be elsewhere too.' It was his turn to be embarrassed. 'Present company excepted, of course.'

She smiled, and this time there was nothing forced about it.

Over on the veranda, Aunt Helen chatted with Admiral Frost and her father. They were part of a small group. John Hammond of the trawler company was with them, and she recognised the manager of the National Provincial Bank, and Tom Wintringham, timber merchant. It looked like a party, but it was nothing of the kind. It was Helen Frampton's method of oiling the wheels of industry.

Ruth saw Arthur marching over to them, a scowl on his face, though he smiled broadly when he caught her looking at him.

'Your brother dragged me off on some half-baked tour of the garden looking for some elusive chap that seemed to have *disappeared*.' His tone was jolly, but his demeanour oozed irritation. He bared his teeth in a smile to Proctor. 'Nice to meet you, old chap. Ruth, I said we'd meet Mother in the marquee.' He bent his elbow and she reluctantly took it, keeping as much of a distance between them as she could.

Proctor gave a small bow. 'It's been a pleasure,' he said, looking only at Ruth.

Arthur turned sharply and led her away, spoiling the afternoon once more. If Henry and Proctor could make the break from what was expected of them, perhaps she could find the courage to do the same.

10

Ruth's twenty-second birthday would be memorable for all the wrong reasons, not that those she loved hadn't made the effort. At Meadowvale House, Mrs Murray had dressed the breakfast table with flowers from the garden and used the fine china as opposed to the everyday. Her father had bought her a gold bangle, the inside engraved with *To my beloved daughter, on the occasion of her birthday, 14.8.14*. She had delighted in it, admiring the symmetry of the date before slipping it onto her wrist. Henry had bought her a box of handkerchiefs edged with Nottingham lace and, in his absence, Charles had left his own gift. She opened the navy-blue box and peeled back the white tissue paper to discover a silver frame containing a photograph of him in his uniform. He looked so handsome and gallant, and for a time she couldn't speak.

Henry leaned over to look. 'He looks quite the officer, doesn't he?'

'He does.' She handed it over to her father, who stared at it and handed it back. He was still smarting from Henry's defiance in joining the trawler section, no doubt thinking he would never see such a photograph of his younger son.

There had been ructions when they'd got home from Saxon Hall late yesterday afternoon and Ruth had tried to calm things, to put forward both points of view. But even as she had intervened, she'd kept thinking of Philip Proctor, and how he too had found the courage to choose for himself. Had it not been her birthday, she doubted her father would have held back from spitting out barbs over breakfast, making Henry quite aware of how disappointed he was. They were being civilised, but it was an uneasy atmosphere as they sat at the table that morning.

Ruth propped the frame on the table in front of Charles's empty chair. In a couple of hours, all three of them would be outside Doughty Road Barracks to watch him march his men to the station, the train taking them to their camp in Belper, Derbyshire.

'What time do we need to leave to see Charles off, Father?'

He had been deep in thought and glanced at the wall clock. 'Half past ten. They march at eleven.' He got up from the table and came to her, kissed her forehead. 'Happy birthday, darling. I'm sorry I am not in a more cheerful mood.'

She reached for his hand and squeezed it. 'None of us are, Father. We will get through it as best we can.'

* * *

Doughty Road was thronged with people, young and old, and the police walked along to maintain order, not that people were doing anything but waiting, small children a little impatient perhaps, but nothing unruly for such a large gathering.

A constable waved her father's car into a suitable spot and when they got out, Ruth walked beside him, Henry close behind, searching for Daphne. She found her to the left-hand side of the barrack gate.

'Not the best of birthdays, my dear, but many happy returns.' She kissed her cheek and as she pulled away, Ruth saw how changed she was from yesterday. She was there to see Charles leave, but if she cheered him on his way, it would only be for courage's sake. They were both afraid for him, though neither would admit it to the other.

Ruth acknowledged Mr and Mrs Willoughby with a handshake, and they also wished her the very best for her birthday, then she took her place beside Daphne. Henry and her father stood with the Willoughbys. Ruth was glad they were there, for, to some extent, they healed the gap that might have presented itself between her father and Henry. Her father might be disappointed, but he was still proud of his son.

'Have you waited long?' Ruth asked Daphne.

'Ten minutes at most. I wanted to come earlier, but Father wouldn't have it. He was right, I suppose, for I will only glimpse Charles as he marches past. I will not be able to go to him.' She reached out for Ruth's hand. 'Speak of something normal, something of the everyday, Ruth. I don't want to let my thoughts take hold. They are racing already.'

She understood only too well. They talked of the party, how charming Lieutenant Proctor had been, how lovely Millicent had looked, that she was sweet on an officer she had met there.

'She's far too young of course, Mother would have a fit, but... we have to enjoy what days we have, don't we?'

Ruth smiled, fearing the conversation was getting melancholy too soon and changed the subject. 'Only a few weeks until we have our exam for the St John Ambulance. I don't feel very confident about it.' As rumours of war gained strength Daphne had enrolled in earnest, encouraging a reluctant Ruth to join her.

'You'll sail through. You are always so precise, so careful.'

'That's a polite way of saying "slow",' Ruth teased.

From behind the barrack gate they heard a sergeant major bellowing orders and the great arched doors were opened to allow a procession of men, a blur of khaki. The hammering of boots was thunderous as they marched along, and people waved and cheered, but try as she might, Ruth couldn't cheer her brother's leaving.

The two women leaned forward, and Henry came to stand beside them. 'He's there, three groups back.'

They shielded their eyes and followed Henry's pointed finger.

Ruth held out one of her new handkerchiefs, keeping the other for her own use. 'Do not weep, Daphne, though I know you want to. Let his last sight of us be our smiles. They must leave knowing we are strong, that we can cope while they are away. As the fisher wives do.'

Daphne took the handkerchief from her, gave a small nod of understanding, and the two of them swirled them in the air as the men marched past, their faces wreathed in smiles, their hearts breaking.

* * *

They were all quiet in the car when they made their way back to Meadowvale House. Father went into his office with Henry, and Ruth went to her room, wanting to be alone, not wanting to talk or appear to be brave. Henry would be next, and although there were no army fatalities so far, there had already been many lives lost at sea.

She tried to read, but could not focus, picked up her needle-point and put it down again. Her sketchbook and pencils were on her dresser and she took them and went outside, hoping that the beauty of being in the garden would soothe her worried heart. There she remained until a light shower made her retreat to the drawing room. It was after two and that evening they had been invited to dinner at Saxon Hall. She would rather have remained quietly at home, but Aunt Helen had insisted, making such a fuss that Ruth had conceded.

She had been listening to the gramophone when Arthur arrived bearing a huge bouquet of red roses, and the very sight of such an ostentatious offering set her on edge, that, as she had suspected, it was not just for her birthday.

'Happy birthday, darling,' he said, handing them over to her. He leaned forward, his lips pursed, and she was glad that the flowers were between them. He moved and she raised her cheek for him to kiss it.

'How very generous of you, Arthur. You shouldn't have gone to such expense.'

'A mere trifle to what you shall have in the future.' His words set her heart racing and she pressed the bell and called for Mrs Murray.

'Oh, how beautiful, Miss Ruth.' She smiled at Arthur.

'Could you put these in water, Mrs Murray. I will deal with them later.' She hadn't wanted Mrs Murray to leave but could think of no good reason for her to remain.

'Shall I take a seat.'

'Yes, of course. Forgive me, Arthur. I am distracted today.'

He didn't acknowledge her comment, made no queries about Charles, only sat down, crossing his legs and spreading one arm along the back of the sofa as he reclined. He smiled and it irritated her. There was no hint that he might have considered how she might be feeling today. Did she really want to tie herself to such a self-centred man?

'I didn't expect to see you so early in the day. I thought with your father so overloaded, you would not be able to leave the office.'

She could tell by his expression that her comment had annoyed him, but she couldn't help herself. He had annoyed her yesterday, with his excuse that he was needed to run the office, that there weren't other men equally capable of doing so. That he was more important than either Charles or Henry. She thought of her father, the strain he had been under, that he had not only lost men, but ships – worst of all his sons, leaving to fight for king and country. Arthur Marshall had brought her flowers for how it would make him appear in her eyes; he hadn't been thinking of her at all.

'You're rather prickly. Is something the matter?'

'Charles left this morning.'

'So he did. It slipped my mind that it was today. To Derbyshire, I believe. Did they get off all right?' He didn't wait for her to reply. 'I suspect they did, the military are very precise, aren't they? It will all run like clockwork.' He smiled, pleasantly, to reassure her, but it only served to irritate her more. She had little enthusiasm for small talk.

He began pulling at his collar and she could tell he was building up to something, his nervousness exacerbating her own anxiety.

Not wanting to look at him, she walked to the window, pressed her hand against the frame. Would Charles be at camp now, his men settled? How long before they went to France to support the troops?

She heard Arthur get up, move about. She focused on the willow, the leaves dropping into the small pond in the corner of the garden.

'Ruth.'

When she turned, he had moved to the centre of the room and was on one knee, a small red box in his hand. She gasped, pressed her hands to her mouth. Didn't he understand that it was all wrong, the timing – everything?

Arthur interpreted her horror as delight. 'Darling.'

She took her hands from her mouth, held them in front of her. 'No, don't. Don't, Arthur. Not today. Please.'

It took a moment for him to register her words and he slowly got up from the floor, wiped his hand across his mouth.

She moved again, stood behind the gold velvet chair and grasped the back, wanting something between them.

'I don't understand.' He held the small red box in the fingers of both hands and looked at it, then at her. Confused. 'It's your birthday. I wanted it to be special.'

'It's not the right time. Charles has left, Henry will leave shortly. We should wait.'

'But when I asked for your hand...' His voice had a sharp edge to it, that things hadn't gone as he had planned, and she became a little afraid at what she had done. 'Your father was in agreement.' He looked again at the box, and she willed him to put it back into his pocket. 'Is he short of funds?'

'No more than yours,' she countered. Had he not listened to her at all? 'It's war, Arthur. I am worried about my brothers, my father. I don't want to marry while everything is in such turmoil.'

He threw up a hand. 'Then we'll have a long engagement.'

He moved towards her, and instinctively she stepped away from him. Her hands were beginning to shake and she gripped the chair tighter.

'I'm sorry, Arthur. But today is the wrong day for something like this. I feel too sad.'

'And a marriage proposal will not make it better?'

He looked pathetic, but she couldn't find it in her to relent.

'Nothing will make it better.'

She heard her father's car pull in the drive, Henry speaking to Hawkins.

'I'd better go.' Arthur walked to the door, took hold of the handle, then turned. 'Happy birthday, Ruth.'

She heard him in the hall, briefly speaking to her father and Henry, the front door close. Knowing he had left, her entire body began to shake violently, and she made her way to the sofa and sat down. Her father came in, followed by Henry.

'Arthur was in a hurry to leave.' Her father looked at her with concern. 'Everything all right, my dear?' He sat down beside her and took hold of her hand. 'Why, you're trembling, dear girl.'

His grip was firm and it steadied her somewhat, though the thought of what she was about to reveal made it worse. She glanced to Henry, who was hovering by the door, and knew at once that he understood the circumstances for Arthur's hurried departure.

'Arthur was about to propose.'

'About to?' Her father patted her hand with his free one.

'He got down on one knee, but I stopped him before he could ask.'

Her father didn't comment but kept her hand in his. It made her feel a little braver.

'It was all wrong. Any day would be better than today. Saying yes wouldn't have made me feel better about Charles leaving. He shouldn't have come.'

'He was thinking of you, surely. To make things extra special – for your birthday.' Her father did not sound convincing, it was as though he was repeating something he had been told.

'If he was thinking of me, then he would know how I'd be feeling.' Would her father guess that it was an excuse, and a small one at that? It would be too complicated to admit that she no longer wanted the relationship to continue.

Her father sat back. 'When he has licked his wounds, he will realise how upset you are and will ask again.'

She looked to Henry.

'He might not ask again,' Henry commented, taking a seat. 'Ruth might not want him to.' He was offering her a chance to speak of her feelings, but she was too afraid to take it.

'Don't be ridiculous, Henry. Ruth knows what a good marriage it will make.' Her father patted her hand and got up. 'Have a rest, dear. We don't have to be at your aunt's until seven.'

* * *

Ruth had thought the day couldn't get any worse, but she had been mistaken, for when Hawkins pulled the Wolseley up to the entrance of Saxon Hall, she recognised the Marshalls' Rolls-Royce parked in the drive.

'I thought it was just going to be family tonight,' she said to her father.

'That's what your aunt told me. Possibly Cyril is here on some business with Jack. I shouldn't think he'll stay once he knows guests are expected.'

She hoped he was right, but something told her he was not.

Henry caught her hand as they walked up the steps. 'Don't worry. I'll stick to you like glue.'

Her aunt was in the hall when they arrived, the butler having been told to alert her the moment their car appeared in the drive. She took Ruth by the elbow and led her to one side, while Kingston helped her father off with his coat.

'What on earth has gone on?'

'Aren't you supposed to wish me many happy returns first?'

'Happy birthday.' Her aunt gave her a tight smile. 'I am not in the mood for your truculence, Ruth. Arthur said you turned him down.'

'I didn't turn him down at all. I stopped him from asking.

There's a difference. I asked him to wait.' She freed herself from her aunt's grip.

Henry was ready to come over, but she gave him a quick look to deter him.

'Well, that's not when he said a few moments ago.'

'He's here?' Her mouth was suddenly dry.

'Of course he's here. With his parents. This party was to celebrate your engagement.'

'And not my birthday?'

'Well, yes, of course, but the engagement was the main celebration. The uniting of the families.'

'And you didn't think to wait. For me? To ask?' Ruth clenched her fists. 'Didn't think to include Father in your plans.'

'Your father relies on me as regard to your future, he always has.'

'Not always.' She was incensed. It was as if her mother had never existed. Her father was as much to blame, handing over so much to his interfering sister.

He came over to them. 'Is there a problem?'

Ruth was close to tears. Over her aunt's shoulder, she could see Henry, standing by the entrance door. If she wanted to leave, she knew he would go with her without a moment's hesitation, and knowing that she had his support, no matter what, gave her the strength she needed to challenge her aunt.

'You rather put the cart before the horse, Aunt Helen.'

'Could someone please tell me what's going on?' her father questioned.

Henry came closer.

'Aunt Helen anticipated that I would say yes to Arthur's proposal. This is not a family gathering for my birthday, as I thought, but a celebration of my engagement – or rather non-engagement.'

Her father frowned. 'Is this true, Helen?'

'No, of course it isn't. It was for Ruth's birthday – to begin with. But then you told me Arthur had asked for her hand in marriage, and I happened to talk to Arthur and discover he was thinking of proposing on her birthday – which I thought, rightly or wrongly, was a lovely gesture on his part.' She let out a long sigh. 'I thought we could celebrate and expand the dinner.'

'The Marshalls are here?' Her father looked apologetically to Ruth, then turned to Helen. 'And you didn't think to inform me?'

Her aunt did not like being in the wrong, especially not in her own home. 'I hadn't expected Ruth to reject Arthur.'

'I *didn't* reject him,' Ruth repeated.

Henry stepped forward. 'Do you want to go home, Ruthie.'

Their father considered his son. Henry had defied him once and Ruth knew he wouldn't hesitate to do it again. But Richard Evans was not angry with him, it was his sister who had crossed the line this time.

'You have presumed too much, Helen. And I too am at fault, because I allowed you to. But Ruth is an intelligent young woman and perfectly capable of speaking her mind. If she asked Arthur to wait, he must respect that – and not make it into something else, to put Ruth in the wrong. What kind of man would do that? I rather think Ruth is right to wait.'

Her aunt's shock was visible, but was nothing to Ruth's own. Perhaps the day had also been too much for her father, for he turned to her.

'Would you rather go home, Ruth? We will leave together.' He looked to Henry, who nodded his agreement.

The two men looked to her for her answer. Their unity gave her renewed strength, and though she felt embarrassed, she was not afraid.

'No, I have done nothing wrong. Only asked a man I thought cared for me to wait.'

Her aunt closed her eyes with relief and led the way to the drawing room, where her guests were waiting.

'Well, this is going to be awkward,' Henry grinned and put out his arm for her to take hold of. It would be awkward for all of them, but best to face the difficulties that lay ahead rather than avoid them.

11

The front bedroom at Park Street was hot, cooled only by the breeze through the open window. Alec Hardy gently pulled out a drawer to find a clean shirt, not wanting to wake Letty. Stella had woken in the early hours and climbed into bed beside them. It had taken all his willpower to draw back the sheets and leave them, but he needed to get down to the docks and get back to work.

Letty made a small noise and he twisted to look at her. She gave him a sleepy smile, rubbed her hand over Stella's downy head, then moved to sit up. The child mumbled but did not stir.

Alec slipped on his grey shirt, sat on the bed while he buttoned it, and Letty ran her hand over his back.

'Where are you going?'

He leaned across and kissed her, not wanting to tell her that he'd made up his mind. These last few days had been the longest time they'd spent together since they were wed and, as much as he loved her, a man had to be doing. Letty ran the house and had made it home while he was away earning. Most of the women did the same, the good ones, keeping it all going. He had to bring the big money in, had to feel he was contributing, not sitting on his arse doing nowt useful.

'There were rumours last night,' he told her. 'I want to find out for meself if they're right. The owners are trying to negotiate with the admiralty to get the fleet back to work. Admiralty rules – they can fish, but only by day, and they have to keep sight of land. It means things will start moving, but when they do, there'll not be enough work for all of us. No deep-water fishing.'

She felt for his hand, and he squeezed it tightly.

'While I'm here, we've no money coming in to speak of and we haven't got savings to burn. Not when we've all worked so hard these past two years. And I'll not touch the money set aside for a trawler.' He had a good bit put by from the sale of the *Stella*, and more he'd earned since. But that was for the future, when this ruddy game was done and dusted. 'I'll be at sea, Let, whatever way I choose, and I'll do more good in the trawler section of the RNR. I can't wait to be called up. I'm better giving my place on a trawler to men too old to fight. People like Puggy and Tosh. They'll keep the fishing going until it's time for me to take me chance again – and I'll do me bit keeping the seas safe fer 'em to fish in.' He kissed her cheek.

He could secure a position as warrant officer – the navy's term for skipper – for, thankfully, he'd met the minimum requirements, being the age of twenty-five and two years as skipper. He knew she wouldn't plead for him to stay, that wasn't the lass's way. She would take what came and make the best of it. He'd never had to fret about her like some men did, who never knew what their missus was getting up to while they were away earning a crust.

She reached up and fastened the studs of his collar. Her silence unnerved him; she normally had so much to say for herself.

'Aren't you going to say somats?'

'What *is* there to say? Every woman in the country feels as I do,

I shouldn't wonder. They don't want their sons or husbands or brothers to fight. We're all going to have to make difficult choices and sacrifices, aren't we?'

She eased herself away from Stella, her nightie about her bare legs, and he pulled her close.

'I'll get called to go in the end. Might as well get meself front of the queue.'

She smiled, but her eyes brimmed with tears she would not shed, not while he was around, he knew that. But he understood her fear.

His mother would take the news less well. She had already lost a husband and a son. But he had to fight for what was right. They all did.

Dorcas was already up when the two of them went down into the kitchen. Alec watched her while she moved around, filling the kettle and putting it on the stove, the old pine table sprinkled with flour where she kneaded the dough, the blackened loaf tins already greased. She'd had those tins years; they had given them bread since he was a boy and it surprised him how many memories they aroused. It might be his mother, and now his wife, a different kitchen, a different town, but some things were constant and as such gave comfort.

He pulled at the dough, tore a bit off, and his mother slapped his arm.

'You'll get belly ache.'

'No doubt I will, Mam, but t'will be worth it.'

She smiled indulgently, and it hurt his heart to think he would not know when he would see her face again.

He squeezed her shoulder and kissed her grey head. He was glad to be leaving them here, and not at the mucky old hole at Mariners Row that Mam and Let had made homely while they had lived there – but it was a worry all the same.

Letty pulled her apron from the hook on the back of the pantry door and wrapped it around her. 'I'll see if there are eggs,' she said and went into the yard.

Dorcas put the dough into a large bowl and covered it with a cloth as he'd seen her do a hundred times before. Sometimes bread was all they'd had to eat when his father died – bread, and the fish he'd caught while on the boat with his uncle. It seemed such a long time ago. He was a man now, had his own family to care for and, God willing, he'd be spared to do it.

Letty came in from the yard, her hand to her apron, the sunlight catching her brown hair, giving her a halo. The lass deserved one, for she had put up with his mother when he had taken her away from her own – and his mother was not an easy person to live with, he knew that. At the table, she peeled away the cloth and placed five eggs in a small bowl. 'One for each of us. They are good girls.'

He grinned. 'The way you talk to 'em sometimes, I think you're chatting to lass over yon wall.'

'Daft as a brush,' Dorcas said, but not unkindly.

Letty was past taking offence. They had their ways and she had hers, and somehow they managed to brush along beside each other, more for Letty's tolerance than his mother's.

'They understand a kind word and manner,' Letty told them. 'Why would they lay eggs for me if I went out cursing and screaming. Hens are the same as people. They recognise a kind heart.'

He sat down at the table, cocked his head and listened. 'Aye, aye, looks like I'll not get me breakfast in peace now.' The tread of small feet could be heard on the bare wood of the stairs and Alfie came in, clutching Stella's hand. 'Now then, boy Alfie, ready for your breakfast? And your sister too, no wonder.' He drew his girl onto his lap and kissed her small head, her skin smelling of sleep, of her mother to whom she had lain so close.

'Are you down dock again today?' his mother asked as she slid a plate in front of him.

He looked to Letty, who shrugged. Best to get it over with. His mother would not be happy, no matter when he told her.

'I am, Mother.' He coughed a little, wanting the words to come out clear. 'I'll be signing on for the RNR.'

Dorcas paused. 'I thought you might. I'd hoped you'd be home a while longer but...' She let out a long sigh, wiped her hand on her pinny and turned to get dishes for the children, for herself and Letty.

Hope, it was a powerful thing. Hope for a fair sailing, hope for a good catch, hope for a safe passage home.

When she looked up, he smiled at her, and she somehow found the strength to return it. He knew it was hard on all of them, but especially his mother. She had no family to go back to, only the one Letty and he had made together.

'Alfie, lad, you'll be the man o' the house and look after Nanny Dorcas and Mrs Letty now, won't you?' He looked to his daughter. 'And our bonny girl, Stella.' He tickled her tummy and she giggled cheerfully, making them all smile. Ah, the power of a child to soften life's hardest blows. God willing, they would be blessed with more.

Alec took his time at the table with them, and closed his eyes for a moment or two, listening to the children's chatter, the gentle chiding of Letty, and his mother's clucking. She was like a hen too, a carpy old hen that Letty had won over with her kind words and deeds.

Dorcas scooted the children upstairs to get dressed and Letty got up, scraped the crumbs onto the top plate and took them out into the garden. Alec followed her outside. His mother's empty braiding pole was fixed across the scullery window. On fine days, she would sit out there with her rope and expertly weave the nets and cod ends that would be collected at the end of the week. He had wanted her to stop doing it, there was no need when they were doing so well, he and Letty, but she would not hear of it – and now he was glad of it. It paid a pittance, but it had kept many a wolf from their door when his father was lost at sea. But, more than that, he understood why she hung on to it, holding on to the old ways, old memories that were of comfort. Like the bread tins, and the photographs on the mantel.

At the bottom of the yard, Letty was in the coop giving the scrapings to the hens, who pecked the earth about her feet.

'We're not there yet.'

She frowned and he stood beside her, putting his arm about her shoulder. Beyond the gate was an alleyway, and beyond that the short backyards of another terrace of houses. It was a small patch, but she had made good use of it, digging the soil and planting seeds. She was a smart lass, not just in businesses, but in the way she ran the home – and all the while letting Dorcas think she ruled the roost.

'Your farm,' he explained, 'or your smallholding. I promised you'd have your land one day, Let. We're not there yet, but we're getting closer.'

She slipped her arm about his waist and laid her head against his shoulder. He wanted to protect her, save her from any heartache – but to protect he had to fight.

'One step at a time,' she said. 'We'll get there by and by.'

He kissed the top of her head, warmed now by the sun, and wanted to linger there but knew he had to leave. He released her.

'I doubt I'll go today, but I can't promise 'owt. If I do come back, we'll tek the kiddies to the park over the way.'

She nodded. Wiped at his chin. 'Egg.' She smiled, though her eyes glittered with tears, and he pulled her close once again.

'I'll be back. Don't you worry about that.' He felt her head move in agreement, but the two of them knew it was only words to comfort.

'I wanted to talk to you about Alfie.'

He released her, still holding on to her hand.

'He can't go on calling us Mr Alec and Mrs Letty,' she said. 'Not when you tell him Stella's his sister. He's confused.'

'Aye.' He tried to bite back his smile, knowing what she was going to ask but letting her ask anyway. 'And what were yer thinking?'

'That we adopt him and announce it as such in the newspaper. That he can call us Mam and Dad, as Stella does. If he so wishes. He's called me Mam a couple of times, then come over all embarrassed. He remembers his mother, but if we explain things to him...?'

He nodded, taking his time so she knew he had thought it over. And he had, so many times. The poor lad had been rejected by his own flesh and blood. 'You don't think the Lewises would object.'

It got her fire up, as he had known it would. 'What? When they'd wanted me to take him to the workhouse. His own grandparents.' She opened the panel to the coop and let them both out.

He took her arm and pulled her to him, smiling at her, kissing her nose. 'I love the lad as if he were my own flesh and blood. You do what's necessary. That's fine by me.'

'And you'll tell your mother?'

So, she was still worried about his mother's approval?

He held on to her. 'It's our family, Let, yours and mine. It's what we choose to do.'

She didn't look convinced.

He took hold of her hand. 'We'll tell her together. She'll as like make a song and dance about it, but that's her way. She wouldn't know what to do with herself if she didn't have nowt to complain about.' He grinned at her. 'Best get it over and done with, then she'll have all day to burn herself out.'

* * *

In the end, Letty was surprised. Dorcas didn't make the fuss she had expected, and she wondered whether Alec had talked it over with her beforehand, or whether, as she suspected, Dorcas had grown to love the boy too, in her own mysterious way.

'I'd always thought it foolish, to tell the truth. He calls me Nanny Dorcas and Stella his sister and you two daft 'app'orths Mr Alec and Mrs Letty. I don't know what the pair of you were thinking.' She threw her hands in the air. 'But far be it for me to interfere.'

Letty hadn't known whether to laugh or cry as she looked to Alec, his lips beginning to twitch, his eyes to crease, and in the end the two of them burst into laughter.

Huffing and puffing at the pair of them, Dorcas turned away and stepped into the pantry where they heard her muttering away to herself.

'Best we go and tell the lad,' Alec said, his eyes full of warmth.

'Hadn't we better wait till I write to the Lewises?'

He shook his head. 'You know what their answer will be, Let. They don't deserve consideration. Get that advert put in the paper today.' He walked into the hall and leant on the banister. 'Alfie,' he called upstairs. 'Come down, lad. Me and Mrs Letty have got some news.'

12

For almost the entire length of Cleethorpe Road, men stood and waited, for want of something better to do. They sat on walls and leant against railings, and if Alec had stopped to talk to them, he'd have never made it more than a few yards. As it was, he knocked for Puggy, his third hand, and the two of them moved at a quicker pace as they chatted, merely giving a nod of the head or a small lift of the hand in acknowledgement to those they passed.

'They couldn't make the pressure valve go up any higher if they tried, Puggy old mate. Waiting like this is like shovelling more coal on the devil's furnace.' His companion was thickset and thick-necked, and he tugged at the kerchief about his neck to loosen it as they walked.

'Well, if they don't let us fish, I'm all for fighting.'

'Someone's got to fish, Puggy or we'll all starve.'

He shook his head. 'I can't believe they won't let me. Forty-three I am, and still got plenty of strength.' He flexed his arm to illustrate his point. 'What's to be done but just letting the trawl go and hauling 'em now and again – and no fish in 'em. They'll take no effort at all. I've been doing it man and boy.'

Alec sympathised. The cut-off age of forty for the RNR was ridiculous, for many a man in his sixties still skippered the trawlers. They were tough men, used to being awake hours on end with little or no sleep when they were on the fish.

He slapped him on the back. 'We've all got our roles to play in this. Happen they'll change their minds in a week or two.'

Puggy grunted his response. No one had any idea of what would happen, or when, and as the days dragged, gossip was rife.

Alec tried to ignore the whispers and concentrate on facts.

'Any news of what's happened to the *Juniper* or the *Alice Grey*?' Puggy asked. They were Hammond trawlers and, as skipper, Puggy probably thought Alec would be more likely to have firm information.

'Both taken for minesweepers. They can't convert 'em fast enough, sending 'em all over the ruddy country to get 'em sorted.'

'Aye, Doig's shipyard is taking on extra men at a rate,' Puggy told him. 'If I'm pushed fer work, I can try that, though what I'll be good fer, I dunno. I'd rather be on the fish.'

He recognised Puggy's restlessness. Alec never knew what to do with himself when on land for a more than a few days; his mind and body unable to settle. He knew nothing else but the sea. For some, it was to make a living, but it was more than that for him. He relished the challenge, and pitting his wits against the elements made a man feel fully alive. He made for Hammond's offices, but when he saw the crowd outside and the door closed knew it was pointless to hang about.

'Come on, Puggy. I'll stand you a brew at Solly's café.'

* * *

Skipper Harris and his boy, Ben, were seated at a table by the window and called him over. Alec ordered two mugs of tea at the counter and pulled out a chair next to Puggy. Alec had sailed with them when he first came to Grimsby, and when the skipper had got a new ship, he'd put in a word for him with the Hammond gaffers. Not long after he'd got his skipper's ticket, Alec took command of the *Black Prince*. The certificate of competency was in his breast pocket now. He carried it always, as the other men did, ready for the off.

'Glad you never took out a loan for a ship now, Hardy?' Skipper Harris asked.

'Aye. It would be burning money while it sat in the dock waiting for the buggers to make up their minds. I wouldn't have had the money for that.' He'd been narked when Letty had urged him to hold back as rumours of war escalated, but thank God he'd listened to her or he might have lost everything. 'Bet the trawler owners won't get compensation for that.'

A man behind them at the next table leaned back and interrupted, 'Never mind trawler owners in their big houses and their fat bank balances. What about us daft beggars who only just get by on what they pay us.'

'Pay yer plenty that you can stand a pint or three at the Albion,' Alec countered. 'What you've put over that bar would have bought shares in a trawler.'

The man was a shirker, and Alec wouldn't have had him in any of his crews. Word soon got round who was worth having on board and who wasn't – and the café was always the best place to find out the details.

They chatted for a while, Ben busily sketching on a flyer he'd pulled from the noticeboard behind him. The lad was never without a pencil or a scrap o' paper and drew what was about him – people, ships, ropes, and any other small detail his eye alighted on.

Alec drained his mug, slapped Puggy on the back. 'I'll be away to the dock office.'

'Yer fer the reserve?' Harris asked.

Alec nodded. 'Bugger all this fer a lark.'

'I'll come with you,' Puggy insisted, getting to his feet. 'If I kick up, they might take me on.'

Alec laughed. 'Only if you need the walk.' He slapped Puggy's belly. 'Need to get a few of them pounds off you, you'll never git in a uniform.'

* * *

At the dock office, they waited in line while the clerks took details. It was a slow process and Alec and Puggy yarned to the men in front and behind. He recognised many of them, even though he might not know them by name.

'Isn't that the Evans lad over there – young Henry?'

Puggy looked over to where Alec had directed. 'Aye. I wonder what he's about.'

'Probably on some errand for his father,' someone behind them butted in.

Alec doubted it. Word had got about what a lad he was, that he didn't set himself apart and expect to be treated different. He admired that, for many an owner's son had thrown their weight about. They had a bit of posh schooling and thought they were a cut above, but from what he'd heard, the lad didn't duck the tough stuff.

'His father should be proud of him,' Alec replied. They had come in to dock on the same day, he remembered that.

'I doubt it.'

Alec frowned and Puggy explained.

'His father ain't one fer goin' backwards. Young Evans there, his grandmother had a market stall for years. All her money went on her kids. Got 'em schooled and pushed 'em hard. Yer know his sister is married to old Frampton, who owns newspaper.'

'Aye, and a lot else,' someone piped up. 'Trawlers, chandlers, a finger in every pie. That's why he's so fat.'

There was a burst of laughter, but Alec didn't join in.

'Good luck to the lad. At least he's willing to do the graft.' Alec watched him. The lad was talking to someone with stripes and shiny buttons.

'Probably don't have to queue like us mere mortals,' someone commented.

'He's here, isn't he?' Alec said, putting an end to the conversation. 'And that's what matters.'

13

Ruth's birthday dinner at Saxon Hall had been endured but not enjoyed by those gathered about the table. Nothing untoward was said, by Arthur or his parents, no one would be that bad-mannered. It might have been more enjoyable if someone had been, enabling them to clear the air – and the misunderstanding. As it was, her aunt had fought valiantly to recover the situation, repeatedly stating how wonderful it was that they had all come together for Ruth's birthday. They had toasted her good health and Henry had stood to toast Charles, who had left with his company that morning, for other than his own immediate family, everyone else seemed to have forgotten. Ruth couldn't have been more proud of him, and by the expression on her father's face, he was of the same mind. For his part, Arthur had been charming enough on the surface, though Ruth was still smarting at the fact that he had exaggerated the situation into something more than it was. But as she had watched him converse with her Uncle Jack she had known she had been right to wait. She hadn't been brave enough to give him an outright no that afternoon, but if he asked again, she knew she would not accept.

The following morning, a letter arrived for Henry giving details of where he was to present himself for training. He was to attend the local office of the Naval Reserves with his kitbag and his paperwork for onward departure the following day.

'So soon,' Ruth said when she told him. 'How did Father take it?'

'He is resigned to it now. I think Arthur's behaviour – and Aunt Helen's – far outdid anything I could do.' He flopped onto the sofa and the cushions sighed. 'It seems good can come from bad after all.' He grinned at her. 'You did well last night, Ruthie. It can't have been easy, especially as Arthur had exaggerated the details. The rat.'

She didn't disagree. 'I could bear it because I knew I could leave at any time, that you and Father would have left with me. It meant everything.'

'Father would have pounced on Arthur if he'd have said even one wrong word.'

It was not an exaggeration. 'He was annoyed with Aunt Helen, wasn't he? That she hadn't informed him of her intentions.'

'*Intentions*. You were ambushed, good and proper.'

The doorbell ringing interrupted them, and Henry paused, the two of them listening out for who it might be.

'Aunt Helen,' Henry mouthed, getting up from the sofa and pulling at his trouser legs to smarten them.

She did not come in directly, but they heard Mrs Murray go and fetch their father, heard him go to the hall.

Henry leaned against the door, trying to make out what was being said. 'I can't quite grasp what they're talking about,' he whispered to Ruth as she came beside him.

'We both know what it's likely to be.'

Her father raised his voice to its normal volume and the two of them rushed back to their seats and carried on where they had left off, seconds before their father and aunt joined them.

Henry got up immediately. 'Aunt Helen. How lovely to see you. And we get to thank you personally for such a wonderful birthday dinner. Don't we, Ruth?'

Ruth made to get up, but her father motioned with his hand for her to remain seated.

'I'll have none of your facetiousness, Henry. I've come here to talk to Ruth.' She peered down her long nose at her niece.

Ruth did not flinch as she might have done a few days ago. Having her father and brother's support gave her strength that had previously eluded her.

Aunt Helen looked to Henry and Richard. It was evident she expected them to leave, but her father held out his hand for his sister to take a seat, and when she did, he sat down, as did Henry.

'I've come to see if I can smooth things over.'

'To apologise, surely,' her father countered.

Her aunt bristled with indignation and sat straight-backed on the edge of the sofa. 'Richard, I have already apologised for not including you in my plans, but, to be fair, you have always left things to me and...' She took a slight pause. 'I know how pressed you are at the moment – but then we all are. Jack had three more trawlers requisitioned this morning.'

'I should imagine the newspaper circulation is up, though, Aunt Helen, so that will be of some compensation,' Henry replied.

Aunt Helen swivelled her head to glare at him and he retaliated with a disarming smile. For once, her father did not step in to caution him and Ruth could only chew at the inside of her cheek.

Her aunt turned back to her brother. 'I thought I was being of assistance. And I thought Ruth,' she directed her words to her niece, 'would have appreciated the double celebration.'

'You thought wrongly,' Ruth informed her. 'As did Arthur.'

'Well,' her aunt was uppity, 'you've been stepping out with Arthur for so long – what is it, two years, three? Why would it cross his mind that you would refuse him.'

Ruth spoke through gritted teeth. 'I. Didn't. Refuse. Him. I asked him to wait. I was upset with Charles leaving. If it hadn't been for Father and Henry making an effort, I would not have marked the day at all. He didn't understand, and it seems, neither do you.'

Her aunt got up. 'Now look here, young lady—'

'Sit down, Helen, for heaven's sake, and listen to her.' Her father waved his hand up and down. 'Don't you understand, her brother's leaving was not cause for celebration. Neither was it for me.'

Helen sank back onto the chair. No doubt she had expected her brother's full support and it not being forthcoming had unsettled her. 'I was thinking of you, Ruth, of securing your future. You know what it means to the family, to have Marshalls in our camp.'

It was her father's turn to interrupt. 'That's quite enough, Helen.'

'It's all right, Father,' Ruth said, quietly. 'I know Aunt Helen's intentions are genuine. But it is Arthur who has made a drama out of all this, not me. I explained the position, but he did not listen.' And neither had her aunt. 'If he didn't think of my feelings yesterday, and only of his own hurt pride, then what kind of future would that be?'

Her aunt was about to reply, but her father got up. 'Now is not the time nor the place, Helen. Ruth is still feeling raw from yesterday. As are we all.' He picked up Henry's instructions from the mantel. 'And now we have Henry leaving us in the morning.'

She pursed her lips but did not argue and got to her feet. 'I believe Arthur intends to ask again. I will speak with him.'

'I'd rather you didn't,' Ruth told her. 'If he wants to apologise, he must be a man and do it of his own volition.'

Her father showed his sister to the door.

'Good for you, Ruthie,' Henry encouraged. 'Stick to your guns. It was bad form of Arthur, through and through. The ball's in his court.' He took hold of her hand, and she felt his strength flow into her. Would she still be strong when he left in the morning?

* * *

At eight o'clock, Henry's bags were set by the door and Ruth waited for him in the large entrance hall. He'd insisted that his father and sister didn't come to wave him off, wanting their goodbyes to be here. It all felt rather hurried, like enough thought hadn't gone into it; but there was little time for thought these days. The British Expeditionary Force was already in France and the losses were beginning to be reported. Trawlers had not returned, entire crews lost, and no one knew if they had been taken prisoner or, worse still, drowned. People had been stranded in Europe, desperate to get home, and boats had been chartered to rescue as many as was possible. Ruth daren't even imagine how frightened they must be. She daren't imagine too much at all, for her thoughts were liable to run into the darkness and poke about there, dislodging the many demons that she had kept at bay.

Henry came swaggering down the stairs, his hair flopping forward. He brushed it back with his hand and pulled on his cap. 'Reckon I'll be the best-looking bloke on the ship, don't you, Ruthie?'

She forced herself to smile. For all his bravado, she worried more for him than she did for Charles, who she knew would not take silly risks. 'You'll look smart. If you put your collar right.' She flicked her hand to make him turn his back to her and she straightened it, picked a stray hair from his jacket.

When he turned, grinning at her, she could not smile back. She felt to warn him, as she had done countless times, not to get into any trouble, but knew it was a wasted effort. More than once, she had sneaked him upstairs and bathed a bloodied nose or lip, smelling the ale on his breath. She had wondered whether her father had known of it and had chosen to turn a blind eye, putting it down to boyhood exuberance. Henry would not be so lucky in the Navy, and she thought now that the rigours of life at sea, with rules and discipline, might be the making of him.

He opened the door and picked up his bag. The chauffeur came forward and took it from him, placed it in on the luggage rack at the rear, and Ruth went to fetch their father from his study. She discovered him sat back in his leather chair, his hands a steeple and resting under his chin, his eyes closed. His desk was heavy with papers and buff folders that never seemed to diminish; he didn't appear to have touched them for days.

'Father,' she said gently.

He opened his eyes, stared blankly at her.

'Henry is leaving.'

He got up and made his way to the door, and she followed him back into the hall.

Mrs Murray had joined them and handed Henry a tin. She tapped the lid as he took it from her. 'For the onward journey.'

He eased the lid and his eyes creased with delight as he inhaled the fruit cake. 'I doubt very much it will last long. It smells delicious. Thank you, Mrs Murray.' The housekeeper had always had a soft spot for Henry, who'd often found sanctuary in the kitchen when he was in trouble with their father. She treated them all kindly, but Henry was her favourite.

Ruth took the tin and added it to his kitbag.

'Father.' Henry held out his hand and their father grasped it with both of his. The business with Arthur Marshall had brought them closer, uniting them against her aunt's interfering, Arthur's thoughtlessness.

Ruth watched them, awkward and restrained, and felt this was when they most needed their mother, for she was sure she would have embraced him, made her father do the same, building bridges that Ruth had never been able to construct, much as she'd tried. They were used to holding back and this occasion was no different to many others, when the boys had gone off to school, Father shaking hands with the boys and telling them to work hard and do well.

She thought again of the women on the wharf, of how easily they had embraced their men, how arms had gone about shoulders in comfort. Once, she had been like that, all of them had, when Mother was alive. The Evans children had been affectionate, with each other, and with their father. As she'd got older, her aunt had cautioned her to have restraint, that such outward display was unseemly, and Ruth was suddenly filled with fury at her, for changing the way their mother had done things in her home – and with her father, for allowing her to. Things would have to change, and now that her aunt had overstepped the mark, Ruth had an idea that they could return to their own way of doing things.

Henry came to her and kissed her cheek, held on to her hand, and she felt as if her insides were crumbling as he pulled away. She must not cry, must not. He took one last look about the hall, lingering on their mother's portrait for a time, then walked away from them.

A shadow of foreboding made her shudder. 'Henry!' she called out, rushing towards him. He stopped, and came back to her, and she threw her arms about him, relieved to feel his arms tight about her. How she had missed his hugs, her father's familiar warm embrace. The years had set them apart, not drawn them together, and Ruth was overcome with sadness.

He whispered in her ear, 'Live your own life, Ruthie. Make me proud... but most of all... be happy.' He released her and kissed her cheek, walked back to the car and got in.

As the Wolseley drove off, Henry turned briefly, waving through the small rear window, and she left her father and ran down towards the gate and out onto the pavement, watching until the car became smaller and moved out of sight.

Her father was still in the hall when she returned, staring up at the portrait of his beloved wife. Had he been thinking the same as Ruth? He did not move when she came to stand beside him, and she slipped her hand in his and was rewarded with a tight squeeze. It was a small comfort, the best he could offer, the best she could, for she dare not speak, lest the tears fall.

Mrs Murray came out to them, rubbing at her nose with a handkerchief, unable to disguise the redness about her eyes. 'Would you like coffee, Mr Evans?' she asked.

When he did not reply, Ruth answered for him and asked for it to be taken into the drawing room. He sat down and she opened the French windows onto the garden and let the scent of late summer waft over them. The leaves on the horse chestnut had begun to turn gold and the lawn was still brown in patches from too much sun, but the birds still sang and the bees still buzzed lazily about the roses and hydrangeas.

Mrs Murray placed the tray on the low table, poured the coffee and handed them to father and daughter, then left the room, pulling the door to behind her.

'Well, what a week.' Her father sipped at his cup, eased back into his chair.

Behind them, the grandfather clock kept its steady rhythm and listening to it helped Ruth steady herself, stopped her thoughts from galloping.

Her father gazed into the middle distance. 'If your aunt

smoothed the way and Arthur asked again...' Another sip, a swallow, a pause. 'Would you accept him?'

She detected no anger in his tone, and at first she hesitated. But hadn't Henry told her to live her own life. She thought again of Lieutenant Proctor. Of the women on the wharf who had collapsed in grief. These last few days had been turmoil – first happiness, then relief that Henry had come safely home; her sadness at waving Charles away, and Henry; the tension around the dinner table last night. Was this her opportunity to do something different? It hadn't been the right time for Arthur to propose – but she knew there never would be a right time. She thought of Colin Wilson and the mission. To live her own life... was it within the realms of possibility? Her father looked to her. 'I don't know.'

He smiled; his eyes full of warmth. 'Your mother was my entire world, you know. I loved her very much.' The pain of losing her still hurt him, after all these years, and although he had been encouraged by Aunt Helen to remarry, he had not pursued anyone – though a man of his wealth and status could take his pick. Was he offering her a way out?

'I want to be someone's entire world too, Father. But I also want them to be mine. I don't think Arthur Marshall is that man.'

He nodded, sipped again at his coffee, then placed it on the table, sat back and closed his eyes. 'I don't think he is either.'

14

As Alec had thought, the *Black Prince* had been requisitioned and two days after he registered at the docks he received his instructions to take ship and crew down to Lowestoft to be fitted out as a minesweeper. When he left, Letty had no idea how long it would be before she saw him again. At least when he was fishing, she knew more or less when he would return, but this was different and she tried to comfort herself with the fact that she was not alone, that so many women would be saying goodbye to their menfolk. Her way of coping was to keep busy, but with little trade and the shop takings down, she needed to think of other ways to generate income.

She'd not heard anything from the admiralty about Parkers being on the approved list of suppliers, but she was hopeful. Alice Wiltshire, on hearing of Letty's appalling treatment at the admiralty offices, had promised to contact her sister-in-law to see if she could have a quiet word in the appropriate ear. It had helped that Letty was known to Helen Frampton, for she supported her work at the mission and was part of the Ladies Guild. It was a question of waiting, and as far as she was concerned, no news was good news. Alec would be paid by the admiralty, but it would take time for it to come through and she couldn't rely on Parkers' income alone. Milly had been put on short hours and they'd trimmed things down to the bone. It would do for the short term, but Letty was thinking further ahead. This war could go on for months and if it did, it wouldn't be long before the bills piled up, and worse, they might not be able to afford the rent. She'd had half an idea ticking over in her brain, expanding on it in the early hours while she lay awake, trying not to fret over Alec.

Leaving the children with Dorcas, who was only too glad to have something to occupy her, she made her way to Parkers. Norah was dusting the counter, making sure everything was in place before they opened that morning and Letty leant on it before her.

'Can we gain access to next door?'

Norah was puzzled. 'Websters?'

'Yes. I want to have a look about the place. I have an idea for it.'

Norah grinned. 'You do surprise me.' She tucked the duster under the counter.

'I'd like to get in there today, before someone else snaps it up.'

'Who, Letty? No one will take it with things as they are.'

'Which is exactly why we must. We'll get it at a good price if we strike now.' She'd already worked out what a fair rent might be for the place. It had been neglected this last year or so, but it wouldn't take long to smarten up, and she could do it gradually, as she had done with Parkers. It had worked once and there was no reason she couldn't make a success of an additional business. 'Do you know where Mr Webster lives?'

'Somewhere off Railway Street, I believe,' Norah mused. 'Wolfie will be along soon enough, he'll know. What will you do with it?'

'I was thinking of turning it into a small café. For breakfasts and the like. The men are always in here, under our feet, talking of the football and anything else they can find to argue the toss about. We can do hot drinks and soup, mebee a stew one day. It doesn't matter what we do with it, Norah. The war won't last forever, all we have to do is survive, then we can expand the premises.'

'Whatever for, lass?'

'For the future, for us, for my children.' She had never wanted any sons to go to sea and she was doing her damnedest to put things into place, so they didn't have to. They would get an education, they would have choices that Alec hadn't had, and although he might protest, might dream of his own ship and his son beside him, as he and his father had been, she didn't want that to be the be-all and end-all. She tried to explain it to Norah.

'And what else, lass?' Norah said kindly, knowing that it wasn't the entire reason.

Letty looked at her. 'Because... because I need to do something. Anything. I have to keep busy. I can't bear to think, Norah. My mind gets too knotty with Alec and...' She leant back against the counter, feeling her eyes begin to fill with tears, and she wouldn't look up until she had blinked them away. She didn't want Norah to know how frightened she was, how worried for them all. They couldn't easily turn Parkers' present premises into a cafe, but she knew she could do something next door without going to too much expense. It would take little work to get it up and running and she'd still be able to keep an eye on them both, for although Percy was much recovered, he was still frail, and caring for him had impacted Norah's health. The elderly couple had got through the bad times before, but they were not as strong, or as young, as they used to be.

Norah took her by the shoulders, gently but firmly, and when Letty wiped away the one unruly tear, she swallowed down her misery and looked up with a wobbly smile.

'Now then, Letty Hardy. Don't you go thinking like that. Let's wait for Wolfie, *then* we'll get the key. There's no harm in looking.'

Norah had not told her she was being silly, or reassured her that nothing would happen to Alec, she knew better than to offer Letty false promises.

Wolfie arrived, then went off to fetch the key for Websters. He let them in through the back door and waited while Norah and Letty looked about it. It was narrower than Parkers, but she could see where she could make it work and how it could be adapted. She would use the back room as a kitchen, upstairs as a storeroom – although if it was successful, she could put tables up there too.

The two women went back to join Wolfie.

'Would Mr Webster rent it to us, Wolfie?' Letty asked.

'I din't ask, just said I wanted the key and he gev it me. I thought you'd mebbe need to see it first. Din't want t' put me foot in it.'

Letty looked to Norah, who smiled encouragingly.

'Only one way to find out.'

* * *

Mr Webster lived in a run-down two-up two-down that backed onto the railway sidings and hadn't seen a lick of paint for years. His wife had died some years back and he had neglected the house to keep the business going – but he could do it no longer. The man was stooped over so badly that he had to tilt his head to look up at Letty.

'I came to return your key.' She placed it into his grubby palm. He stared at it, then squinted at her. 'Wolfie Turner borrowed it on my behalf.'

He nodded, and invited her in – though she'd rather have stayed outside and warmed herself in the sunshine.

The house was cold and damp, little light coming in from the street, for the window had been mostly blocked by planks that had been propped against it. Numerous periodicals and old newspapers were piled high about the room, and here and there were wooden crates full of old tools, bits and pieces of clocks. A delivery boy's bicycle was laid against a beautiful grandfather clock and on the oak table sat a tin bath, full of empty bottles.

Mr Webster had a hacking cough and rubbed at his mouth with a grubby handkerchief that can't have helped matters. His son had died suddenly, not long after Letty had come to work at Parkers. He had two married daughters; one lived in North Shields, the other in Hull.

Letty took care where she stood, fearing one wrong step would send the whole lot tumbling about her. He brushed at a pile of books and a cloud of dust erupted about him, forcing him to another bout of coughing. When he at last caught his breath, Letty smiled at him, eager to get her business over and done with and get out into the fresh air.

'I came to ask what your plans are for your shop?'

He squinted at her.

'Next door to Parkers'.'

He frowned, then bobbed his head. 'You his wife then?'

Letty didn't understand.

'Mrs Crowe?'

Letty went cold. Gilbert Crowe had got here first. No wonder he had been smirking at her more than usual the other day.

'My name is Letty Hardy, I work with the Parkers.' She had met Webster only a handful of times and it was understandable that he wouldn't remember her, but his response had thrown her. 'I didn't realise Mr Crowe had already spoken with you.'

'Spoken, aye, and bought the shop. My girls will have the

money by the end of the week, so he says. It's not much, but at least I can leave 'em summats when I'm gorn.' He gave a small laugh. 'Which won't be long now.' He looked up at her, his eyes rheumy and clouded, and started another bout of horrendous coughing and wheezing. He was a pitiful creature, but here and there she could see the small touches that this had once been a lovely home – a framed needlework sampler, photographs in mahogany frames, which she took to be his wife and children. 'There's not a problem is there,' he queried. 'Only I was counting on the money being in the bank be Friday.'

'No, not a problem, Mr Webster.' She tried to hide the disappointment in her voice, but it was such a blow. She had been so certain of getting the building that she hadn't had the slightest thought that anyone else could have been interested. She had underestimated Gilbert Crowe. She wouldn't make the same mistake again.

Webster leaned closer, peering at her, and she caught the full force of his sour breath, tried not to show her discomfort.

'Did he say what he was going to do with it?'

'Storage, he said. I'n't going to bother with getting it up and running again. Well, he wouldn't have the skills, would he? He only knows baccy and fags. Aye, storage.' He flicked his hand at her. 'You're the lass what did Parkers' winder, made a display, like. I 'member that. Yer did a grand job, aye, yer did that. Coulda done with a lass like you to help me. My lasses went off with their menfolk. When my boy died, there din't seem no point going on with it. Crowe came along at the right time. Got it for a song mind, but it was cash I needed and cash I got.'

At least he would see his daughters right before he died. It was a blow to her, but not for him. She couldn't resent that, even though she loathed that it was Gilbert Crowe who had thwarted her plans. 'I'm so sorry to have bothered you, Mr Webster, but thank you for giving me your time.'

He saw her to the door. 'Give me regards to Norah and Percy, won't yer.'

She said that she would and, sick at heart, made her way back to Parkers. She couldn't have bought the shop, but she might have leased it. Still, that Crowe had bought it filled her with unease. Now they were sat squat in the middle of him. And what on earth did he want to store? Surely there was enough room in his own shop for whatever he needed.

* * *

When Letty returned, Norah could tell something was dreadfully wrong. 'What on earth's the matter, lass.' Her temper was up, there was no doubt about that, and instead of the fear taking hold, it was clear that anger had won.

Letty slapped her bag on the table and folded her arms across her chest. 'I'd like to wring the bugger's neck.'

'Letty!' It wasn't like the lass to use bad language. Norah pulled out a chair and indicated for Letty to sit upon it, and after a few seconds of glaring at it, she did.

'I'm sorry, Norah.' She let out a long sigh, her voice shaking with her anger, her fists clenched. 'He's trying to squeeze us out. I know exactly what *he's* up to.'

'Who, lass? Who's trying to squeeze us out? Surely not Mr Webster?'

Letty shook her head. 'Gilbert ruddy Crowe, that's who.'

She told Norah of her conversation with Webster. Norah gripped the back of the chair. She might have known he'd be ahead of the game, and it upset her to see Letty so distraught. There had been plenty of opportunity to take on Websters. The old man had often threatened to give it all up when his wife died, but it hadn't crossed her mind. They could barely keep their own shop going, let alone think of taking on any other commitments before Letty came along.

'I never thought to ask.' Norah pulled the chair out and sat down. 'Oh, Letty.' The lass was so downhearted. 'Perhaps it's just as well. You've got enough on your plate as it is.'

Letty put her elbows on the table and drew her hands through her hair. 'But I could have made it work. I could have brought a little more our way to see us through. I don't know how many times I've walked in here and found it full of blokes talking to Percy. I thought we could knock through, put a door that linked both premises – and they could have done all their talking in there.' She gave Norah a rueful smile. 'Might as well make a bob or two instead of giving tea away for free.'

Norah pressed her hand to her knee and got up.

'You'll have other ideas.' That Letty would wasn't in question, but it would be harder to make things work so easily. She could see the girl's thinking.

'What I'd like to know is where a man like Crowe got the money to buy the shop? Cash Mr Webster said. Cash!'

Norah had thought the same thing. 'It would be a mortgage. I doubt it's all cash.'

'Maybe so,' Letty replied. 'But if he has got the money, I'd be surprised if he came by it by any honest means.'

'Fair means or foul, he's got it. Did Mr Webster say what he was going to do with it?'

'Storage.'

Norah screwed up her face.

'My thoughts exactly,' Letty said.

Norah made a pot of tea and handed Letty a mug to take in the shop for Percy. At the sink, she looked out over the wall that divided Parkers' yard from Crowe's. No doubt the lass was right, and Gilbert was trying to squeeze them out. He might have already done so had Letty not come along and bought them time. But with things as they were, he might yet be successful, and there was nothing much they'd be able to do about it.

15

The following week, the embargo was lifted and what trawlers were available were allowed into the North Sea to fish during daylight hours and within sight of land. The relief was palpable and the comings and goings of the docks picked up speed, although somewhat constricted by the admiralty rules and regulations. But men, and women, were back at work and there was a sense that the town could finally let out its long-held breath.

Three more Evans trawlers had been requestioned and in that same week came news of the loss of two more Grimsby trawlers that had been out fishing in the North Sea – the *Grimsby Rose* and the *Neptune*. Details were sketchy and they pieced together what they could. The ships had been sunk and the fishermen taken prisoner. It hollowed Ruth's stomach to think how close Henry had been to suffering the same fate.

The streets were ripe with gossip, the newspapers filled with scant detail. The Earl of Yarborough, whose eldest son, Lord Worsley, was in the Royal Horse Guards, had given land at Brockelsby Hall for the army's use and it had been filled with tents to house the hundreds of new recruits that had answered Kitchener's call.

As Proctor had said, the army were outnumbered compared to the kaiser's force and reinforcements were needed. Any man between the ages of eighteen and thirty could now enlist to serve his country and they flocked to the recruitment offices in droves – entire streets of men joining up at the same time. There was an air of excitement about it to the youngest of them, that they were going off on some huge adventure, akin to the stories they'd read in books and comics when they were boys. They were still boys, most of them. Lawyers, clerks, and those used to a more comfortable life had bedded down with labourers and porters.

The weather was still warm, with only occasional showers, but winter might prove unkind. Barracks would take time to build, and the wood was not as readily available as it had once been, the imports not forthcoming since war was declared. It was imperative that the trade routes were kept open, and the minesweepers were working long hours to ensure their safe passage.

Since her brothers' departure, the house had felt different, it was quite unlike the emptiness Ruth had felt when they were away at school. Each night, when Ruth went to bed, she pressed a hand to their bedroom doors and whispered a goodnight as she passed, as if her wishes would reach them wherever they were.

Arthur had not contacted her since her birthday, and she had no intention of making the first move. He had twisted what had happened between them to put her in a bad light. It had been ungentlemanly and ungallant. Her father was in full agreement and that had been enough to sustain her.

Ruth brought the post to the breakfast table and set it beside her father who was reading the morning edition of the *Herald*, holding on to the two letters addressed to her. 'One each from Charles.'

Her father glanced at the letters in her hand as she took a seat beside him.

'Nothing from Henry?' Her father took up his knife and slit open the envelope, began to read.

'Henry was never the letter writer. He was not so good with words as Charles.'

'Not the written, but the spoken is a different matter. I wonder how far his smooth talking is getting him thus far.'

'I'm sure he has written. His letters may have been delayed.'

'He's not written to you?' He glanced at her as she withdrew four pages from an envelope.

'No. This is from Lieutenant Proctor.'

'The second this past week.' He raised his eyebrows.

'It is. I look forward to them.' They were full of the small details he noticed with his artist's eye. 'He's a very interesting man.'

'So interesting that you turned down Arthur?'

His remark made her laugh. 'Oh, Father. I don't think of him that way at all. He's years older than I am. Fifteen at the very least.' It was enough to enjoy his company – and not to be stuck with Arthur. Even though things had been uncomfortable since she'd given him her answer, she would rather that than a lifetime of it.

'There was twelve between your mother and I.' He looked at her from under his reading spectacles, removed them and rubbed at the bridge of his nose. 'What are your plans for today?'

'There's a meeting at the Bethel Mission Hall. A new league has been founded – the League of Help.' The inaugural meeting had been held at the town hall and women had turned up in great numbers. Many had to be turned away and had waited outside for news. It had been decided to create small groups to encompass those who willingly offered their services. Aunt Helen had been the first to offer to establish one at the Bethel Mission Hall on Tiverton Street. The Ladies Guild met there every fortnight to sort through the donations for the benefit of the Fishermen's Mission.

It was merely a matter of adding one more committee to Aunt Helen's substantial list of worthy causes.

'Aren't there more than enough places of assistance already?'

'Not in the present circumstances. There is more need than ever. It's not only helping those who need food and clothing, but also for any support required, at any time. It could be nursing, cleaning—'

'I very much hope that you will not be carrying out such menial tasks as cleaning.'

'And I very much hope that too, not that I'm unwilling to do what's required, but I suspect there will be women there who cannot contribute much else.'

Her answer satisfied him. Lord forbid that she should be seen to be doing such work. Once, she had helped change beds at the mission, a pillowcase here and there, not much. They had been short-staffed, and when Letty had volunteered, so had she. It had come to her aunt's attention, as everything usually did, and she had been reprimanded and told to remember her position – as if she would ever be allowed to forget.

* * *

Her father had the chauffeur drop her off at the Bethel before continuing on to his offices. Ruth made her way into the hall at the back of the chapel, the volume of chatter increasing as she drew closer. Rows of chairs had been set out, facing an area at the front where two tables had been positioned, each with a chair, one with a sheaf of paper and a pen, a pot of ink – where Aunt Helen stood talking to Lydia Barton.

Things had cooled between them since the debacle last week, and Ruth had avoided her as much as possible. Her aunt would not mention anything of it here, but it had not been forgotten, and she would not give up on her plans for her niece so readily. Helen Frampton was simply biding her time.

Women of all ages were already seated and talking among themselves. Many of them Ruth knew from her work with the mission, the Hewitt sisters and Mrs Barton among others, but there were new faces too. Details of the meeting had been placed in the newspaper and word of mouth was as good a way for spreading news as any. Still, the number assembled was surprising, with all the other efforts going on in the town.

About the room, trestle tables had been set up and abutted three walls. Each was piled high with clothing and food donations, lengths of fabrics and skeins of wool. Another was entirely filled with boots and shoes of all sizes.

She walked over to Aunt Helen, who excused herself from Mrs Barton to talk to her niece. 'Ruth, I'm going to nominate you for secretary to keep the minutes. You have a good clear head on you.' There was no question of anyone disagreeing. Her aunt's reputation for getting things done was not founded on rumour.

Helen Frampton turned back to those gathered and clapped her hands for attention. Those women still standing took a seat and the room fell silent, apart from the tail end of a conversation that petered out on the back row. No doubt her aunt had given them an icy stare.

Letty Hardy was seated at the end of the second row and caught Ruth's eye, smiled.

'Ladies, first of all, thank you for your attendance this afternoon. We are living in extraordinary times and, as such, we must take extraordinary measures. As things progress, there will be great need for all manner of things – things that don't easily fall into one of the welfare funds already available. I hope that with your agreement we can fill those gaps, whether that be with food, clothing, and supplies' – she gave a sweep of her hand to indicate donations already collected and heads turned to satisfy curiosity – 'or to give support in any way we can.' She paused, clasped her hands in front of her. 'There is much to discuss. My niece here, Ruth Evans' – Ruth looked out at the faces, some women leaning forward and sidewards between the rows to take a good look at her – 'will take the minutes of this meeting. Unless anyone has any objections?'

Ruth could only see the back of her aunt's head, but she knew exactly what expression she was using, the 'see how little you have to do. I have it all in order' expression.

Mrs Barton got to her feet and Ruth caught Letty's eye. If anyone were to challenge her aunt, it would be Lydia Barton. Permanently clothed in black, she was a force to be reckoned with and Helen's money and status was no deterrent. Mrs Barton would question anything, and anyone, as she saw fit. She had lost her husband, brother and son when their ship was lost and knew only too well the suffering that might lie ahead for many of the women gathered. Her stern countenance hid a kind heart, for she was the first to come to the aid of families in need, but there was not a sentimental bone in her body. Sentiment didn't fill an empty tummy or clothe a frozen child.

'I don't see anything wrong with our present system, Mrs Frampton. We collect and sort here, and distribution is made from the mission building at Riby Square.'

'I agree, but these are challenging times. The mission takes care of the men, but it is the families of those men who will be in greater need. There is no longer enough space, and Mr Wilson's plate is already too full. As more trawlers are taken by the admiralty, there will be less available for fishing. Therefore, the men remaining, those who cannot serve due to age or ill health, will be left to crew what boats remain. We must be prepared to help in whatever quarter we can.' She paused again, looking along each row. 'We must not forget the women who are left behind. And the children. Ships have not returned, men too. There have been rumours that many have been taken prisoner of war. Ships in harbour in Germany when war was declared have not come home. Might never come home.'

There was a whispering and mumbling.

'What about the mission work?' It was Rosa Hewitt.

Helen's answer was firm. 'We go on as we have always done. But we must also spread our net wider, just as Jesus Christ told his disciples.' She waited for the women to stop talking. 'There will be gaps, we have no idea what is going to be needed but we can be willing to do anything that is required. Not just in money or words, but in action. Harold Street school is being converted into a hospital, the pupils distributed among other schools in the area. There will be cleaning and scrubbing to do; there will be a need for cooking simple meals and the provision of refreshment. The Manchester regiment are already arrived in Cleethorpes and are guarding the coast down towards Tetney and beyond. The army will need our support, as will the men away from home. Like the fishermen.'

Mrs Barton screwed her mouth and Ruth held her breath. Would her aunt's answer be sufficient to stop any more questions? It was not – and they came thick and fast. Where would they hold their meetings, how often would they meet, would there be a rota, how would it be funded. Ruth, taking it all down in shorthand, was glad that she had persevered with her studies.

As they continued, the hatch doors into the kitchen opened, and a red-faced Mrs Higgins and Mrs Green stood like sergeant majors in front of a regiment of sturdy cream cups and saucers.

Helen Frampton sucked in her cheeks. 'It seems our meeting is over. For the time being. We'll have tea, a most welcome break. Is that all right with you, ladies?' She turned to the two women behind the hatch, who gave her a quick nod of acknowledgement, leaving Helen Frampton in no doubt as to who was in charge. 'If you can come forward and give your details to Miss Evans, when you are available, and what assistance you can give, we can create a rota. We will also make a list of needs as they occur – bedding, clothing, food, et cetera.'

She spoke to Mrs Barton as the women got to their feet and began to move, quietly helping themselves to tea, Mrs Green loudly explaining where the milk and sugar could be found.

Letty placed a cup in front of Ruth and took a seat beside her, taking another sheet of paper and a pencil to speed up proceedings.

When at last the line had ended, they sipped at their cold tea. There was no shortage of willing volunteers, many of them with sons already serving, many of them of few means but willing hands and strong hearts. As Ruth had taken each name, she had thought of the many who would benefit from their kindness and her thoughts had gone to the woman at the docks when Henry had arrived home.

'The woman you helped a few weeks ago, with the small children...'

Letty paused, the cup to her lips, lowered it again and waited for Ruth to go on.

'I wondered how she was. The children?'

'Mary Owen,' Letty replied. 'Not too good the last time I saw her, but friends and family are rallying round. Neighbours. If she can't manage, members of the family might take one of the children until she gets back on her feet, other than that...' Letty sipped at her tea, replaced it on the saucer and pushed it on the table in front of them. 'The children's home.'

Ruth felt the words in the pit of her stomach. She knew of these things, of course she did, wasn't that what their work supporting the mission was all about? But to be witness to it, to see the blow fall, register the pain.

'That would have been my boy Alfie's fate when his poor mother died. She was desperate that he wouldn't end up there.' Letty beamed. 'I placed a notice in the paper to say that Alec and I were adopting him. He's Alfie Hardy now.'

'Oh, Letty, that's such a kind thing to do.'

'Ah, it was the right thing to do, and I find most folk are kind, many of them barely keeping their heads above water, but they help when they can. Look at what a turnout we have today.'

The two of them looked about them, at the women who mingled, some of them, perhaps for the first times in their lives, with others not of their class. War had already broken down so many barriers, and that could only be to the good. Weren't they all equal when all was said and done? Ruth had sensed it that day on the wharf, waiting for Henry, but in the turmoil that had followed, walls that had previously divided them had come tumbling down. There was movement that hadn't even been considered before.

'I'm also fortunate to have a good husband. If he hadn't been in agreement, it would have been a battle,' Letty added.

Ruth drank her tea and was quiet for a time, the noise of the women's chatter filling the silence. A good husband. It was so important. Over the last few days, she had reflected on Arthur's reaction to her asking him to wait. Had he been unreasonable? Had she? She had decided it wasn't about being unreasonable, it was being kind and considerate of others. Arthur had been neither. No, he would not make a good husband – not for her anyway.

'I admire these women, the ones who are left behind.' Ruth stared down into her empty cup. 'I never truly knew what it was before, to wait for the return of someone you love. To be afraid.'

Letty gave a small shrug. 'It's something you get used to, though – constantly living in fear, or learning to adapt, to keep busy.' She smiled. 'But there is no alternative.' She got up from her chair. 'There will be many more women waiting now. We won't be alone in that.'

Ruth thought of the fine gathering at her aunts, of the young men in uniform, so handsome and smart, so willing to go to war. How many would return? She tried to shake her head to dislodge the panic that filled it. Would Charles be any safer on land than on the ocean? All around her were women wanting to help, as always, yet there was an earnestness about them that hadn't been there before. Money would not soothe the pain of loss, but it would make them more comfortable in their misery.

* * *

When the meeting was over and a date arranged for the next, chairs were cleared away, and an army of women tackled the washing up.

Letty handed over her list of names to Ruth as Aunt Helen joined them.

'I'll put these in two ledgers, Aunt. It will be as well to have a spare.'

Her aunt nodded her agreement, turned to Letty. 'How is young Stella?'

'Thriving. Thank you for asking, Mrs Frampton. My mother-in-law is caring for them. She is better occupied than not, and there is not much braiding work available at present.'

'Jolly good. All working together makes the difference.'

'It certainly does, and I have reason to thank you.'

Helen Frampton frowned.

'I was not making much progress with the admiralty,' Letty explained. 'Mrs Wiltshire said she would mention it to you.'

Helen nodded. 'She did.'

'I wanted you to know that we received notification yesterday that Parkers is now on the approved list of admiralty suppliers.' Letty beamed.

'Oh, that is good news,' her aunt replied, genuinely pleased for Letty. 'We all have to help each other where we can.'

'I doubt we might have got it but for your good interventions.'

Aunt Helen looked to her niece and said kindly, 'Not all my interventions are so well received, but I do the best I can, if I can.' It was the nearest to an apology Ruth would get.

Behind them, Mrs Barton was instructing the newcomers in methods of sorting the clothes, and with the aid of the caretaker, more trestle tables were brought out and the work began. Helen Frampton gave them an approving glance.

'And what next, Mrs Hardy?'

'To the mission. To assist with letter writing.'

Ruth leapt at the opportunity. 'I'll walk with you. I told Mr Wilson I would take dictation.'

'Whatever for?' Her aunt could not disguise her surprise.

'Mr Wilson's monthly article for the *Toilers of the Deep* magazine will be due.' His commitment to the magazine of the Mission to Deep Sea Fisherman had been a bind. He had mentioned more than once how much he struggled with it. Her help was merely a contrivance on her part.

'Oh,' her aunt replied, pulling a face for Letty's benefit. 'I rather hoped you would come with me to the *Herald*. I need to deliver my copy for tomorrow's newspaper.'

Ruth did not feel in the mood to defend herself over her words to Arthur, but there would be little point objecting.

'You can collect two ledgers at the same time. For the details.' She looked to the papers Ruth held at her chest, then smiled at Letty. 'Best to get these things done sooner rather than later.'

'Oh, I agree,' Letty said. 'A few minutes' work can turn to hours if you let things slip.'

The three of them walked to the entrance and Ruth and her aunt got into the waiting car. Ruth watched Letty make her way down Tiverton Street and wished she were walking with her.

'I heard this morning that you were at the mission on the day of my garden party. Alone,' Aunt Helen said as the car moved off. 'And that is why you were late.'

It was not what Ruth had expected at all and it took time for her to gather her thoughts.

'Have you not learned that there is little goes on in this town that doesn't reach my ears one way or another. People love to gossip – and cause trouble. It occupies them when they have so little else to do.'

'I waited there for Henry,' Ruth replied. 'I lost him in the crowds. I thought it safer there than outside.'

Her aunt tossed her head. 'And what good did that do?' She turned her piercing gaze on her niece. 'You could quite easily have walked over to the *Herald's* office.'

'I knew you wouldn't be there,' Ruth countered. 'You were at the Hall, preparing for the party.'

Her aunt gave a slight shake of her head. 'People will think you only help at the mission so that you can spend time with Mr Wilson, that your intentions are somewhat, unseemly.' Her aunt lowered her voice. 'I am beginning to think your asking poor Arthur to wait was for another reason entirely to the one you gave.'

Ruth was incensed. It was 'poor Arthur' now – but at least her aunt hadn't repeated the lie that she had turned him down.

'It was not for that reason at all,' she said through gritted teeth, 'and you know it.'

Her aunt lifted her shoulders. 'Don't think I haven't been aware of the way you flutter your eyes at him when he comes to speak with us. That it hasn't escaped my notice that you make the slightest excuse to accompany me, or your father, to the mission. Using Letty Hardy as a chaperone for your devious intentions. Does she know?'

Ruth cheeks burned with anger, but her aunt hadn't finished.

'Mark my words, dear girl. Nothing good will ever come of crossing that particular line. You have a duty and obligation to this family. Throwing yourself at a man who is not your class is not the best use of your life.'

'I am not throwing myself at anyone,' Ruth gasped, appalled by her aunt's dismissal of the port superintendent. That she had feelings for him was something else entirely. 'I am there to help, as Letty does.'

'Dear Lord.' Her aunt sighed heavily and turned to her. 'You have a brain, Ruth, when are you going to start using it?'

'When would I be allowed to?' she snapped.

The car stopped and her aunt swept into the offices of the *Grimsby Herald*, Ruth following at a distance. While she waited, Ruth walked towards the print room, watched the great rollers turn as they delivered newsprint, sheet after sheet. Could the written word conquer the spoken, sway opinion? Her aunt's column was a frequent rallying call to the town, to stir the hearts of its people, but she could not stir her own.

After a few moments, Aunt Helen returned with two ledgers, one for general use and one for her own. She handed them over.

Ruth was curt. 'Thank you, Aunt Helen. I will have them completed by tomorrow.'

'I'll have my driver take you home,' her aunt said firmly, heading towards the door, but Ruth was no longer in the mood to be amenable.

'That's very kind of you, Aunt Helen, but I promised to help Mr Wilson with his article, and I would not go back on my word.' Her aunt was about to protest when Ruth added, 'And whatever you think, I enjoy Mrs Hardy's company. It will not be unseemly if she is at my side.'

Her aunt was thin-lipped. 'Very well. It is your decision.'

It *was* her decision, albeit a small one. Not as earth-shattering as asking Arthur to consider her feelings, but it was step in the right direction. Henry had outwitted their aunt's machinations and Philip Proctor had carved his own path. Perhaps she too might one day find herself living a life of her own choosing.

Down in the lobby, Ruth requested a glass of water and waited to calm herself before making her way to the mission. The heat had left her cheeks and she hoped Letty might not notice anything untoward. She crossed the main road to the mission, only to be told by the desk attendant that Mr Wilson was out on calls. A simple phrase, one that made reasonable the substance of the calls. He would be passing on the news that a man was lost at sea – a husband, a brother, a son.

She asked of Letty and was informed that she was in the dining room.

'Would you like me to escort you, Miss Evans?'

'That will not be necessary. I know the way and I don't want to take you from your post.'

She borrowed a pencil and sharpener and made her way to the room at the back of the building.

Letty was at her usual table by the window, sitting opposite a young lad who was talking, and she was writing down his words. Ruth slipped into a chair at the next table and placed her ledgers down. She watched Letty as she worked, hearing her aunt's accusations that she had used Letty as a chaperone. She had been bruised by her aunt's words but only because she was right – in part. For Ruth enjoyed Letty's company, regardless of Colin. She was always so positive, always searching out opportunities, and Ruth admired her for it.

When the boy left, and no more men were forthcoming, she went to sit beside Letty. It was a wonder her aunt had not been disagreeable to their friendship, Letty not being of the right social class. But Letty was respected among both fishermen and their wives, and Ruth had half a mind that Helen recognised her own strength in the young mother. They had met when Colin had become port superintendent. It was a position of great prestige, for Grimsby was the largest fishing port in the world by all accounts, and the well-being of a huge part of the town rested on his shoulders. He had status – but that was not enough for Aunt Helen's satisfaction.

'I was sorry not to walk with you. My aunt wanted to talk to me.'

Letty smiled. 'It wasn't at all obvious.'

Ruth relaxed. If she could confide in anyone, it would be Letty. There were a couple of men sitting over by the door and the men from the kitchen were preparing things for supper. No one would hear them.

She lowered her voice. 'Letty, what would you do if you had feelings for someone and you weren't sure how they felt about you?' She had an inkling Letty knew who she was talking about. She had often caught Ruth's eye when Colin came to speak with her, couldn't have failed to notice how flustered she became when he did.

Letty considered her question. 'It depends who that person was.' She looked directly into Ruth's eyes. 'I would look for small signs when I was with him, what attention he paid me, or didn't.' Letty paused. 'It depends on so many things. It wouldn't be the same for someone of your position. You would have to choose more carefully than I.' She glanced out of the window, back again.

'But then we all have to choose wisely, don't we? Marriage is a commitment. I wouldn't want to be with someone I didn't love. Who didn't make me laugh, who was unkind.' The men setting out the cutlery for the evening meal and briefly looked their way. 'In the end, I suppose it's what you're prepared to give up?'

Ruth frowned, not understanding.

'When I met Alec, I didn't for a minute imagine that falling for him would mean leaving Lowestoft. My family have a small farm and I have grown up in a full house, with brothers and sisters – and not much room for all of us. I knew the land, the fields and the crops, the animals and the birds, I knew nothing of a fisherman's life – but I was prepared to learn. Because I loved him.'

She went quiet, her thoughts with her husband, and Ruth waited for her to continue.

'When Alec first talked of moving here, I was afraid, I can't deny it. Worst of all was leaving my family behind. It was difficult – more than I had ever thought it could be.'

'But you succeeded,' Ruth urged, wanting so much for Letty to tell her it had all been worthwhile. 'And you're happy?'

Letty thought for a minute or two before she answered.

'It was a shock to discover I would spend more time with my mother-in-law than with my husband. We had difficult times, still do. Things are better – though they are not perfect. But I love Alec and we are a family now, with Stella and Alfie. We pull together and try to work things through, hoping the good times will get us over the bad ones.' She held Ruth's gaze. 'Nothing in life is easy. But if...' She stopped talking, looked about her. 'I don't have your life, your comforts. Something of what you are considering...'

Ruth urged her to continue but Letty would not.

'Happiness doesn't last forever, and we all have our ups and downs. Some folks get more than their fair share of the downs. Money can make a lot of things more bearable. But not all.'

Ruth understood. She thought of Mary Owen and women like her. If she chose Colin, she might lose her allowance. Her aunt would certainly intervene. But she loved him, and if she knew he felt the same, she was sure, like Letty, she could weather the storm it would create.

16

Alec had been a week in Lowestoft, waiting for the *Black Prince* to be made ready for war. There had not been room in the dry dock in Grimsby and ships had been sent elsewhere to get them converted to minesweepers quickly and efficiently. The fishing gear had been unloaded, save for the warps and enough coal, water and provisions to last for seven days. He had been given his charts and sailing orders and made his way south, hugging the coast, the crew on the lookout for mines that might have drifted nearer the shore.

It was an odd feeling to be home, for this was home, the streets as familiar to him as his own hand. And no matter that it was changed temporarily, the place scattered with uniforms, the harbour filled with trawlers painted grey, one day they would leave, and it would go back to the rhythm he knew so well. He had missed it more than he'd realised.

There had been time to meet with his aunt and uncle, with his cousins, and a few old pals. He headed for the beach village, or the Grit as it was known to the locals, walking the long narrow streets, the scores, that ran down to the sea. Streets he had run as a lad, waiting on the cliff for his father's ship to come in. His mother was different then, she laughed more – and though she delighted in Stella, Alfie too, he had not heard her laugh as she did when he was but a boy. He had forgotten those carefree days. They had ceased the day his father was lost and he, at fourteen, had taken on responsibility for his mother and Robbie. He blamed himself still for Robbie's death, watching the boy fall overboard, guiding the boat home, and walking the path to tell his mother the news, his uncle at his side. He'd doubted he would ever hear her laugh again and it saddened him more than he could ever find the words to say. Stella had brought her happiness but not laughter.

In his pocket, he carried the letter from Letty telling him of her plans for a café. She had hoped for the shop agin Parkers, but Gilbert Crowe had beaten her to it. There had been a few choice words about that, and he had smiled when he read them, hearing her voice as clearly as if she were with him. The man would not get the better of her and she was already looking for something else. Alec didn't doubt she would find it. That the lass had settled so well, had found her feet, *and* looked after his mother reassured him. He patted his breast pocket, feeling her close. He had written back, told her to use some of the money they had saved for his ship. If he got through this caper, God willing, a few good trips and he'd soon top it up again.

It was still light, the sun falling lower in the sky, dripping amber over the cobbles and lighting a path toward the shore. The door to the pub was ajar, the windows open and the smell of ale mingled with that of the sea. As he stepped over the threshold, the noise of men's chatter and laughter greeted him, a few turned, nodded in acknowledgment as he pushed his way to the bar and ordered two bottles of beer. He looked about him, peered over shoulders to the corner where he knew his Uncle Eric would be and, once found, went over to him.

A man got up and pointed to the spare space on the trestle. 'Sit yerself down, boy. I was jest gooin'. The missis'll be down 'ere if I don't get a move on.'

Alec took his seat, put the ale in front of his uncle. Though the door was open, it was hot with so many men inside and he looked about him at faces, old and new. 'Reminds me of when the herring fleets are in town.'

'They'll not be here this year, that's fer sure.' His uncle emptied the bottle into his pewter tankard and supped at it, wiped the foam from his mouth. 'Mebee the next too.'

There was a mumbling of agreement from the other men about them.

Old Tom drew his pipe from his mouth and dampened it down with a match. 'Let's hope they git's it all done and dusted as they say they will.'

'Ah, that's pie-in-the-sky talk, that is. Codswallop,' his uncle chipped in. 'We might be back fishing, but we can't make up fer what we've lost.'

'Ah, we'll manage.' Old Tom tapped the side of his brow. 'We've got to use what we've got up top.'

'T'ain't no sense in doing ow't else,' one of the old fishermen chimed in. He was leaning against the mantel over the unlit fire, his head bent to miss the low ceiling. In winter, they would settle by it, enjoying the spit and spark of the logs. As a boy, Alec had sat there with his father, after his first trip, his mother unaware of it, for she would have chased Will Hardy down the lanes and back again if she had found out.

He rested his back against the wall. He had dreamed of spending many an evening with his father here, but it was not to be. Alec had moved to Grimsby partly to escape the memories. And yet here he was finding comfort from them.

He settled a while with the men, catching up on the day's news. The town had been hit hard when the fishing fleet was recalled – the coopers, the braiders, the beatsters finding themselves idle.

'How's business?' he asked his uncle, who had set up as a fish merchant using his half-share of the *Stella*.

'Poor, the prices are high as the fish are so scarce. Not everyone can afford it.' They were all in for a hard time, whether that was on the sea or on land – and not only the fighting men. They were all going to have to fight to survive.

When his uncle was ready to leave, Alec walked with him, along the narrow street and down towards the shore to his cottage. A small lamp glowed in the window, and he opened the door, ducked his head and called out to his wife. Aunt Minnie was settled in her chair by the empty grate and was sewing an elbow patch onto his uncle's brown jacket. In the hearth was a dish of pebbles and another of shells that their girls had gathered over the years. Many a time, he and Robbie had gone with them, returning home with bits of driftwood for the fire. It seemed so long ago now. All but one of their three daughters were married. The youngest to be wed the following summer.

Minnie's face creased with a broad smile. She was a tiny woman, her eyes brown pebbles, and after much fussing, she gestured for him to take her chair.

'Please, Aunt Minnie, I'd rather stand.'

His uncle, who had waited by the door, there not being much room to move, placed his hat on the hook beside him, then took the chair opposite while the pantomime of his aunt insisting and Alec resisting went on. Ignoring his protestations, she plumped the cushion and adjusted the woollen blanket that hung over the back of the rocking chair and made him sit down. A fine ship's clock hung on the wall opposite and the steady tick was soothing. They had lived in the house since long before he was born and the tiny room was as it had always been, his aunt and uncle too, perhaps a little greyer and more stooped, but the same in every other way. Their home had been the only constant in his life, the place he came for solace and good cheer.

'Any news of when your ship will be ready?' his aunt asked as he settled himself.

'The end of the week by all accounts.'

She nodded, considering. 'And you know where yer goin'?'

He shook his head. He wouldn't know until he sailed, and even if he did, he wouldn't tell her. He doubted she really wanted to know, it was merely something to say.

She took the pot from the hearth and made tea, stirred two large spoons of sugar into each mug and handed him one. They talked for a while; she told him of her girls, of the husbands who had left for their own training in Portsmouth. Both the girls had married fishermen. It was the way among them. Most of the people on the Grit were connected to the sea in some way or another, or to the hotels along the seafront on the south pier. He had wooed Letty there, when the wind was wild, walking out along the pier to propose to her in the deserted bandstand. He suddenly ached for her, ached with loneliness for the life they had made for themselves, for Stella's little arms to be about him.

His uncle's eyes were growing heavy, in part aided by the ale, and Alec drained his mug and handed it to his aunt. 'I'd best be away. I'll need to be back at me lodgings.'

She showed him to the door, both uncle and aunt hoping they'd see him again before he left for his duties. Aunt Minnie reached onto her toes to kiss his cheek and he grinned, remembering when he was a lad and the position reversed. 'God bless you and keep you safe, boy.'

Her words warmed him as he left her on the doorstop and began to walk down towards the foreshore. When he turned, his aunt was still at the doorway. She held up her hand and he did too, then thrust them into his pockets and headed down to the water.

Dusk was falling, but there was still light enough to see. He didn't want to go straight back, preferring to wander along the water's edge, enjoying the peace of it, the suck of the tide on the shingle, the rattle of the pebbles as they rolled back and forth with it. The breeze was up and ruffled his hair and he took his cap from his pocket and pulled it over his head.

For a long time, he stood looking out over the water. The sea was different here, the way the light fell, the sound of it, and it was suddenly of comfort as it had never been since his father had died. His father felt close, Robbie too, and for a moment Alec regretted leaving, but only a moment. Here, he would always be tethered to the past and he longed to be free of it.

When he had had his fill, he headed for the score, saw a lass coming towards him, her head held high, her dark hair falling about her shoulders, and from the familiar sway of her hips, he knew it was the girl he'd finished with when he'd met Letty. Becky Drew.

She stopped a few yards before him and waited for him to draw close.

'I'd heard you was back.'

'Aye. While my ship's made ready.'

'Your ship is it,' she teased.

'Yer know what I mean.'

'Aye, I know what you mean,' she laughed.

'Are you away home?'

'I am. Mother will be about for me if I don't.' She pressed his arm and looked at him from under her lashes. 'Come and say hello. Mother will be glad to see you.'

'I doubt that.' Becky had been sweet on him and had followed him about, always at the jetty when he landed. But he had played with her, not wanting to get attached to anyone, not until he saw Letty. His mother had thought Becky the right wife for him, but Alec had chosen different, and was glad that he had.

Her dark curls fell about her face, and she tossed her head to move them. 'Walk with me, tell me what you've been up to.'

The lass hadn't changed a bit. She was trouble then and she was trouble now. 'I should be getting back to my—'

'There's no harm in it, Alec Hardy, is there? You're a married man – and I'm almost a married woman.' She swung her shoulders. 'John Trent is my intended.'

He raised an eyebrow. John Trent was not the sharpest knife in the box. He worked beside his father at the ironmongers at the top of the town. It did a good, steady business, and he would be set to inherit it when the old man was gone, the Trents having no other children. By, the man must have thought all his Christmases had come at once when Becky had set her cap at him, for Alec could not see it happening any other way.

She pulled her shawl about her shoulders, and before he could blink, she linked her arm in his and gently pulled him towards the slope. 'Aye, second best, but you broke my heart. What else could I do.'

'Eh, lass. I never promised owt.' He knew he'd treated her badly. He had been Jack the Lad back then, happy to be with the prettiest girl, the one the other fellas wanted. It was all he'd thought of, until Robbie was lost – and that changed everything.

She started walking, pulling him with her and he saw no harm in it. 'No, you didn't, Alec Hardy.' Even in the low light, he could see the sparkle in her eyes. 'But you broke my heart all the same.' She leaned to him. 'How's your mother? And Letty?'

'Mother is quite well, better in health than temper, but wasn't she always that way.' She knew well what his mother was like and needed no reminder, and he avoided speaking of Letty. What he and Letty had was between the two of them. He knew he should release her arm and walk away, but it was easy to talk of the past, of something other than war, of a time when he was as free as the waves before them. 'What are you doing with yourself?' he asked.

'I help Mother, as I always did.' Her father dragged for cockles and mussels. Becky and her mother would boil them and sell them in paper cones, from a basket over her arm. A pretty girl was good for business and Becky was good at getting them to buy, much to the chagrin of the lads' wives and girlfriends. The lass knew how to catch a man's eye, there was never any doubt about that. 'I hear you have a child?'

He cocked his head to one side.

'Your cousin told me.'

'What else did my cousin tell yer?'

She gave him a coy smile. 'Nothing to tell – or is there?'

Alec stopped in front of her house.

'You do look handsome in your uniform, Alec.' She put her hand to his coat. 'And such shiny gold buttons.' She touched them one by one, top to bottom, flirting with him, coming closer, and by, she was a bonny lass, but she was not the lass for him.

He stepped back, knowing she would lean forward to steal a kiss, aware that curtains would be twitching. 'Goodnight, Becky. Say hello to your mother and father for me. I best be off.' He walked away, his boots clicking on the cobbles, and this time he did not look back.

17

It was mid-September and although things were ticking along, they were not great. Parkers had kept a steady trade when the fishermen went back to fish, but Letty wondered how much the restrictions would curtail their income when winter came. There had been little movement at Websters' empty shop and at one point she'd wondered if the sale had fallen through. If Gilbert Crowe had not had the money he boasted of. But a quick visit to Mr Webster had soon resolved that conundrum. He had been paid in full. In cash.

Norah had suggested that Letty might ask Crowe if she might lease it from him, but Letty had told her she would rather burn her own eyes with a red-hot poker. That Gilbert had pulled the rug from under her had only strengthened her resolve. The more she thought about her idea for a café, the more she knew she could make it work.

The warehouses and shipyards and engineering works were thriving, and buildings were being adapted all the time to cope with the extra demands of the war, on shipping and on armaments. The admiralty had more or less taken over the docks at Grimsby and Immingham, but it was not a naval base and still run by civilians. The shipbuilders and repairs were independent of them but were on a list of approved suppliers. J. S. Doig's, along with other businesses, had increased output in their yards and fitting shops and were working at full capacity. Hours were extended, men working around the clock to make certain the fighting men had something to fight with. Those willing to do overtime had more money in their pocket than ever before and were willing to spend it. If she could find the right premises, she could relieve them of a coin or two.

Most of the cafés were around the pontoon and in the streets off Fish Dock Road, for that was where the fishermen usually congregated, but things had changed, and the perfect opportunity might present itself elsewhere if she bothered to seek it out.

Letty had spent the morning at home, building up the fire in the outhouse to heat the water, and was red-faced, perspiration trickling down her neck.

'It's only going to get worse, mark my words.' Dorcas was elbow-deep in washing, rubbing at her blouse, her knuckles clashing as she did so, plunging the thick cotton into the soapy water and out again, in and out, rubbing and chaffing.

While she grumbled, Letty filled the buckets with fresh water for rinsing, and when Dorcas was satisfied, they each took one side of the washtub and emptied it down the drain. Letty filled it with the fresh water and Dorcas sank the clothes into it, while Letty filled another pail and emptied it on top. Her mother-in-law swilled the clothing and squeezed out the soap, waited for Letty to refresh the water each time. When it ran clear they took the basket of washing out to the mangle and Dorcas fed it through the rollers, while Letty turned the handle. Stella was sitting in another wicker basket with Alfie, the pair of them pretending they were sailing away to Arabia. Letty wished she could be anywhere but listening to Dorcas.

'To my mind, we'd have been better off if we'd stayed in Mariners Row. It was cheaper to rent, and to heat. What's it going to cost us when the cold weather comes, that's what I'm thinking.'

'It wouldn't make that much difference,' Letty ventured, knowing her words would fall on empty ears. Once Dorcas was on a rant, she would not be stopped, and it was easier to let her blow herself out like a gale. 'We're growing food of our own, we have eggs.' It didn't take Dorcas long to look on the black side of a house she'd been so proud to enter – her boy going up in the world, never mind that part of it was down to Letty's industry as well as Alec's earning as skipper. 'Anyway, you hated it at Mariners Row. You played merry hell the first day we got there.'

'Because it was mucky,' Dorcas huffed. 'Not because of where it was.'

Letty didn't want to argue, Dorcas could blow hot and cold, and it was only her fear speaking. She willed herself not to bite back.

They hung the washing on the line and Letty pushed the prop high, wedged it against the terracotta tiles that edged the border. She unfastened her apron and dropped it on the children's heads and set them giggling. It made Dorcas smile, and it was worth it for that, her grumbles forgotten. Alfie lifted it up and peeked out, Stella grinning her gappy smile. Letty urged him to step ashore, and when he had, she lifted the basket and carried Stella into the house, singing her little nursery rhyme as she went.

After giving them both milk, Alfie in his small cup and Stella in a bottle, she settled the two of them in the chairs either side of the range and they eventually fell asleep. Dorcas spread a sheet of old newspaper on the table and began brushing the soil from a few potatoes Letty had pulled up earlier that morning and began peeling them.

'Can I leave the kiddies with you? I need to see Norah about a bit of business.'

Dorcas glanced at the pair of them. 'Aye, they'll be no bother. I wasn't going anywhere.' For all her grumbling, Dorcas had been a great support to her these past months, especially as far as the kiddies were concerned. She doted on Stella, her first grandchild, and had grown to care for Alfie. Their presence softened her mother-in-law in ways that nothing else did.

* * *

Letty didn't go directly to Parkers but instead walked fully around the entire dock area, from the Royal Dock down the riverhead and back again and over by the slips where the boat builders and repair yards were situated, looking for any building that might lend itself to a café. Posters had been pasted on the walls of Doig's and almost every other building, calling for skilled and unskilled men to fill positions in the boiler shops and paint-works. She peered into the sheds, watching men weld and hammer and paint. No one gave her a second glance. Rumours were rife about the infiltration of German spies, trying to discover admiralty secrets, but if anyone was on the lookout for them, no one was interested in it being a female. The thought amused her. It was ridiculous how much men underestimated women.

She walked a little further and saw a hut with a tin roof. During the herring season, it was used to house the Scottish lasses who followed the fish down from the north. As their menfolk moved down the coast, so too did they, arriving on trains that brought them directly into the docks. Their large wooden chests – kists – containing their belongings – knives and clothing, their long oilcloth aprons, their knitting – would be unloaded and taken to buildings like this. They would not be back for the foreseeable future and Letty knew she could make good use of the space.

The door was secured with a padlock and heavy chain, yet she still pulled on it, then walked about the hut, peering into windows, some broken and boarded up. It was dark and cluttered, but she could get an idea of the interior space. Behind her was the noise and clatter of men working, and seeing through the grime and dirt, she began to sense that this was a far better spot for a café. Gilbert had done her a favour – and the thought pleased her as much as she knew it would displease him.

As she made to move away, someone called out to her. 'How do, Mrs Hardy.'

Sandy Brownlow was hauling cans of paint from a wagon outside a warehouse, and when she turned he stopped and tipped his cap to her. His sleeves were rolled up to his elbows, and his shirt was wet with sweat under his armpits and on his chest. He had been a deck-hand with Alec, able enough to keep fishing but too old for service.

She walked over to him.

'What brings you over this way?' he asked.

'Curiosity.' She glanced over to the ship that was being painted grey in the slips. Men worked on a wooden cradle suspended from the rails, a man above calling down to them from the deck. 'You didn't want to stay at the fishing?'

'Not much point. There's few boats left and too many men to sail 'em. I'm home every night after me shift, which is a novelty.'

'And you're enjoying it.'

He considered his answer. 'Aye, I didn't think I would. Not sure the missus likes it. She's been used to ruling the roost herself. We got under each other's feet to begin with, but we've sorted it out.' He grinned. 'By and large.' He pulled off his cap and wiped away the sweat on his brow with the back of his hand.

She pointed at one of the posters. 'Doig's still short of men?'

'Aye, there's orders coming in thick and fast. To convert the trawlers, and to build more. At least there's jobs to be had. Never thought a good thing would come from conflict, but it has.' She knew it wouldn't be the same for everyone, but at that moment she could only agree.

'Do you know who owns the hut? Is it Doig's?'

He shook his head. 'No idea. But Loftis will know. You'll find him down the railway siding. He has a small wooden hut there.'

A sharp whistle made him turn and they looked over to see a man with an overall, his hands to his hips.

'Now I'll be in trouble.' He winked at her, picked up his jacket from the wagon and ambled off.

* * *

Letty found Mr Loftis in his office. When she asked about the building, he screwed up his face. 'Yer mean the hut yon side of Doig's?'

'That's it. It's painted blue, with a tin roof.'

He reached up, taking a key without reading the tag from a board that was cluttered with them, and led the way back to the hut. When the padlock popped open, he pulled back the door and stood aside to allow her to enter. The light from the open door was enough for her to see by and enable her to thread her way through the coils of rope and old lobster pots that were stored there. She didn't need to see much, she could feel it was the right place, just as she had done when she'd first stumbled upon Parkers. It was a sixth sense. She could smell the potential just as skippers had a scent for where the fish was.

She turned to Loftis. 'Is it available for rent?'

He removed his cap, scratched his bald head. 'Don't say as I know.'

'Can you find out?'

He shrugged. 'Depends what yer want it fer.'

She didn't want to tell him. If word got back to Gilbert Crowe he might try to beat her to it, and she'd be damned if she let that loathsome man derail her. 'Could you just ask?'

He looked at her for a time, assessing her, and she gave him a small smile. 'Aye, I can ask. Come back at four.'

* * *

She made her way back to Parkers. Gilbert Crowe was coming out of Websters and slipped the key into the lock. He smirked at her, withdrew the key and swung it around the metal ring that contained others, taunting her.

'Making sure it's all secure, Mr Crowe. I don't blame you. There are some unsavoury types about these streets.'

He tugged at the front of his bowler hat, bared his yellow teeth. 'I hear you was after the place.' He looked up at the frontage, then at her, clicked his tongue. 'You'll have to move quicker if you want to outsmart me.'

Letty faked a smile. 'I doubt that very much. You've not done much in the time you've had it.'

'No need to rush. I'm not desperate, not like some.' He walked up to her, leaned into her face.

She resisted the urge to lean away, his foul breath reigniting the memory of when he had attacked her one night, thinking she was Alfie's mother. In the darkness, Sally Penny had knocked him unconscious with a rolling pin before he could do any damage, thinking him just another customer, but Letty had known who he was, even if no one else did.

He tilted his head towards Parkers' doorway, slipped his long fingers into his lefthand waistcoat pocket. 'Biding my time, that's all, Letty Hardy. Just biding my time.'

He walked away, whistling, and for two pins she'd have pushed him into the gutter. But he would have enjoyed knowing he'd made her lose her rag and she wouldn't give him the satisfaction. Well, she thought as she went into Parkers, he wasn't the only one biding his time. She'd get the better of him yet and when she did, she'd relish every minute of it.

Percy had gone out for a pint with Wolfie and Norah was at the counter serving, wrapping a man's purchases in brown paper. Letty walked up and placed her finger on the cross of the string, hardly able to contain her excitement. Norah eyed her with curiosity as she tied the knot and snipped off the excess with her knife. Letty was almost bursting by the time the customer left.

'What's got you all of a lather?' Norah observed wryly.

'I think I've found somewhere.' She lowered her voice. The walls that divided them from Crowe's were thick, but she wouldn't put it past him to have a glass to it. She wouldn't put anything past that man. 'It's over by Doig's.' She couldn't stop grinning, though she was trying not to get too excited in case she couldn't secure it. 'It's a bit of a mess right now, but oh, it will be perfect.'

Norah listened while she told her of the building and her plans for it.

'But how will you manage, with the kiddies? You've already got so much on your plate, lass.'

She knew what Norah meant. Trade was slowly picking up in the shop and elsewhere things were beginning to move again. Things had been adjusted, allowances made, and the town had begun to move forward – just as she wanted to do. It seemed to Letty that they had survived squall and thankfully stayed afloat.

But it was early days, and anything could happen. If it did, she wanted to be prepared for it.

'Alfie will be at school. Dorcas might have Stella for me and if she doesn't, there's a creche at the orphanage.'

'I can't have that. You can't leave Stella there.' Norah sank onto the wooden stool behind the counter. 'We should have kept the lass on.' She looked at Letty. 'Mebee, we can get her back.'

'There'll be no need, not to begin with. I'll get along fine as I am. If I need to, I can get a lass to help me.'

Norah's worry was evident. 'Don't take on too much, Letty. You never know when to stop.'

'I don't like being idle,' she said to reassure her.

Norah sighed. 'You wouldn't know how.'

* * *

Letty hurried back to the house to get some money. If a deposit was needed, she wanted to have it ready and sign any paperwork there and then.

On her way, she saw Mary Owen's children outside the Red Lion.

'Is your mother in there?'

Emily nodded. The three of them were grubby, their hair tangled, the baby's nappy sodden with urine and heaven knows what else. Letty ran a hand over the toddler's cheek and smiled at her, pulled on the door and went inside.

A thick pall of smoke hung about the room and spilt ale had made the floor sticky. Mary Owen was on one of the banquette seats, a glass in her hand, her cheeks ruddy, her eyes glazed.

'Letty Hardy. I never thought I'd see you in here.'

Letty sat beside her, removed the glass from her hand. 'Time to go home.'

Mary shook her head, getting tearful.

Letty got up and pulled Mary to her feet. 'The kiddies need you,' she whispered.

Mary gave a small nod of her head and after a little persuasion left the pub.

'I'll walk with you.' Letty picked up the baby, her sleeve suddenly damp and tried not to think too much as her arm warmed accordingly. She smiled to encourage the children, began to walk, and Mary, to her credit, picked up the toddler and walked beside her, Emily close behind. When they were nearer to their home, Letty stopped at the chip shop and bought three pennorth of chips with scraps. She handed Emily the parcel to carry and the child's face brightened with anticipation.

At the house, she spread open the newspaper on the table and the children ate greedily. She blew on a chip and handed it to the baby. Mary sank into a chair, ignoring the food.

'Thanks, Letty. For the chips.'

Letty found a plate and put some chips on it and pushed it into Mary's hands. 'Eat,' she instructed.

'I'm not hungry.'

'Eat anyway. It'll soak up the drink.'

Mary picked at the food while Letty stood over her.

'Hasn't your mother been?' The house looked tidy enough. 'Your neighbours – don't they look in on you.'

'Now an' again, they do. Nosey buggers. Telling me what I should be doing. As if they know how I feel.' She flung out her arm. 'Then there's me Mam telling me it's about time I pulled meself together.' She began to cry. 'But I can't. I can't think straight. It ain't that easy.'

Mary's mother, Edna, was kindly enough, but not one to tolerate too much drama, and she already had another daughter in the same boat. Letty imagined Mary had pushed her to her limits.

Plenty of women lost their husbands and were left with young kiddies, but the majority of them put their children first, not a bottle of ale.

'Come to the mission, Mary. You'll have company at least,' Letty told her. 'There's help out there for you and the kiddies, to get you back on your feet. You can't leave them standing outside a pub while you drink yourself to death.'

'*Help*? Can they bring my Lennie back?' she snapped.

Letty sighed, shook her head. 'Drink won't make things any better.'

Mary stared at the wall. 'No. But it will make me forget. And that's all I want to do.'

18

'Are you mad?' Dorcas threw her hands in the air. 'A café. How will you pay for that, and how will you run it with Parkers – and the kiddies. Don't be daft, lass.' She shook her head, began picking up the clothes that were on the airer.

'I know what I'm doing.' Letty had braced herself for Dorcas's tirade. 'The dock is busy again.'

'There's only half – nay, perhaps a quarter of the boats out there.'

'Yes, but that's not everything on the docks. The wood yard is open again, and the boatyards can't get enough staff. Doig's is still converting trawlers to minesweepers, as are many of the other companies at the graving dock and the slips. There are hundreds of men up there, all hungry for something to eat – and not all of them want fish and chips.'

Dorcas sat down at the table and rubbed one hand over the other, looking at her gold band while Alfie slunk into the chair. He knew to keep out of the way when Dorcas was ready to erupt.

'It will bring in more money. You were only saying this morning about the rent.'

Dorcas tutted. 'Aye, well. It's a lot to bring in each month. We could have gone for something smaller. Cheaper.'

'I'm glad to see the back of Mariners Row,' Letty replied. 'As were you only a few weeks ago.'

'A café,' Dorcas muttered, then lifting her head asked, 'And how will you pay for it?'

Letty knew that would be her first response. Alec had already written to let her know she could dip into their savings for it, but she wouldn't touch Alec's money. To do so would be tempting fate.

'I have enough for two months' rent. A little put by for things I'll need – but I'll not need much. I can get plenty of second-hand bits and pieces from Jack Tapper's yard. He'll have the things I need – a bench or two, a few pots and pans, mugs and the like. I don't need new, I can make do with what he has in stock and add to as I go.' She looked at the clock. There was plenty of time to get things sorted before she had to be back at Loftis's office. 'I haven't got it yet,' she told Dorcas. 'I wanted to rent the shop next door to the Parkers, but it's been sold.'

'Oh, aye,' Dorcas said, fighting not to appear too interested.

'The chap the other side of the Parkers bought it,' Letty enlarged, not wanting to give Dorcas too much information. 'I didn't move fast enough last time and I'm not going to miss out on this.'

She took down her tins from the top of the dresser and counted out the cash. She wouldn't need more than a pound or two.

'How much is it going to cost you?'

'Not much, I shouldn't wonder. It's only fit for storage.'

Dorcas got up and picked up a dishcloth, wrung it out, her forearms bulging, and began wiping the table with big sweeps of her hand. 'Huh, only fit for...' She stopped her wiping and stood upright, the cloth held in her fist, her hand to her side, and eyed Letty.

Letty carried on counting out the money. When she had what she thought she needed and a little bit more, she smiled at Dorcas, half expecting her to object. 'Would you look after the kiddies while I go back. I've only got until four.'

Dorcas shook her head. 'It's your money you're wasting.' She looked to Alfie. 'Come on, boy Alfie. 'Spect yer hungry and yer sister too.'

Letty could've hugged her, but she didn't, knowing that Dorcas would push her off and tell her she was soft. 'Thank you, Dorcas. I'll be as quick as I can.'

She flew out of the door and back down to the docks. She could call in Jack Tapper's yard on the way back. He was open 'til late and not a man to let a bit of ready cash pass him by.

* * *

Letty came back with the keys, and a rent book. Alfie was reading a comic that Percy had bought for him, and Dorcas was bathing Stella in the tin bath. 'She sicked up her milk,' Dorcas said by way of explanation.

'Is she all right?' Letty put her things on the table and removed her hat and coat, draping them over the back of a chair.

'She is now.' Letty half expected Dorcas to remind her that her first duties were as a mother, but Dorcas only said, 'It'll be something or nothing, nowt that a good night's sleep won't put right.' She took the child from the bath and swaddled her, handed her to her mother, then picked up the bath to empty it.

'Let me.' Letty got up.

'Sit yerself down, catch your breath, since you've been runnin' about like a headless chicken.' She muttered something under her breath, barged the door open with her backside and went out into the yard.

Alfie looked to Letty and she smiled to reassure him.

'Have you been all right, Alfie, love?'

'Yes, Mam. Nanny Dorcas told me a story about her boy Robbie. He went to sea on a boat called *Stella*.'

At the mention of her name, his sister looked about her.

Letty rubbed her hand about his face. He had stumbled over calling her Mam to begin with, shy and clumsy, but over time, his awkwardness had faded and now he never called her Mrs Letty. She had not heard a word from the Lewises – but then she hadn't expected to. 'I should imagine Nanny Dorcas liked that,' she told him. Dorcas never spoke of Robbie to her, nor her husband Will, but she obviously enjoyed talking about them to Alfie. The boy was a blessing to them all.

A few seconds later, Dorcas bustled back into the room, having hung the tin bath on the nail in the yard and wiped her hands on the corner of the towel that was wrapped around her granddaughter. From the pile of clothing she had removed from the airer, she pulled out a nightdress for Stella and gave it to Letty. She eyed the rent book Letty had left on the table, raised her eyebrows. 'You've got it sorted, have yer?'

'Most of it.' She told her of the things she'd had put by at Jack Tapper's. There was still lots to do, but she had secured the rent, and that was the most important, and perhaps the easiest, for there was still so much to do before it could open as a café.

Dorcas took down a pan and poured fresh water into it, put it on the stove to boil. Letty had no sooner got Stella into her nightdress than Dorcas handed the child a bottle of the cooled water to settle her tummy.

'I still think it's a daft idea. But then you've always had daft ideas. You and my lad, both of yer.'

Letty wanted to tell her that her daft ideas had worked so far, but she didn't want to tempt fate. There was a mountain to climb yet, and she needed all the help she could get.

19

The *Black Prince* was no more. The trawler had been painted grey, the name and number obliterated and replaced by an official number, painted in white, two feet long on each bow. She would now fly the white ensign to signal that she belonged to the Royal Navy. Alec felt as if he were masquerading as something else too, with his navy uniform and his brass buttons. He was not a fighting man, but he was willing to do what was necessary until he could go back to what he loved, to what he knew best.

They had left Lowestoft at the end of August paired with another ex-trawler and now minesweeper, the *Artemis* – a Hull ship with a Boston skipper, the work tedious and dangerous. From first light, they moved through the trade routes, channels that had been marked by buoys, keeping the lanes clear for merchant ships to move in safety, allowing the fishing vessels that remained to get on with their work. A steel cable was stretched between the *Prince* and *Artemis* who kept a steady course as they cut through the waves, hoping to catch the mines on the cable, sending it up to the surface where it could be dealt with. If they were in shallow water, they might drag them along to be despatched with. Alternatively, out would come the rifles and the men would line the rail, firing at the horns on the outer surface of the mine to detonate it. It had none of the pleasure of the rifle range at the fair.

Alec couldn't remember the last time he'd been in church, but he'd never prayed to God as much as he had these past weeks. They had already cleared forty mines and still there were more. There must be hundreds of the blighters. The Germans were using U-boats to lay them, and as fast as they cleared an area, it could once again be littered with the bastards.

Alec looked out over the bridge, steering a steady course, and blew down to Cookie in the galley to send up a brew. There was no thrill of the catch, no searching the places for shoals of fish, or dropping the lead line. Below him on deck, men stood at the rails, keeping a lookout – for the horns of floating mines that had come adrift, or the dark shadow of a U-boat. The hours spent watching an endless horizon could drive a man crazy.

He saw Lieutenant Proctor coming up the ladder to the wheel-house and as he opened the door and ducked his head, squeezing through the opening, Alec called down for another brew. Each minesweeper had a naval officer on board as third in command, to assist and advise of naval procedure and protocol – but the skipper was in charge of the ship.

'Change of watch,' Proctor said, closing the door behind him.

Alec shifted his cap to the back of his head and saw Proctor twitch, then grin. He was a good 'un, and apt to turn a blind eye if their cap badges weren't directly to centre. A couple of the lads did it on purpose, but most because they were not used to the strict naval discipline. What did it matter if yer badge was a bit skew-whiff, as long as you did your job properly.

'By 'ell, I'm glad of it,' Alec told him. 'When we're fishing, we have a few hours here and there while we're steaming out and home again, otherwise we're on the fish day and night, and the men can go for hours on end – but this game...' He blew out over his top lip. 'Rots your brain, it does.'

Alec didn't know what he preferred: standing watch or going below. He couldn't relax, always tense, listening for the sound of something catching on the trawl, or, worse, the hull. They had already witnessed the loss of a ship, blown to smithereens, and moving over to find only wreckage and a body or two. They had been brought aboard and taken to shore as soon as was possible. Poor buggers. It was best to block it out. Not think on it, only of the next few minutes, the next few yards.

'One more day till we put in at North Shields. I'm more than ready for three days ashore.'

'More than we ever got as fishermen,' Alec replied. 'Forty-eight hours. If you were lucky. Then back to sea.' What he wouldn't give to be doing that again.

Cookie came up from below with two mugs and handed them over to one of the deckies, who held them with one hand and shinned up the ladder. They were all meant to be called seaman this and seaman that, but the lads couldn't get the hang of it and carried on as they always had, calling each other by their surnames and nicknames.

Proctor pushed down the window and the lad passed the mugs through. Proctor handed one to Alec. 'It's a difficult life. Especially for the families. When we are on manoeuvres, we can be away for months, but we are home for weeks. I possibly see more of my family than you ever do. I don't think I could do what you and your men do. It's relentless.'

Alec didn't argue. He'd tried to work out how many days a year he spent with Letty and the kiddies, his mother. Two days in every three weeks, hoping for a chance for longer. Yet when the trawler was in for a refit or repair, he was anxious to be away again, knowing time ashore was not bringing in the money. The gaffers didn't like ships idle, or men, and there were plenty more to choose from if he decided to take an extra day at home. He wanted better for his family. The new house was a start. Letty would have her land and he would have his ship, perhaps a fleet. Dreaming of the future kept him going.

'You got family, Proctor. A wife. Kiddies?'

He sipped at his mug, swallowed, shook his head. 'My father died long ago, my mother lives with her sister and her husband in Sussex.'

'Admiral Frost?' Alec nodded. 'I had heard. There's not much you can keep quiet on the docks.'

Proctor laughed good-naturedly. 'Not much else to tell. My father was a naval man, as was his father, and his father before him. I enjoyed my time, but I'd had enough. I followed the family trade, as we all do, most of us. When the time came to sign up for more, I chose not to.'

'That must have gone down well with the Admiral.'

'It wasn't without its difficulties.'

He didn't say any more, and Alec didn't press him. What a man chose to do was his own business. Would he have gone fishing if it hadn't been his father's trade, and his father's before him? It wasn't down to choice in the end, it was all they knew; and so it followed. Letty didn't want any sons to go to sea, he knew that, it was a bone of contention between them. They no longer talked of it, there being no sons, and Alfie would make his own decision. It was different for him.

Alec drained his mug and took Proctor's with him as he went down to the deck. He didn't go below directly but stood by the rail looking out over the water. A shout from port side made him start and he hurried beside Nobby Clarke, who was pointing to the right of him, about fifty yards off the bow. There was a black shape which neither of them could quite make out, but they had to assume it was a mine, first, last and always.

A light flashed the signal to the *Artemis* and the engines slowed. Staffy came to, handing out rifles that were passed along the men who lined the rail, and they began firing at it. They heard a clang of metal but no explosion, no sign of leakage as it drifted closer. Alec felt bile rise in his stomach.

Staffy climbed the ladder on the funnel and stared out as the waves washed it nearer, then shouted down to them. 'Barrel.'

Alec cupped his hands about his mouth. 'Repeat.'

'Barrel.' The man came quickly down the ladder. 'It's a barrel. Flotsam. I can see the curve of it and the metal bands.'

As it came closer, they let out a collective breath that Staffy was right. But they couldn't take any chances.

'We don't know that the blighters haven't laced it with something. Best blast at it till it disappears.'

They did so, lifting and firing, until the barrel broke open and sank. Alec slapped Staffy on his back, looked up to Proctor on the bridge, gave him a thumbs up and went below.

He rolled on his bunk, fully clothed, not removing his boots in case he needed to move sharpish. It was hard to settle. His nerves were shot to pieces, as were everyone else's. Watching, always watching, aware each moment might be their last, aware things might be left undone, unsaid. He must write to Letty, to tell her he loved her, Stella, Alfie too, as if he were his own, that should anything happen to him she must use the money to buy the house. He could rest easy knowing they were cared for, that she would not struggle. And even though Letty and his mother didn't always see eye to eye he knew they would take care of each other.

He thought of Becky, how she had teased him that night, and knew he had made the right decision. Letty was not flighty, he would never have to worry on that score. Letty was as steadfast as a lighthouse; she was his lighthouse. Alec closed his eyes, picturing her dear face, and eventually fell asleep.

20

The wounded were seated on chairs that had been spaced evenly about the room at the rear of the Bethel Mission Hall. Rosa Hewitt was applying a sling to her younger sister Lucy's arm and Ruth was knelt on the floor fastening a splint to Daphne's shin, her skirts up about her knees. It did not matter, for they were all women together, and though they were only practising, they needed to know how to treat the wounded – any wounded. So far, the battles had been fought in France and Belgium, and on the ocean, but they all feared invasion by land or sea.

Daphne sat up, resting on her forearms, and squinted at Ruth's progress. 'Have you heard from Charles?'

Ruth stopped winding the bandage and looked up. 'Lie down. Be still. If that's at all possible. The tension in your leg has changed and I won't be able to dress your wound properly.'

Daphne sighed, lay back down again.

'Nothing since last week,' Ruth told her. 'The post is difficult. It's all difficult.' She tried not to think of how bad it might be in France. She scoured the newspaper each day to discover what was happening, half wanting to know, half afraid of knowing, but no matter the saying, ignorance was not bliss. It made her more fearful. She felt safe with facts. Men were being killed and the ships sunk at a rate. The reality of loss in towns such as Hull, Grimsby and Boston already hitting hard. News came every day of crews who had not returned home, and more than 1,100 men had lost their lives when the Royal Navy battle cruisers *Cressy*, *Hogue* and *Aboukir* had been sunk in the North Sea. 'Henry has finished his training and is being assigned a ship. Unlike Charles, he was never the letter writer. He has a silver tongue but not a silver pen.'

Daphne sat up again and Ruth tilted her head on one side, glared at her, irritated. If the time came when she would need to bandage someone, she wanted to do it correctly. But Daphne was too agitated. She had been like it when she'd arrived. 'What will you do when you pass this exam?'

'*If* I pass it,' Ruth corrected her.

'You will. You're always so careful, and you pay attention.'

Ruth finished the dressing and remained on her knees. It was important to do something that would be of comfort, to lessen the pain – but if her patient were real, she doubted she would be so calm. She got to her feet and waited for Mrs Whittaker to inspect her dressing, tried hard not to giggle at Daphne, who was forcing herself to lie still. She could understand why Charles had been attracted to her, regardless of her father's wealth or good standing. Daphne was everything Charles was not, as light and joyful as he was sober and serious. She excelled at sports, could equal any of their number at tennis and was always the first to suggest a game of sardines, or a day out at the river.

'I intend to work at the mission,' Ruth said as they waited their turn. 'Men are being brought in almost daily with some injury or another – and at least I will be of use.' She so wanted to be of use, not just to the men, but to Colin Wilson, to show him, to show her aunt, that she could adapt to that life, that she was suited to it.

She had thought long and hard about what Letty had said, about what she would be willing to sacrifice, and when she left here, she would make sure Colin knew that too.

She stood back to allow Mrs Whittaker to approve her effort and when she had done so, Ruth undid her work, rolled the bandage and dressing in preparation for Daphne, and they changed places.

Ruth settled herself on the floor, pulling up her skirts about her knees. Daphne took hold of the dressing and gripped Ruth's shin.

'I'm going to join the VADs – the Voluntary Aid Detachment.' Daphne pressed the splint to Ruth's shin. 'I hope to go to France. To be with Charles.'

It was Ruth's turn to sit up. Daphne pressed her shoulder and made her lie down. Ruth stared at the ceiling at the cracks where the paint was flaking, holes where the rain had come in leaving brown rings around the damp patches, holes where nails had pierced the plaster when they hung the Christmas decorations for the children's party. Would there even be parties this year? What was there to celebrate? She didn't want to contemplate it.

'You won't be with Charles.' How would Daphne find him, how would anyone find any one at all. The battlefields were vast, the line stretching down from the coast of France to the border with Spain – the Western Front. A person could search for ever and still not find the one they loved. Ruth thought of Colin, of the time she had first seen him, in this building, when he had stood in front of the congregation, his cap under his arm, and addressed them all. She had experienced feelings then that she had never felt for any other man, before or since.

'But I'll be on the same soil.' Daphne stopped rolling the bandage. 'Closer.'

Would she do the same if it were Colin? She believed she would.

'But there is so much to do here, Daphne. There are already more widows and orphans than we can support. There is campaigning to do – for supplies, for money.'

Daphne finished the dressing and pressed her hand to Ruth's arm. 'And there are the older women to do it – the Hewitt sisters.' She looked about her and leaned close to Ruth's ear. 'Most of the people in this room.'

Ruth lay still, an image of Daphne roaming the fields of France searching for Charles in her head. She wanted to sit up, to move, to disturb the images before they disturbed her, but she had to remain until Mrs Whittaker gave her approval.

When Daphne's dressing had been passed as adequate, they got up and took their seats for instruction. The chairs were reorganised, and they faced the blackboard, taking notes as Mrs Whittaker delivered her lecture: The Organs of Circulation. There were twenty of them in the room, and there would be twenty more in the following session. Women young and old had come forward, everyone wanting to contribute in whatever way they could for the war effort, to support the boys.

Ruth looked to Daphne, so earnest, taking in Mrs Whittaker's every word and making notes. It hadn't crossed her mind to leave, only to remain and be where she felt she was most needed. Perhaps she was wrong.

* * *

When the lesson ended, they gathered their belongings and made to walk back towards the town, crossing the invisible border into Grimsby and walking along Cleethorpe Road. The weather was on the turn, summer truly over, and the wind that blew in off the sea had a chill to it. Winter would be on its heels – and what of the men in France then, of the men on the minesweepers, and those still fishing?

Newspaper vendors were on almost every corner calling out to passers-by. 'Lord Worsley killed in action.' The boy held up a copy in one hand and took pennies with the other.

Daphne hurried to him, took out her purse and paid for a copy, and the two of them stood to one side of the pavement. Daphne read the beginnings of the report to Ruth. 'The Earl of Yarborough's son has been killed in action in Zandvoorde while serving with the Royal Horse Guards.' She read a little to herself, then folded it, tucking it inside her bag that held her notebook. 'Oh, his poor wife. She was meant to open a garden party this summer but had to cancel because he was called away with his regiment. How very tragic. And for his parents. Just dreadful.'

The Pelhams' generosity would be a painful reminder, for The Grimsby Chums, local men who had answered the call to arms, were nestled in the woods about their home, Brocklesby Hall, for their basic training, before going elsewhere. There had been a shortage of serge material and hundreds of Post Office uniforms had been supplied until the serge could be obtained. It had been overwhelming; the call had been answered by so many.

Daphne began to walk again, stopped. 'When will it all end, Ruth. When?'

Ruth knew she didn't require an answer and perhaps both their thoughts had turned to Charles, to Henry – to the boys they knew who were already serving or had enlisted. It was a little too close for comfort.

They walked on in silence, weaving between people as the streets grew busier, then Daphne began to pick up the pace, Ruth striding to keep up with her.

'We must do more.'

'We're doing everything we can,' Ruth said, hoping to calm her.

'We help at the mission, with the relief fund. We have the Ladies Guild, the League. We're taking our first-aid certificates.' She reeled off the measure of their days. 'It doesn't seem to amount to much, but without it, life will grind to a halt and there'll be nothing worth fighting for.'

'It's not enough though. When young men are dying.' She gripped Ruth's gloved hand, stilled her. '*Our* young men.'

Ruth wriggled her hand free. 'Don't, Daphne. I can't dwell on what Henry and Charles, and men like them, are facing. It paralyses me. I feel helpless and I don't want to be helpless.' They began to walk again. 'We must keep busy, keep things going, so that when they come home, life will go back to how it was before.'

'But don't you understand.' Daphne was earnest, and of all things this was the most unexpected. 'Things will *never* go back to how they were before. Never.'

The world was full of holes, spaces where the young men used to be, in the shops and offices, at the docks and the warehouses. There were no young men lingering on corners, promenading with their girls, no dances, no parties. Life had paused, like a children's game, and when the music stopped, someone had removed all the boys.

Ruth briefly closed her eyes and pictured Charles, somewhere in France, Henry on the North Sea. If she could see them in her mind's eye, then she knew they were safe. It was all she had, and she would keep thinking of them, hold them in her heart and in her head.

'Where to?' Daphne asked.

'I'll keep walking. I'm meeting Mrs Hardy at the Mission.' The lie came so easily that it shocked her. She would have liked to talk of her feelings for the port missioner but was in no doubt that Daphne would try to talk her out of it. Daphne was a young woman with a sound sense of what was and was not respectable in their social circle. But then her friend was lucky, for she had fallen in love with the right man.

'I rather like Mrs Hardy. She's a shrewd woman,' Daphne said, showing interest as they navigated the crowds that were spilling from the streets that led away from the docks, many of them stopping to call in at the public houses that dotted along the main road.

Outside the Saracen's Head a small girl was standing with a toddler that couldn't have been more than eighteen months, a similar age to Letty's Stella. The toddler had fallen asleep on the pavement and the girl was huddled against the wall. She was familiar, though Ruth had no idea why until the child looked straight at her.

A woman staggered out of the entrance door, the worse for drink. Daphne took a step back, disgust clear on her face, and sidestepped about them, but Ruth could not take her eyes off the child. And where was the baby? She shuddered.

'Sorry, missus, didn't see yer,' the woman said, straightening up.

Ruth was overwhelmed with pity. The woman had been well put together when she had last seen her, her children cared for. It was hard to believe it was the same Mary Owen, but she knew it was. Grief had made its mark, and a deep cut at that.

Daphne had walked on and, realising Ruth had not, turned and waited. Ruth could not forget the sound of the woman, her cry of pain, the hollowness of her own insides when she'd heard it on the wharf.

'You can't spare a few coppers, can yer, lady? For me girls. They've had nowt to eat all day. Lost me husband, I have.' She clutched her hand to her breastbone and her face crumpled. 'And me babby's gone. The good Lord saw fit to take her from me.'

'Oh, how truly dreadful. I am so sorry for your loss.' Ruth opened her purse and gave the woman two shilling pieces, wondering whether to give more, when Daphne came and took her by the arm.

'Dear Lord, Ruth,' she said as she guided her away. 'What on earth are you thinking of, you'll have every beggar on the street after you.'

'It was for the children.'

'I doubt the children will see any of it,' Daphne muttered as she led her away, down towards the tram stop.

Ruth could not erase the child's face from her mind and after Daphne had ceased her berating of her friend's outrageous generosity, Ruth told her of what she had witnessed the day Henry came home from sea. 'Only a few weeks ago, I doubt that woman would have set foot in a public house alone. Her name is Mary Owen. She was waiting for her husband, nicely dressed, her children clean and tidy beside her. He didn't return and now she has lost her baby. I can't bear to see what it has done to her.'

Daphne pulled her arm and linked it to hers. 'It will worsen as the war continues and women like Mary Owen will be on every street, on every road. But you can't help all of them.'

Ruth slowed her pace. 'None of us can help all of them – whether they are soldiers, sailors, women or children. But if we all help one or two when we can, it might make a difference.'

'You're right, of course,' Daphne agreed. 'I only hope she spends the shillings you gave her wisely.' The tram came to a stop in front of them and Ruth released her arm. 'I suppose we must do what we can, where we can,' Daphne said, kissing her cheek before she stepped up onto it. That their ways of doing so might differ was irrelevant, as long as they did something to hold things together, instead of being bystanders while things fell apart.

* * *

Across the road, Helen Frampton watched her niece and Daphne Willoughby from a window on the upper floor of the *Herald* offices. Daphne was an excellent partner for Charles, she would ease the way as a good wife should. That was what Richard needed for his company.

Young Henry had outfoxed them this time, with his joining of the trawler section. It was a filthy job and she half admired him for not taking the easy route, if there was one to be had. If only Ruth could be made to see that marrying well was a way of securing her own future. It was not too late to resolve things with Arthur Marshall.

When the tram moved off, Ruth waited until it was out of sight, then turned and walked around the corner to Orwell Street. Helen shook her head in despair. She knew exactly where her niece was going. Oh, the silly, foolish girl. Couldn't she see that it would never work. It wouldn't do at all.

21

Ruth considered that the best way to go into the mission unnoticed was to walk in confidently as Henry had done at Saxon Hall. She thought of that day, how he had left her and told her to have an adventure, to take a chance. Here was such an opportunity. Was she brave enough to take it? There was only one way to find out. She took a deep breath, put a smile on her face and entered, asked to see the superintendent and waited in the lobby, bold as brass. And even though she hoped she gave the appearance that she was confident, her heart was beating wildly. There was no way of knowing how long she could maintain it, and as she waited, panic began to rise and she thought it a mad idea. She was about to make her excuses when the man behind the desk spoke to her.

'Miss Evans. Would you feel more comfortable waiting in Mr Wilson's office?'

Her relief was immediate, and he led the way to the superintendent's office, leaving the door ajar.

She sat down, looking again at the painting of the founder, and Ebenezer Mather stared back, accusingly this time, as though he could see through her pretence.

'Miss Evans.'

At the sound of Colin's voice, Ruth got up, hardly able to contain her excitement at seeing him. 'Mr Wilson,' she lowered her voice to a whisper. 'Colin.' She saw him hesitate, glance to the door. The man at the desk was booking someone into a room and two men were arguing about who was first in the queue. 'I have counted the seconds.'

He frowned. 'Miss Evans?'

'Ruth,' she corrected him.

He shook his head. 'You shouldn't be here, alone. People will think badly of you. There has already been distasteful gossip and I would not want...'

She went to him then, took hold of his hands, was thrilled when he didn't withdraw them. 'I cannot keep away. The other day, when I came. There was so much I wanted to say.' She wanted to make him see that it was all right, that no matter what anyone said, her father, her aunt, rumours, she didn't care. She wanted to be at his side, to be on the same soil, as Daphne had said – yes, that was it, on the same soil. Everything was changing and the world they had known, so stable and secure only a few months ago, was no more. Husbands, brothers, sons had already been lost.

'Miss Evans.' He stepped forward, and she closed her eyes, waiting for his lips to touch hers, but he did not oblige, and wondering why, she opened them to see her aunt beside them. She sprang away, the colour and heat coming to her face, her neck.

'Do forgive my tardiness, Mr Wilson,' Aunt Helen said, directing her speech to Ruth, her voice louder than necessary. 'I had to go back for the ledgers and told my niece to come ahead of me. Thank you, Ruth.' She took a seat at the desk and Colin made his way to the other side of it. Helen Frampton handed the ledgers to Ruth, who took them, her hands trembling. 'We had made a comprehensive list of items at the last meeting of the Ladies Guild and wanted to reassure you that we are doing our very best to make certain you have everything you need.'

Mr Wilson could not look at her, and Ruth could not look at her aunt. For a good five minutes, they went through a charade of shortages, of wants and needs, and try as she might, Ruth could not find her voice, or speak up. If only they'd had had a few more moments. She knew he would have told her he felt the same. Ruth stared at the blank pages of the ledgers.

Presently, her aunt got up and Colin followed suit. 'Thank you for your precious time, Mr Wilson. I understand just how busy you are. It's very good of you to see us.'

Ruth got up, put out her hand and he gave it the briefest of shakes. He walked with them to the door, Ruth stepping out into the lobby, her aunt following.

'Oh, and before I forget, the fundraiser.' She smiled at Ruth, and at the man behind the desk. 'Would you wait in the lobby, dear.'

Ruth dare not argue. The man looked down at the booking-in ledger as Ruth waited in the lobby. She moved to the window and stared out onto the street, her throat thick with fear. Colin had mentioned distasteful gossip. Weren't there more pressing things for people to talk about?

Shortly afterwards, her aunt came out, all smiles, chatting away to Mr Wilson, who once again shook her aunt's hand. 'Mrs Frampton. Miss Evans.' He gave her only the briefest of glances, opened the main door and waited for them to leave, closed it behind them.

Her aunt did not say anything until they were across the road and in the *Herald* offices, and from the window Ruth realised how her aunt had known she was there. She waited by it while her aunt gave instructions to her secretary, then came in and closed the door. She poured a glass of water and sipped from it, then took a seat behind her desk.

'Sit down, Ruth.'

'I'd rather stand.'

Her aunt considered her, and Ruth felt like a small child again. She turned away, looked down into the street below, at the newspaper sellers and the people going about their business, then to the mission. She had been so close – and when he had looked at her, she knew. It was as Letty had said, the small signs, the look in his eye, the touch of his hand, the feel of it on her skin.

'There's no point my asking what you were doing at the mission.'

Ruth didn't answer. It was best to let her aunt have her say, and she knew better than to argue when she would never win.

'I've had my suspicions for a while but thought you had more sense.'

Ruth swung round.

Her aunt was glad to have her attention. 'And I see now why you asked Arthur to wait. To keep him dangling while you had your little flirtation with Mr Wilson.' She touched the frame of her husband's photograph. 'You are letting your heart rule your head.'

Ruth was about to defend herself, but her aunt put up a hand to stop her.

'Hear me out.' Ruth stared down at her hands. 'These are strange times, emotions are stirred, we are fearful of the future. I understand.' Her tone softened. 'But we *must* think of the future, Ruth – and your future in particular.'

If only her aunt was concerned for her happiness instead.

'I agree. It is my future.' She looked directly at her aunt. 'And I don't want to spend it with Arthur.'

'And I...' Aunt Helen corrected herself. 'Your father will want you to make a good marriage.'

'And what is a good marriage? A happy one? Or a strategic one?' At that moment she wasn't certain of the answer, but it wasn't her aunt's life they were talking about. She walked to the door. 'I'd rather I choose for myself.'

'Very well, Ruth.' Her aunt pressed her palms to her desk. 'Then I very much hope that you'll be able to deal with the consequences.'

22

Stella was sitting up in the pram, peering around the hood that had been put up to protect her from the wind. 'She doesn't like that, does she,' Dorcas said as they crossed the road. 'What a neb she's got on her, proper nosey little article. We'll have to watch her when she gets a bit bigger.'

'I have to watch her now.' It had been a palaver fastening Stella's leather reins, but Letty wouldn't have it otherwise. The child was a scamp.

The boiled water had settled her stomach and Letty had been able to get a good night's sleep. She was glad of it, for it would be a marathon trying to get everything done on her list. Alfie was at school, the house was clean, the washing and pressing done, and there was very little braiding work to keep Dorcas busy. More was the pity. Letty had been on her way to check over the hut to assess what amount of work was needed before she could open, and make a start on it, when Dorcas had invited herself along. Stella wasn't the only one with her nose in everything, and Letty prepared herself for a barrage of criticism.

There was nothing about the hut to brag about, it was practical and functional – and that was all it needed to be. She hoped excitement hadn't clouded her judgement and she had underestimated the work it would take to get it up and running – and the cost. Balanced at the foot of the pram was a bucket and some old rags, a block of soap and a bag of soda. She'd borrowed brooms and other larger items from Parkers, needing to save where she could until the money started coming in.

She manoeuvred the pram down the side roads and out towards the slips, and pointed out the building to Dorcas as they neared it. Dorcas passed no comment, simply pursed her lips and nodded. Letty dealt with the padlock, and pulled open the door, letting the light flood in. Once they were inside, she pushed the pram hood down and Stella's eyes were everywhere, as were her grandmother's – but still Dorcas said nothing. Letty wished she would. She was used to sparring with her, deflecting her barbed words, but her mother-in-law's silence was even more unsettling.

As Letty unloaded the pram, putting the cleaning materials by the brushes and dustpan she had loaned from Norah, Dorcas strode about looking up and down, went to the windows and rubbed at them with the side of her fist, looked out, around, up and down. Letty caught her eye. 'I know it's bare and dirty, but a bit of elbow grease will soon see to that...'

'A bit!' Dorcas exclaimed.

'Nothing I can't fix with soap and water. A lick of paint.' She picked up a broom, and began sweeping, steeling herself for more criticism. If her mother-in-law had come to gloat, hopefully she would get it over and done with, and then leave her to it.

Dust and dirt swirled about, and she stopped to open a window, afraid the dust would catch in Stella's throat. When she turned back, Dorcas had picked up the broom and was sweeping the larger bits of rubbish into the corner.

'You'd best get a bucket of water and damp down this dust while our Stella's about,' Dorcas told her. 'I assume there is water?'

Letty couldn't have been more surprised if Dorcas had walked stark naked down Freeman Street on market day. There had been no hint of her coming to help and Letty hadn't dare ask. She picked up the bucket.

'There's a tap outside. Puggy is going to bring it inside for me. I've a number of things coming from Jack Tapper's at the end of the week. I plan to open on Friday.'

Dorcas rolled her eyes, stopped sweeping. 'The good Lord preserve us.' She shook her head, began sweeping again. 'Get a move on, lass. We haven't got time to hang about.'

* * *

For the next three days, Dorcas came with her to the hut and each day they cleaned and scrubbed and painted. Letty had posters made and Wolfie and a mate pasted them about the docks, on walls and lampposts. They were putting the finishing touches to the tap and making a counter for the stove when Jack Tapper's cart arrived. Wolfie and Puggy had rounded up a few mates to help unload it, taking the items into the hut and putting the trestle tables and benches where she wanted them. Dorcas washed and dried the sturdy mugs and plates, Stella fastened in her pram at the side of her, watching the comings and goings as intently as her grandmother. The pair of them missed nothing.

Letty went out to settle up with Jack Tapper and when she returned, Dorcas was handing out mugs of tea, the men settling themselves among the tables to enjoy it. The sight made her close to tears. Little more than two years ago, she had arrived here, afraid and filled with apprehension. She knew nothing of this life, of docks and trawlers, the fishing – and Dorcas had been on her back the entire time. But here she was, among friends. The sight of the old sea dogs gathered about as she had imagined was almost too much to take in. As if that wasn't enough in life to be grateful for, Dorcas had been at her side all week. And she had worked harder than any of them.

Dorcas released Stella from her pram and she began toddling about the floor, begging to be up at the table.

Wolfie swept her up and set her beside him.

'Get yer drink, lass. Have five minutes, cos you'll not get it once yer doors are open.' All week, men had come and peered around the door to satisfy their curiosity, to ask when it would open, to wish them well, glad there would be an escape, away from the warehouse and the yards. Their words had been enough to spur her on when each day ended and she was bone-tired, Dorcas too, and the walk home seemed to have lengthened.

Letty took her tea and sat down, cupped her hands about the mug and looked about her. It was her very own business. Hers. She looked to Dorcas, who gave her a smile, as if to say, 'Well done, lass,' and Letty could have burst into tears there and then. She listened to the men talk, their laughter and jibbing of each other, their gentle teasing, these big rough men so gentle with Stella, with Letty.

Wolfie winked at her, looked out of the window. 'Kenny Oakes is outside with his wagon, Letty. Will you be wanting me to do anything?'

A second ago, Letty had felt she could do no more, but now a shaft of excitement recharged her. 'Only if he needs any help.'

Wolfie went outside and there was the sound of a ladder being propped against the metal, then hammering. Dorcas looked across at her, but Letty could only smile. It was best to wait until it was done.

The hammering stopped and Wolfie stuck his head about the door and called to Letty.

'Mr Oakes wants you to come and check all is in order.'

Letty got up and took Stella in her arms. 'Dorcas, perhaps you could come with me.'

It was cold on the wharf, the wind coming in sharp off the sea. Dorcas grumbled as she walked to Letty, who was standing with Wolfie and Mr Oakes. All three were looking up at the front of the building. Dorcas twisted to see what they were about and stopped dead in her tracks.

'What do you think, Dorcas. Will it do?'

It was a while before Dorcas could respond and then it was merely a nod.

Letty smiled. 'You've done a grand job, Mr Oakes, and so quickly too. I'm sorry to have sprung it on you.'

'Eh, it were worth it. It looks grand.'

The sign above the tin hut declared that it was now Hardy's Café in blue lettering on a cream background.

Letty turned to Dorcas.

'Hardy's,' Letty, said. 'I think it looks wonderful, don't you?'

Dorcas stood for a while, looking up at the sign, opened her mouth, closed it again.

Letty waited, knowing it had met with her mother-in-law's approval, though she would never admit to it.

Dorcas took a hankie from her pocket and rubbed it under her nose, took hold of Stella. 'That cream paint will be mucky in no time,' she called over her shoulder as she went back inside, leaving Letty not knowing whether to laugh or cry.

23

The station platform at Grimsby was already overflowing with soldiers and sailors, and now the VADs were scattered about among them, waiting to board the train. Ruth had travelled to the station in the Willoughbys' car, Daphne's parents wanting to see her off to her training in Yorkshire. They had stepped back to allow the two friends to talk and waited by a bench, never taking their eyes from their daughter's face.

Daphne squeezed Ruth's hand in thanks as she handed her a small, neatly wrapped gift. Ruth had wanted to get her something to carry with her, something personal and practical, and had opted for a compact leather notebook, a small pencil attached to the side, and embossed with her initials. 'Thank you, my dear,' Daphne said as she removed the paper, admired it, then tucked it into her handbag. 'You know, it's not too late to reconsider, Ruth. They are desperate for volunteers.'

She had thought about it many times, wanting to break free of the restrictions she felt held her here. 'I couldn't leave Father.' She was aware of the burden Excel Trawlers had become without Charles at his side, let alone all the other men who had left. There was more to do and less men to do it and she tried to be of help to him where she could. They couldn't all leave, could they? But most of all she wanted to stay because of Colin, to be on the same soil, as Daphne had put it. She had told her father of her feelings for the port missioner, before her aunt could fill his head with what was expected of her and what was not. He had cautioned against it, told her to really think things through before she shared her feelings with this man. He had explained the consequences of committing herself. 'His work will become your work. Are you prepared for that?'

'I am. As long as he feels the same way about me, then I feel I can endure any hardships.'

He was thoughtful. 'You will not have a comfortable life, such as you are used to. Living in an apartment in a mission building does not afford much privacy. He will be on call at all hours – as will you. Mr Wilson arrived very suddenly, he might be moved again. You will have to move with him, leave your family and friends behind.' His voice cracked a little. 'If you have children, what then? Please think on these things, darling. Don't act hastily to prove your aunt wrong. That is not the path to a happy life, nor a happy marriage. You have to be certain.'

She'd given his comments much thought these past days, deciding she could get used to the discomfort, that she could get used to most things – all except the leaving. Then Father would have no one and she wasn't sure she was ready to leave him yet. Not while the boys were absent.

As more people boarded the train, the platform became clearer and Ruth could see down the line as it curved away in the distance, the crossing gates just visible. 'Don't you wish we could turn back time, Daphne, to stop the clocks at summer, when we didn't have to be brave.'

'It's not about being brave, my dear. I'm as scared as anyone else. It's about love.' She kissed Ruth's cheek. 'You will write?'

'Of course.'

Daphne picked up her bag, ready to join the other VADs, and her parents took it as the signal to come forward. They held her close and the three of them remained where they were as the train pulled out of the station. Daphne gave a final wave, then withdrew from the window.

The Willoughbys offered to take Ruth home and she thanked them but refused, wanting to be alone with her thoughts.

She took a seat outside the booking office and watched more travellers arrive and trains pull in. There were wounded being helped down, those with crutches, some with bandages about their head. Disfigured. Who knew what Daphne would face when she finally got to France. She had gone for love. Could love give Ruth courage too? The brave ones had left, those who could answer the call stronger than she was.

She walked home. It had begun to drizzle, and droplets fell from her hat, but the air was fresh, and the walk gave her time to clear her head. Like Daphne said, she could always change her mind.

In the porch, she removed her hat and shook it to clear the moisture, then closed the door, placed her hat on the dresser in the hall. She was hanging up her damp coat when her father came out of his study.

'Where have you been?' He was not unkind, had simply forgotten, as he so often did these days.

She checked herself in the mirror, patted her hair into place, and talked to him via her reflection. 'To the station. Daphne has left with the other VADs.'

'Ah, yes, so I recall.' He rubbed at his eyes with thumb and forefinger, smiled at her. 'I thought you might have been with the

Guild. Isn't it today that Mr Wilson leaves. Or have I got that wrong too?'

Ruth turned away from the mirror. 'The port missioner?'

He put his hand in his pocket, pulled out his watch and checked the time. 'I thought your aunt might have mentioned it, being the president of the Guild...'

She didn't hear the rest of what he said as she grabbed her coat and hat and tore out of the door, leaving it wide. He called after her, but she wouldn't turn back, not this time.

* * *

At the mission, she waited outside to catch her breath, her heart pounding. The tram had stopped on Freeman Street. There had been some sort of accident, and not wanting to waste a moment, she had alighted and hurried the rest of the way, almost running for part of it, one hand to hold her hat in place as she had not stopped to secure it with a pin. It was most unseemly, but she no longer cared if people stopped and stared. Half of her hoped that father had been confused, half of her knew her aunt had a part in all this.

The man at the desk was dealing with someone and she slipped behind him, not waiting to be shown to the office, knocked on the door and went it. Colin Wilson and a middle-aged woman were standing to one side of his desk, examining the record books. They looked up and stood more upright as she entered.

'Mr Wilson.' It was all she could say.

The woman looked at her and Ruth felt as if her insides were peeled away. She was a comely woman in her mid-forties, and she stood with her hands clasped in front of her, a watch suspended from her black blouse. Her abundant hair was drawn back from her head in a generous sweep, and though her gaze was intense, her expression was kindly. 'Oh, forgive me.' The woman turned to Colin.

'Miss Evans, this is Miss Sheldon.' The woman held out her hand and gripped Ruth's firmly. 'Miss Evans and her family are fine supporters of the mission work. Her Aunt Helen is president of the fundraising committee, and of the Ladies Guild…' He looked to Ruth as he spoke. 'In fact, I don't know what we'd do without her.'

'Ah, Mrs Frampton,' Miss Sheldon said, making a slight movement with her head. 'We have already met.' She didn't enlarge on it, waiting for Ruth to explain her call.

'I heard you were leaving?'

His eyes met hers. 'Yes. I have been called to take over another mission. Miss Sheldon is to take my position. I know you will be of great assistance to her – as you have all been to me.'

Miss Sheldon did not interrupt but neither did she leave, and Ruth felt the seconds ticking away like a steam train in her head.

'I thought it might be rumour. There are so many.' She had hoped with all her heart it was. She smiled at Miss Sheldon, willing her to leave them, just for a few minutes, but the woman was steadfast, and if she had any thought about Ruth's sudden appearance, her countenance did not betray it.

'No. It's not a rumour.' His tone was flat and matter-of-fact. 'Once I have shown Miss Sheldon around the building, I will hand over and travel to my next post. I leave tonight.'

'Tonight?' she gasped, gave the pretence of a cough to conceal it. Her throat became thick with regret, with words of love that she had never spoken. She fought to regain her composure, aware that she had revealed her true feelings in front of this woman. There would be no opportunity to talk to him alone, and she dare not request it. She had no courage at all, and that was why she had stayed. She was not like Daphne, nor any of the other girls who had left on the train that day.

Miss Sheldon smiled at her, not in malice, but in understanding, and stared down at the ledgers on the desk in front of her. It gave them a moment to communicate, if only with their eyes and not their words.

Somehow Ruth found her voice and, as steadily as she could, said, 'Then I wish you well – and Godspeed.' She held out her hand and Colin took it, pressing it hard. She wanted to weep at his touch, but there would be plenty of time for regret and sorrow later. 'I shall leave you to your work,' she managed to say. 'There must be much for you both to do. Miss Sheldon.'

The woman looked up. 'I hope we at the mission can still count on your support, Miss Evans?'

Ruth forced herself to reply, though her throat was swollen with misery. She managed to nod her head, feeling the tears begin to gather. 'Of course.'

Miss Sheldon put out her own hand and took Ruth's in a firm grip. 'Then I look forward to the next time we meet.'

24

Outside, Ruth gulped for air, her heart pounding, her chest tight. What chance would she have to say goodbye, to ask him to write, to tell him her feelings, that she would give up everything to be beside him. What a fool she was, a damned silly fool.

She walked, aimlessly, not really watching where she was going, felt people push into her as they moved across the streets and the crossings. She waited, hearing the train, the clatter of trucks, but not seeing it. Someone stopped her, took her hand, and for a brief moment, she thought he had come after her.

'Letty.' She looked down at Alfie, tried to smile, and his innocent blue eyes almost undid her.

'Ruth, are you all right, my dear?'

She managed to nod her head, bit down on her lip, but could not stop the tears. The sight of her kindly face was too much.

Letty clasped her other hand in hers. She couldn't move, only watched as Letty looked about her, then guided her into St Andrew's Church. An overwhelming scent of beeswax greeted them, and the cool quietness instantly calmed her. Flowers were set either side of the aisle, the colours blurring as her eyes clouded, the tears spilling onto her jacket, and she had no willpower to stop them. Letty directed Alfie to sit along the pew and handed him a small piece of rope, and he occupied himself tying knots that the old sea dogs had taught him. Letty gently pressed her to sit down on another pew, handed her a handkerchief and settled herself beside her.

'What on earth has happened. Is it bad news?'

Ruth couldn't speak.

'Is it Henry? Charles?'

She managed to shake her head. 'It... It... I...' She dabbed at her eyes, pressing the kerchief to them, blocking out the light. 'Colin. Mr Wilson.' The tears came again, and she gulped for air, then pressed her lips together, fearing the dam would burst, and when Letty put her arm about her shoulders, she leaned into her and sobbed, quietly, so her shoulders racked with the pain of it, of being too late. When she had cried herself out, she remained there, Letty's arm about her. They were close in age, but Letty seemed so much more capable, stronger, and she felt like a child, little more than Alfie. Eventually, she sat up, dabbed at her eyes with the damp handkerchief and rubbed at her nose. Letty's face radiated warmth, and Ruth felt safe here, away from the noise of traffic and bustle of the streets. It was the Fishermen's Church – but then many a church laid claim to that title. There was one on every corner, or so it seemed: Methodist, Baptist, Church of England – but it was all the same God. Was the good Lord watching over her now, or had he abandoned her?

* * *

'Now then,' Letty said, taking hold of Ruth's hand. 'Tell me what's brought all this on? If you feel able to, that is.' The woman was distraught, so heaven only knew what had happened to make her so.

'Colin… Mr Wilson is leaving the mission. I didn't know.'

'Neither did I,' Letty said. 'That's rather sudden. I haven't been able to get there for a while, I've been too busy with the café.' She glanced to Alfie who was absorbed with his knots. He'd been at school all day and would be hungry. 'When does he leave?'

'Tonight.'

Ah, that explained the tears.

'It must have been a shock.'

'It was.' Her voice wobbled, but she did not cry. 'You know how I feel about him?'

Letty nodded. Colin was a good man, upright and honest. Letty had long thought he had harboured feelings for Ruth. It was clear to her, so there was no doubt it was also clear to Helen Frampton.

Ruth looked about her, whispered, 'My aunt walked in on us, a little while ago, when I was just about to share my feelings, but if she hadn't, I know he would have said something, as would I.'

Helen Frampton wouldn't have liked that. She was a powerful figure in the town. It would not sit well that her niece was falling in love with a lowly port missioner.

Light shone through the stained-glass windows casting colour about the highly polished pews. Alfie looked at her, grinned, held up the short piece of rope with a beautifully even sheepshank knot. Wolfie and the other men had been so kind to him, the Parkers too. He was loved and it had helped him blossom. She truly believed that love could overcome all things. Could make things right.

'Didn't you get chance to speak with him at all?'

She shook her head. 'Miss Sheldon was there, the new port missioner. What could I say in front of her? That I love him, that I want him to stay?' She clasped hold of Letty's hand. Ruth's were limp and soft, not hardened as her own were from washing and scrubbing. Ruth lived a different life and Colin Wilson would have considered that before making any kind of advance towards her.

'He would not stay, Ruth. He will want to do his duty, as other men are doing. He will go where he is sent, where he is needed.'

'I would go with him if he asked.'

Letty squeezed her hand. 'I know you would, perhaps that's why he never took things any further.'

Ruth's brow furrowed. 'That's what Aunt Helen said. That I couldn't live that life – but I could. Just as you have changed your life for Alec, for love. I could do that.'

Letty regretted her words. It wasn't only her love for Alec that kept her going, not entirely. Sometimes it was just sheer will and bloody-mindedness, for the nights without him were long, the days longer. She had made vows, vows she intended to keep. For better, for worse. 'It's not the same, Ruth.'

'Isn't it? Haven't you given up your entire way of life, your family, for Alec? Do you think I could not do the same?'

Letty didn't bother to explain, it would be of no use.

'I don't even know where he is going,' Ruth said, miserably. 'I was too afraid to ask. Miss Sheldon will think me a fool.'

Letty considered how best to help. 'Why don't you write to him. I could deliver a letter this evening before he leaves. No one would think anything of it, not even the new superintendent.'

'Would you? Would you do that for me?' Ruth appeared more hopeful.

'Of course.' Ruth withdrew her hand from Letty's, dabbed at her swollen eyes, sat more upright. 'Come to Parkers with me. Norah will have a pencil and paper. And she will be discreet.'

25

The crews of the *Prince* and *Artemis* had been glad to go ashore to let off steam, a chance to forget their duty and let loose. The pubs had been welcoming, the townspeople making sure that their time there was a good one. They had been invited into homes for meals and left many of them with gifts of sweaters and socks. The local newspaper had a fund going and tobacco and cigarettes found their way into many a pocket. It had been a relief not to stand watch, to stare out over the grey waters of the North Sea and instead look upon the bonny lasses that were about. A pint or two had been welcome, but one of the young deckies had not known when to stop and had fallen badly and broken his ankle. Alec and Proctor waited on the deck for his replacement.

Alec pushed up his cap and laughed when the familiar face appeared atop the ladder. 'Well, if it isn't young Mr Evans.'

The lad grinned, saluted both Alec and Proctor.

'At ease, Evans,' Proctor told him.

Henry came forward and shook his hand, then Alec's. 'Well, it's virtually home from home,' he told them. He was much changed since the last time Proctor had seen him, but then they all were, like it or not. Things they had seen could not be unseen.

They set off at dawn, the clouds low and a dense fog that didn't look like it would shift anytime soon. They moved out to their section of the water, the *Artemis* to the port side. The line was stretched between the two ships and they proceeded in the familiar arrangement, zigzagging across the water, other pairs to the fore and aft of them, five pairs in all. It would not be an easy day. But none of them were, fair weather or foul. The winter weather patterns were on their way and the work would become more difficult.

Proctor was on deck, Alec in the wheelhouse and he watched Evans as he worked with the other deckies. He looked like a boy who had been brought up to work the trawlers, not one who had the privileges he was born to. They were all of them equal, each one depending on his fellow crew member. He knew from Ruth's letters that her father had been unhappy that his son had not applied for the officer status that would have been open to him, allowing him to move at speed through the ranks. Looking at him now, he wondered if the lad regretted it, then thought not – what did rank matter on the minesweepers. A mine or a torpedo cared not what status a man held.

When the watch was ended, Proctor waited on the deck for Alec to join him, while the mate went to take over at the helm.

'I never thought I'd see the Evans lad on a ship of mine. Not as deckie anyhow.'

'But he'd been on other ships. His father's?' Proctor vaguely remembered Henry telling him at the Framptons' party that he'd come in on his father's last trawler. He had been on a summer trip. Had told him of what he'd witnessed. Mostly, he remembered his sister, how enthusiastic Henry had been when Proctor had said he was an artist. His sister painted too, Henry had told him, as he'd dragged him over to meet her. Proctor had forgotten much of the day, only the time he'd spent with Ruth stayed fresh in his memory. The way she had looked, like a creature from a pre-Raphaelite painting, the sun about her golden hair, the colours of her dress, the lilt of her voice. He could hear it when he read her letters.

They went down to the mess, which had been converted from the fish hold, and took their seats at the table, as they waited for the grub's up from the cook. Another youngster, Nobby Clarke was seated next to Evans and beside him Staffy. The three of them were talking animatedly and stopped when Alec and Proctor came to join them.

'At ease,' Alec said, grinning.

Proctor knew that when he was about there would be no naval orders given, that Alec would slide in beside his men and talk as if they were on a fishing trip to the far northern waters off the Russian coast. Over the past weeks, they had found an easy way of working together, their mutual respect for each other's way of life a marker.

After they had tucked into a bowl of stew and wiped the bowl clean with bread, plates were gathered up and replaced with mugs of tea. Staffy sat back, his eyes closed, his hands resting on his full belly, while the others chatted.

'What ship were you on before, Evans?' Proctor asked. There had been no opportunity to chat during the watch, each man keeping a trained eye on the waves and what might be washed towards them.

'The *Autumn Rose.* We were torpedoed off the Dogger Bank.'

'Everyone rescued?'

He shook his head and stared into his mug, drank a little of the tea, his cheeks pouched before he swallowed it back. 'Me and two others the only survivors. We managed to scramble onto some wreckage and hang on.' He stopped talking, then looked up at them. 'A patrol picked us up, took us ashore.'

The *Prince* had had its share of narrow escapes and they had witnessed more explosions than he cared to remember. They too had picked up survivors and put in for the shore before turning back to carry out their duties, each rescue a reminder that next time it could be them.

'Your sister didn't mention it.' Henry looked to him. 'We have corresponded since we met at your aunt's party.'

Henry smiled, nodded. He was quieter than he had been then, his youthful exuberance tempered by all he had seen and done since. Training was three weeks, no more than that. The *Autumn Rose* would have been his first posting. It must have been a shock to encounter attack so soon. But then men had been caught on their first voyage. It was nothing to do with skill, more fate. Destiny.

'I was never the writer. She understands.' He was solemn. 'Others don't.' He grinned at Proctor. 'Put a note in for me next time you write, she'll appreciate it.'

He told him he would. He liked Henry Evans, very much. He was a good solid chap, not a shirker as some men were and always willing to do more than his fair share. Though a few might know of his background, he seemed uncomfortable talking about it and quickly changed the subject.

'Have you got a lass yer sweet on?' Staffy asked, opening one eye. 'She'll expect you to write a line or two.'

Henry grinned. 'I haven't, and if I did, she'd be disappointed. What about you, Staffy? Have you got a lass you're sweet on?'

The men around the table erupted into laughter, Staffy too, who pretended to bat Henry about the ears.

'Them days is long gone, 'Enry. I've got five kiddies, two of 'em lasses. An' it won't be long afore I have to keep an eye out for lads like you.' He turned to Nobby. 'And you?'

Nobby nodded. 'Ethel, her name is. We've been walking out since we was fourteen. I promised her, when I have five hundred pounds saved then we'll marry.'

'Five hundred pounds?' Henry repeated.

'Not a penny less,' Nobby said firmly. 'I want to look after her like a queen – or what sort of man would I be? When I gets back to the fishing, I'll get my skipper's ticket. I'll be a quid or two behind yer, skipper.'

Alec laughed.

Henry nudged Nobby with his elbow so that tea slopped over his mug.

'Let's hope this war ends soon, Nobby. You'll be an old man walking her down the aisle on navy pay.'

At one time, Proctor might not have got the joke, but he had soon learned that the fishermen were taking a twenty per cent cut in pay to sign with the RNR, *and* losing out on their share of the catch, to boot. A successful skipper could earn a damn good living for himself. Such a sum would be beyond many a man's reach, but not a determined skipper. He had grown to admire these men who were already used to such a hard life. Their normal hours were gruelling, many of them working around the clock, missing their breaks if work needed to be done. He couldn't do what they did and respected them all the more because of it. They spent winters in the far north, gutting fish for hours on end in the bitter weather, chopping away ice with an axe to prevent the ship from getting top heavy. The trawlers were strange vessels, high to the forward to cut through the waves, low at the sides, allowing the water that washed over the deck to fall away, and for the men to lean over further to work the nets. They had none of the regimented discipline he'd been used to, but they had a method of their own, and to a man they knew what was required of them and did it – though they might grumble about it around the mess table. They were rough and ready, but he knew he could rely on any one of them. He had much to be grateful for.

26

It took Ruth a long time to compose a letter in the back room of Parkers'. Neither Mr nor Mrs Parker had asked any questions and had gone through to the shop with Letty, leaving Ruth alone with her thoughts and feelings.

She walked back with Letty, somewhat calmer, and waited at the tram stop, while Letty delivered the letter to Colin Wilson and said her own goodbye. Ruth longed to do the same, but a brief goodbye would not suffice, and she very much doubted that Miss Sheldon would step aside for him to do so. That Ruth was in distress when she discovered his leaving would have been evident to the woman, but she'd made no attempt to give them a few minutes alone – why would she do so now?

Letty returned only moments later and joined her at the tram stop. 'He's going to the mission headquarters in Gorleston. It's a promotion. He will be serving the men of Great Yarmouth and Lowestoft. A huge responsibility in such times.'

Ruth clasped Letty's hands, as she would a life raft in a storm. 'Thank you, dearest Letty, for being so kind.'

Letty smiled warmly. 'Don't lose heart. What the good Lord

intends for us doesn't pass us by.' Her words gave Ruth comfort, as had been the intention.

Letty went on her way and Ruth waited for the tram. She stared at the stone façade of the *Herald* offices, at the gleaming windows and the gold lettering upon them, and it crossed her mind again that her aunt might have had a hand in Mr Wilson's departure. She wouldn't put it past her at all.

* * *

In the days that followed, Ruth was in utter turmoil. Letty had delivered the letter, but so far there had been no reply. She excused the absence of one to the fact that Colin would not have had time, for hadn't he struggled enough with his own correspondence at the Grimsby mission? Yet nothing eased her anxiety. Added to which was a heavy dose of guilt. She had told Miss Sheldon she would still assist at the mission and had not set foot in it. In the end, she decided she would go along to show willing, just for a few days, then gradually use her time elsewhere.

She knocked on the door of the superintendent's office, waited until Miss Sheldon called for her to enter. She was seated at her desk, addressing an envelope, and gave Ruth a cursory look and made a small motion with her hand for Ruth to take a seat.

Ruth waited while the woman finished her task. Miss Sheldon had not been there a week, but she had already made her mark. Where there had been chaos, there was now order. The periodicals had gone, books returned to shelves and the desk was clear, save for a blotter and a tray of letters ready for the morning collection. It was not ten o'clock, but Miss Sheldon was already ahead of the march. She dabbed a sponge over the gum and sealed the letter, placed it on a tray.

'Miss Evans. What brings you here this fine morning?'

'I came to help, as I always do.'

'And what do you always do?'

Ruth was taken aback. 'I helped Mr Wilson with his articles for the *Toilers of the Deep*. He would keep notes, then dictate to me. I would make a clean copy to send to the magazine office. I occasionally helped Mrs Hardy write letters with the men.'

Miss Sheldon checked the watch that was pinned to her blouse. 'Yes, he told me how kind and supportive you have been – that your family have been. Your support for the mission is much appreciated – but unlike dear Mr Wilson, I will not need your assistance with the items for the magazine.'

Ruth felt her cheeks begin to warm, her head reeling with thoughts of what Colin might have told her? But then what was there to say? He had revealed nothing of his feelings one way or another. He had not replied to her letter, and standing before his successor, she began to realise that it had all been one-sided, that no matter what she longed for, he had never once given the slightest indication that he had feelings for her – not the kind she wanted him to have. What a fool she had been, to think she had the power to make things happen. She was suddenly angry with herself. For thinking she could break free as Henry had done, and Lieutenant Proctor. It was different for men – and yet, here was Miss Sheldon, a woman in charge of men, responsible for the running of the mission and the safekeeping of everyone in it.

Miss Sheldon was watching her, her grey eyes kind. Perhaps there was a way forward after all.

'I am willing to do anything asked of me,' she said, knowing Miss Sheldon would take her at her word.

She studied Ruth, who once again felt as if she was stripped bare. 'Are you quite sure you mean anything, Miss Evans?' Miss Sheldon got up, came from behind the desk. She was tall for a woman, her bearing giving her gravitas that immediately demanded respect.

Ruth nodded, suddenly unable to find her voice.

Miss Sheldon pursed her lips, picked up the letters from her desk and walked to the door. 'Then follow me. There is much that needs to be done.' She looked Ruth up and down. 'I'll get you an apron to put over your dress, but when you come again, I would advise that you choose something a little plainer, something you can work in.'

'Oh, I can work in this,' Ruth said, staying close as they walked out into the lobby.

The letters were handed over to the man at the desk as they passed, Miss Sheldon not stopping to give instruction, her routine already established. She opened the door to the main building, Ruth at her heels, and led her to the rooms at the back of the kitchen and down into the cellar. Ruth had never been in this part of the building before.

In the cellar, two men were stoking a fire that heated the water tanks and four red-faced women were at large tubs, sleeves rolled to their elbows, two of them washing sheets, the others men's clothing. It was warm, and Ruth imagined that in winter it would be welcome, in summer it would be unbearable. The women acknowledged them with a brief tilt of the head.

'This is the laundry, as you will have gathered. And this' – Miss Sheldon opened a door and went through it – 'is where the brooms, buckets, mops and suchlike are stored.' She handed Ruth a metal pail, a scrubbing brush and some rags, and it slowly began to dawn on Ruth that Miss Sheldon had taken her at her word. She paused, expecting Ruth to object, and when she didn't, said loudly, 'Follow me.'

Off she marched again, Ruth almost running to keep up with her long strides, the scrubbing brush clattering against the pail as they went back up the stairs and into the room the Guild used for meetings. A woman was already there, on her hands and knees, and she sat back on her heels, saw who it was and got to her feet, using her hand to steady herself. The woman was older than Ruth, but she wasn't sure by how many years. She guessed at mid-thirties. She had a round face and soft features, her cheeks plump, hair escaping from the scarf she had tied about her head. She wiped her hands on her apron.

'Mrs Thomas, this is Miss Evans, she has come to help.'

The woman raised an eyebrow at Miss Sheldon, looked to Ruth. 'Best put yer pinny on.' She indicated to the apron Ruth clutched in her hand. 'Spoil that bootiful dress, you will.' She shook her head, undoubtedly thinking as Ruth had of the delicate fabric getting soiled.

'Can you show Miss Evans where she will get hot water and soda, Mrs Thomas?'

The woman nodded.

'Very good. I'll leave it with you. Ladies.' She left, her heels beating a retreat down the corridor.

Ruth coloured. 'I've never cleaned a floor before.'

'Didn't think fer one minute yer 'ad, lovey,' Mrs Thomas said, kindly, 'but there's nowt to it. You'll soon learn.'

She led Ruth to a room at the side of the kitchen and showed her the sink and taps. When the bucket was full, the woman threw in a handful of soda and swirled it about with her hand.

'Nah, then,' she smiled, 'foller me.'

Back in the meeting room, Mrs Thomas pulled up her skirts, showing pudgy knees about her stockings which stopped below them, tucked the rag in the top of her apron and knelt down, dropping the brush in the bucket, shaking off the excess water and working in circular movements. She then took out the rag and dried the excess, buffed it to a shine. She sat up on her heels. 'Like I said, nowt to it. We start furthest from the door. That way, we don't get marooned in one corner.'

Ruth gingerly pulled up her skirts, awkward in front of a stranger, and knelt down beside her, doing as the woman had instructed. She rolled up her sleeves as best she could before dropping the brush in the water and retrieving it. Water splashed about as she shook the brush too fierce, then, realising her mistake, more gently, and began to scrub. Mrs Thomas gave her an encouraging smile and set about her own work.

After a few minutes, her arms began to ache and her knees got sore. She knelt back, watching Mrs Thomas who had covered three times the area Ruth had done.

She looked at her, still on her knees. 'It's harder than it looks, ain't it, but you'll build up yer strength and it'll be nothing to yer.' She got back to her work. 'The name's Ada by the way.'

'Ruth.' It was odd giving her Christian name to a woman such as Ada. She was not used to being so informal, but then neither was she used to scrubbing floors. Her aunt would hit the roof if she saw her – and the very thought of it gladdened her.

'Well, Ruth, what's happened to yer that you've had to come 'ere to do this?'

'Nothing.'

Ada got up, moved her bucket, inspected the floor, then Ruth. 'Nothing? You've not fell on hard times then?'

Ruth sat back on her heels, drew the back of her hand over her brow. 'I told Miss Sheldon I wanted to help. That I would do anything.'

Ada laughed heartily. 'Ah, I'll bet yer did. That were yer first mistake, ducky.' She folded her arms. 'Testing yer, she is. Seeing what yer made of.'

Ruth thought of Daphne washing bandages that were thick with blood. She had written that she hoped to be in France soon, that she had volunteered. Her letters had been full of her work, and the young men, how brave they were – and how damaged. What was washing a few floors compared to any of that?

* * *

When Ruth left the mission in the late afternoon, she could barely walk and made her way to her father's offices, knowing she would have the luxury of being driven home in her father's car. She thought of Ada, and women like her, who worked all day, then worked again when they got home, with no comfort of a car, nor even good shoes, and she felt ashamed of thinking that she could do what they did every day of their lives. She ached with toil and loneliness, but she had survived the day. And if she could survive one, somehow she knew she would survive them all. She had been naïve to believe that she could so easily take to the work that life with Colin Wilson would entail. But she had not given up, and that fact alone filled her with pride, pride she had never felt before. Ada had been kind, she had not laughed at Ruth's ignorance, nor treated her with disdain, and although the work had been hard, they had been cheerful at it. A test, Ada had said. Well, she had seen it to its end, and she would do the same again tomorrow.

27

At six o'clock, when the delivery man arrived at Hardy's Café, he found Dorcas, red-eyed, snuffling loudly, tears running down her cheeks. He stood frozen in the doorway, and seeing him, she held up a knife, shouted, 'Onions.' He laughed, his arms wide, carrying the first of two trays filled with bread cakes.

'What's it today? Soup or stew?'

'Soup.' Once she'd dealt with the onions, she would start on the carrots and turnips. The beef bones had been left on a low heat the previous day, so it would not take long to put it all together. 'Beef broth with veg will go nicely with them there bread cakes of yorn.'

Stan put the tray behind the counter and lifted the lid of the pot on the stove, inhaling the rich stock. 'I might come back for a bowl when I'm done. Will you save me a bit?'

'I will if I can. I'm not promising anything, mind.'

He replaced the lid, grinned at her. 'Suppose I'll have to get in the queue with the rest of the blokes.'

Dorcas gave him a wry smile. He could take his cheek somewhere else. She knew he was a widower, so it was only a bit of teasing, but give a man an inch and he'd take a yard. And the place was full of men, young and old. The skilled men who worked in the shipbuilding and engineering had not been required to enlist, their skills needed to fight the war on other fronts. That was one of the main reasons she'd come here. Oh, she wanted to help the lass, but she wanted to keep an eye on her too. Opening a café was asking for trouble, a woman on her own. Letty was not a beauty, not like Alec's previous sweetheart, Becky, but she was young, and she was attractive – and she had something about her that made her stand out from other women. Dorcas had thought about it many a time while she had sat at her braiding, her thoughts coming together as the ropes did. She hadn't done much thinking of late, nor net making, and there was no time for either once they'd arrived at the café, for it had been busy from the day they'd opened and had continued to be so. One thing was certain, Letty Hardy had a nose for business and wasn't afraid of the hard work it took to make it a success.

The café had been open five weeks and it didn't take Dorcas long to realise that Letty could look after herself. She had a kind word for her customers, but she was not overfamiliar – and if anyone overstepped the mark, she was quick to put them in their place. Dorcas had no need to worry about Letty on that part, and it gladdened her that Alec had made a good match, not that she'd ever let the pair of them know it – especially not Letty.

'Letty and young Stella not here?' Stan asked as he brought in the second tray and picked up the mug of tea that was waiting for him. He had dropped into the habit of stopping for a yarn, and she enjoyed chatting to him while she worked.

'Gone to Parkers to see they're all right. Taken the kiddies with her.'

Stan blew over the mug to cool his tea, took a big gulp. 'I'll say this for her, I've never known a lass to graft like she does.'

Dorcas nodded but didn't comment. The lass was ambitious,

like her Alec, peas in a pod they were. He'd been away two months now and she was glad to be here, for the days passed more quickly – and it was good to be at the centre of things instead of at the edges.

The onions were on the go and she was peeling carrots when a man came in, rat-like with his oiled-back hair, and pointed nose.

'Can I help yer?' Dorcas asked as he walked about, his eyes taking in every nut and bolt.

'Mrs Hardy not here?' He smiled, showing yellow teeth and Dorcas took an instant dislike to him.

'Does it look like she is?'

He looked at the blackboard they had hung behind the counter, the items written in chalk and added or removed as Letty saw fit. To begin with, they had limited themselves to hot drinks, mostly tea and Bovril, and slipped an egg inside the bread cakes. As business had improved – along with their bank balance, Letty had offered pork pies and faggots, Scotch eggs, things the men could hold in their hand. The soup and stew had come with the colder weather and word had got round that it was good. Dorcas took credit for that, for it was her recipe they were coming for.

'We're not open yet.' She nodded towards the clock over the doors for him to look. 'Give it half an hour.'

He ignored her, took one last look about him and made to leave.

'Well, the cheeky beggar,' Dorcas muttered as he walked towards the door. 'What the 'eck is all that about?'

* * *

Letty arrived at the café just as Gilbert Crowe was coming out of it. He lifted his hat, gave her a sickly grin. She gave him a curt nod and went inside, pulling off her gloves ready to start work.

'How long has he been in here?'

'Not long, had a quiz about, eyeballs on stalks, then left.'

'What did he say?'

'Nothing.' Dorcas looked to Stan, who nodded his confirmation. 'Just asked where you was. Who is he, when he's at home?'

'Gilbert Crowe,' Stan said, beating Letty to it.

'The man ag'in the Parkers?' Dorcas looked to Stan, then to Letty.

'The very same.'

'Well, what did he come for? He hasn't been gone more than half a minute. You must have bumped into him. Did he say 'owt?'

'Just being nosey. He wouldn't have come to snoop about while I was here. I suppose he saw me calling into Parkers.' Letty pushed Stella's pram to the side of the counter, removed her outdoor things and put on her apron. She'd left Alfie with the Parkers. Wolfie would see him across the main road, and he'd carry on to his school in Strand Street from there. He would leave with Sally Penny's boys and Letty would collect him when she was finished at the café.

'Probably heard how well you're doing, Letty,' Stan offered. 'I know some of the delivery drivers take a detour to come here.'

'Probably,' Letty said, taking up a pencil and making a list of things she needed to order. 'He wouldn't like that.'

'Plenty to go round,' Stan said. 'It's not as if you're in competition. I mean, he sells baccy and fags.'

'I've a good mind to start selling them too,' she replied. It would be easy enough to do so, and she'd take great pleasure in doing it – but until they got established, she didn't want to rock the boat. A few weeks was no measure of success, it was the years that counted. 'He doesn't like that I'm a woman, Stan.' She corrected herself. 'We're women.' She looked to Dorcas. The success was as much down to her mother-in-law as it was to her. A few months ago, she'd never have imagined that the two of them would be working side by side – and making a success of it. 'And I scuppered his plans.' But he had done the same to her. Though the café was a success, it would have been much easier had it been next to Parkers. She explained about Crowe wanting to buy Parkers for a pittance and being narked that it would cost him much more now that the business was doing well. 'Business is growing again. We've been able to get the girl back who we'd laid off a few weeks ago.' Milly had been only too glad to return. It was another small step forward.

When Stan left and they were side by side, Dorcas peeling carrots and Letty on the turnips, Dorcas asked about the Parkers.

'Norah is coping, as she always does. Milly's a good girl and she knows where everything is.' It had saved her showing someone else the ropes. 'I'm pretty certain Norah will get chance to relax now she's got help.'

'And Percy?'

'Not so good now the weather is colder. It seems to slow him down a bit, but compared to what he was, what was expected of his recovery...' She smiled at Dorcas. 'He's soldiering on.'

Dorcas scooped the chopped carrots in her hands and added them to the huge pot on the stove. 'Stan was saying Doig's is going to keep going through the night now it's got enough men for the shifts.'

'So I heard. I was thinking of taking extra help on here as well as Parkers.'

Dorcas stopped, her hands full of chopped turnip. She turned, dropped them in the pot, rubbed her hands down her apron. 'I know I said I'd only help out for a few weeks, but I think you need me here a bit longer. It'll take time for you to get a replacement.' Dorcas looked quite upset, though she struggled not to show it.

'Replacement?' It hadn't crossed her mind. Letty nudged her playfully. 'I couldn't get a replacement for you, Dorcas. You're a one-off. I was thinking of someone to help *us*. Hardy's the name above the door. That's you and me. Partners.'

28

The following morning, after her day of scrubbing floors, Ruth wondered if she could manage to get up from her bed, if her aching limbs would obey her. Her muscles were tight and sore, her back ached, and when she looked at the rawness of her hands, she recalled every floorboard, every tile. She had been ravenous when she'd returned home, grateful for her food, for Mrs Murray who had prepared it, and for her clean sheets and feather mattress as she sank her weary bones upon them. Though she was more tired than she had ever been, she was also happy. It had taken her by surprise, this feeling of power and agency, that she had broken a boundary, albeit a small one, that she had worked alongside Ada Thomas and not been found wanting. It would be easy to remain in bed, she had volunteered after all, but something had shifted within her, and she knew action would be more productive than thought.

Last night, Mrs Murray had been aghast at the state of her dress, more so when she had told her how it had got that way. 'Whatever was the woman thinking of?' She had stared at the pale blue cotton, the patches of grey where dirt was ingrained.

'I think she sought to test my will. She thought me weak.' Strange as it seemed, Ruth had enjoyed the work yesterday, and the company. Ada had regaled her with stories of the goings-on of the mission, things she had no knowledge of in her capacity with the Ladies Guild. She had laughed as never before and when they had finished the day's work, though tired, Ruth had felt invigorated, more alive than she had ever been – she had the sense that she had embarked on an adventure. Henry would approve. She knew from Proctor's letters that he was now on board the *Prince* with Alec Hardy, of her brother's good health and willingness to work alongside the men. They were both much changed.

'But cleaning floors, Miss Ruth!' Mrs Murray had been unable to let it go.

'I said I was willing to do anything, and Miss Sheldon took me at my word. We are all of us doing things we had not expected. The work is the work.' The irony of her words did not pass her notice as she had handed over her spoiled dress for Mrs Murray to launder. In time, she might have to learn to do that for herself too, for staff had already left: the men to fight, the women taking up better-paid positions. War had advanced the suffragists' cause more rapidly than all of the suffragettes smashing windows and throwing themselves in front of horses on Derby Day. There was a ground swell of change and Ruth was not going to be left behind.

Her father had not been happy about her plans, but she had reminded him of what Daphne was doing, along with other young women of her class who had volunteered. Her brother's fiancée had already been faced with bloodied bandages and disposed of severed limbs, bathed and dressed naked men. It had made Ruth's stomach churn to read of it, imagining Daphne faced with such horrors.

When Ruth left for the mission that morning, she made certain to wear suitable clothing. She had found the plainest, most practical item in her wardrobe, removing any adornment of lace and decorative buttoning. It would suffice for the time being, until she could get something more satisfactory.

Miss Sheldon was in the lobby of the mission when she arrived at eight and Ruth detected the glimmer of delight in the woman's eyes.

'You didn't expect me to return,' Ruth stated as she followed her through to her office.

Miss Sheldon invited her to take a seat. 'Another woman, perhaps not. But I believe you had a point to prove. As did I.' She opened the drawer in her desk and removed a ledger, set it before her. 'Mrs Thomas will have told everyone in the building that you got down on your hands and knees and worked beside her. They will know you are willing to get your hands dirty.'

'It was perhaps foolish of me,' Ruth replied. 'I might choose my words more carefully in future.'

Miss Sheldon smiled, and it transformed her features, adding a softness to her mouth and eyes. 'There are occasions when taking a moment to stop and think saves a lot of heartache. Sometimes we don't know what we are getting ourselves into – and it might not be so easy to extract ourselves from our promises.' She held Ruth's gaze. Was she talking about scrubbing floors – or was she speaking of Colin Wilson? She opened the ledger, took out a sheet of paper and handed it to Ruth. On it was a list of men's names and the ships on which they were serving. Grimsby fishing vessels. The ship's names she recognised.

'These ships were reported missing since the early days of the war.'

'You are correct.' She felt she had impressed Miss Sheldon. 'Missing, believed sunk by mine or torpedo. It appears they were not. Information has been passed on to me, to all of the missions, of local men who are currently held as prisoners of war in

Germany. They are detained in a camp at Ruhleben, six miles to the west of Berlin. We have since learned that these men were ordered off their ships and instructed to get into their rowboats, while those aboard the German battleships and U-boats proceeded to sink them. It is fast approaching the end of October. These men will have no warm clothes as many were captured in the summer months, taken from their ship in what they stood up in. Their families will already be struggling, but at least they have knowledge that their menfolk are alive and, hopefully, will return. Soon, God willing. We are already supporting their families where, and when, we can, and have accessed aid from other quarters. We at the mission have petitioned the government for aid, but there is still much to be done – and things will get worse before they get better.' She opened a lower drawer and set a box of writing materials on her desk. 'This is your work for today…' She looked to Ruth, mischief in her smile. 'Unless, of course, you would rather be with Mrs Thomas?'

Ruth gave a small shake of her head. It was odd, but she felt a sliver of disappointment that she would not be using her physical energy. In the weeks since the boys had left, she had felt sluggish, having little stamina. Walking helped, but the vigorous work she had done the previous day had activated her brain and she felt better able to process her thoughts. It was like waking after a long slumber.

'Good, I was hoping you would be agreeable. Women like Mrs Thomas have not had your advantages in life, they can do no more than cook and clean, but they do it well and I admire them greatly for it.'

'Oh, I agree, Miss Sheldon.'

Another smile. 'It is not done to prove a point, but to support their families – for which they are paid the going rate. Our work here is to help people help themselves, not to remove their agency.'

Ruth wanted to hang her head in shame, but she maintained eye contact with the lady missioner who had kindly but firmly put her in her place.

'Now,' Miss Sheldon said brightly, having got her gentle rebuke out of the way, 'it would be remiss of me not to take advantage of your skills and connections for the greater benefit of the mission. In this respect, I think you are best used to write to our supporters about the country petitioning for donations.' She handed over a buff file. Ruth opened it and saw a list of names and addresses. 'I am hoping you might add to that list. I am not so well connected in this area, and these things take time – time we do not have. The money raised in this instance will benefit the men held in Ruhleben camp. I am tasking you with organising and acquiring the contents of Christmas packages that will be sent to them. I had thought chocolate, cigarettes, reading materials, warm clothing – in the custom of the mission.'

'As they did on the boats when it was founded.'

'Quite.' Miss Sheldon seemed pleased with her knowledge. 'These small comforts have been most welcome in the past.' She got to her feet. 'There will be no more scrubbing. We lead by example. Once those around us have realised nothing is beneath us, they will respect us all the more. It's about earning respect as opposed to being given it, Miss Evans.'

Ruth flushed. 'Do call me, Ruth.'

Miss Sheldon went to the door and, before she opened it, turned to Ruth. 'I am Miss Sheldon, and you are Miss Evans. You will always be Miss Evans in this building.'

Ruth gave a small nod of her head, firmly reprimanded by this tartar of a woman. She had remembered how she'd wanted Mr Wilson to call her by her Christian name, wanting to draw them closer, how uncomfortable it had made him, how she had insisted. She had been wrong to do so and now she knew why.

She followed Miss Sheldon down the hall, the keys on her belt jangling as she led the way and opened the door to a small room. In it were all the periodicals and ephemera that had cluttered the office when Colin was in charge. There was a simple desk and two chairs, one either side of it.

'I thought you could work in here. You will not be interrupted as you would be in my office.' Ruth looked about the room. 'You might like to leave the door open as there is no window.' Miss Sheldon paused. 'It is a pity the new building is delayed, but we must work around what we have.'

When she left, Ruth settled down to work out the numbers of what would be required, an estimate of how much each item might cost. She looked down at the list of Grimsby men interned in Ruhleben, of which there were many. And that was without considering the Boston and Hull men who had suffered the same fate. Any civilians who had been on German soil had also been taken there – diplomats and teachers, musicians and doctors. It was hard to think of them so far from home, how lonely they must be. A small package for Christmas would be most welcome and she was determined to do her best to raise funds for what was needed. She made a list of the women she could contact for contributions, her father's colleagues, cousins far and wide, friends of friends, asking for donations, no matter how small. The list was long, and the letters would take days to write, but if each one produced a shilling or two in postal orders, it would soon mount up, little by little.

She was adding to her list when her aunt strode past. Ruth heard her come to a stop, turn and open the door wide.

'Your father said you were scrubbing floors.' Ruth could see that her aunt was relieved.

'That was yesterday. Today I am attending to other duties asked of me.' The look on her aunt's face was reward enough.

Her aunt pulled the door to. 'Whatever were you thinking off, Ruth. Scrubbing floors like a common charwoman.'

'I found it a fair exercise. And my companion was most agreeable.'

Her aunt glanced at the list she had made, put her hand to it and twisted to look. She did not hear the door open, and Miss Sheldon join them.

'Mrs Frampton. One of the attendants said you had arrived. I was not expecting you.' There was not an ounce of charm in her tone and Ruth dipped her head to avoid looking at her aunt, lest she smiled too readily.

'I came to see my niece. I had heard a rumour—'

'Rumour? Or fact?' Miss Sheldon clasped her hands in front of her and Ruth delighted in watching her aunt being challenged. She couldn't remember it ever occurring before. 'Miss Evans is at her work, and I would rather she not be disturbed.'

Aunt Helen's chest expanded as she inhaled, and for a second Ruth thought she might explode, but Miss Sheldon was too quick for her. The door was opened wide, men heading for the dining room having a clear view inside. Her aunt turned to Ruth, her mouth pursed, her irritation evident. Whether it was with Ruth or Miss Sheldon, she wasn't sure. Perhaps it was both, it didn't matter. It seemed her aunt had met her match. Respect had to be earned on Miss Sheldon's watch and Aunt Helen had a long way to go to earn hers.

* * *

As if Ruth had not had enough of letters, her own were waiting for her when she returned home in time for supper. She recognised Daphne's hand, and flicked to the next, froze when she saw the

Lowestoft postmark and recognised Colin's handwriting. She sank into the chair in the hall, half afraid to open it.

The housekeeper came to greet her, giving the lower part of her dress a quick glance.

'Don't worry, Mrs Murray. There will be no more soiled dresses.'

'I'm pleased to hear it, Miss Ruth. It was quite a shock yesterday. I have managed to remove the stains, but it wasn't the frock, it was more of the indignity. I feel like giving that woman a piece of my mind, I really do.'

'Miss Sheldon knew what she was doing – it was I who did not. Let's say I learned a valuable lesson yesterday.' Ruth clutched the letter, wanting so much to open it and at the same time feeling anxious. It felt light, not heavy with pages as Proctor's were. But then how much notepaper did one need to say I love you?

'Well, as long as you're all right. How's your back, your legs? I bet they're tight. Shall I draw you a warm bath? I could add some Epsom salts. That will ease them a little.'

Ruth couldn't help but smile. 'That would be wonderful.'

Ruth stared at the envelope and when she heard the water running, she slid her index finger into it and withdrew the letter. It was as she has suspected. A page, written on one side only, thanking her for her letter and wishing her well. He expressed a desire to write more, but time was pressing, and his workload was heavy. He hoped she would understand. She did. He was not interested.

She read it many times, hearing the water run into the bathtub, Mrs Murray humming as she prepared the towels and soaps, searching for just one word that she might hold on to, that gave hope. There was nothing. She returned it to the envelope and pushed it into her pocket, and heavy with the sense of defeat, she went upstairs.

29

The explosion reverberated along the wire that tied the *Prince* to the *Artemis*. All men who had been below scrambled onto deck, pulling on their sweaters, no regard for caps or blazers. What did regulations matter at a time like this?

Alec grabbed his binoculars and trained them on the *Artemis*. She had caught it at her port side for the starboard side was intact – a mine at best, torpedo at worst. The engine room must have taken the hit, for smoke plumed from the funnel, indicating a fire. He could see crew on deck, the boat being lowered, and counted the men in. Five so far, of a crew of twelve. The skipper was at the bridge, a man on the ladder, his head tilted – taking orders or giving them? If they could keep it stable, they could tow her in. They were close enough to shore that the ship would limp home, and a salvage was better than a loss. He scanned the horizon searching for shadows below the water, the sight of a conning tower, but there was nothing. It had to be a mine.

Proctor was on deck, giving orders. Evans, Staffy and Nobby keeping watch. This was no time for their own men to take their eye off the sea, for where there was one mine, there was likely to be another, and though they might have wanted to do otherwise, they remained at their posts, scanning the waves.

Alec was in the midst of giving orders to release the wire when there was another explosion and the middle blew out of the *Artemis*, flames leaping through the funnel. The bridge had completely gone. There would have been no time for the skipper to escape. Minutes later, the *Artemis* split in two and Alec gave the order for the ship to go to their aid.

Proctor came up the ladder and Alec shouted out the window to him.

'I'm going close as I can.'

'Our orders are to keep ourselves safe. Wireless for the patrol ship. The boat has been lowered. Orders are that the men save themselves and we must carry on our duties.'

'I'm not leaving men to die if I can do owt to help.'

'Navy orders. They were changed when the *Cressy, Hogue* and *Aboukir* were sunk. We are to take care of our own ship.'

'Own ship be blowed. Men need saving.'

Alec adjusted his course. He was taking a risk with his own ship and crew, but he knew not one of them would leave a man behind if there was a possibility to help. If they heard a mayday call in a gale, they went to assist. It was what they did.

Five men were in the boat and rowing away from the *Artemis* as the two halves began their descent below the waves. The swell was high and the boat rose and fell, rose and fell, as the men fought their way to the *Prince*. Alec concentrated on the boat, shouting down to his crew, listening, watching, as the *Prince* crawled forward, and the men rowed through the waves towards them. As they came closer, Nobby threw down a line. A man reached and missed. The line was thrown again, and this time was caught, and the boat was pulled alongside. When it was made fast, a rope ladder was thrown over and the five men brought aboard, drenched from head to foot and badly shaken.

Alec trained his binoculars to the spot where the *Artemis* had been as the water bubbled up, gulping the trawler down to the depths. He had been drinking with the skipper only three days ago, the two of them sharing plans for Christmas. He had a wife and three kiddies. His stomach turned and he spat the bitter taste out of the window.

Proctor came up to join him. 'It was a mine. Hit the port side. Five men rescued. Those in the engine room and in their bunks didn't have a chance. The skipper was in the—'

'Aye. I saw it happen.' He handed the binoculars to Proctor, who stared out over the water. Alec had seen bits of flotsam on the surface. No bodies. No survivors.

'We need to take these men back to shore.' Proctor returned the glasses.

'A ration of rum in order for the rescued men?'

'Agreed. But not for our men on the watch. We need to get ourselves safely back to port afore we can do that.'

Alec set the course for Lowestoft to report the loss of the *Artemis* and get the survivors to the naval base. It would take a couple of hours in this weather. He could do with a tot of the strong stuff himself, but for now it would have to wait.

30

The *Prince* was guided into port by the tug. It was already dark, the nights longer now that winter had set in. There was a team of men waiting for them when they moored, and the survivors of the *Artemis* were taken directly to the mission to be cared for. Hot baths were ready, and clean, warm clothing, a hot meal and a warm bed. Alec and his crew had been found lodgings with one of the many seaside landladies whose properties had been secured by the admiralty for billets. They had left their kitbags and gone straight to the nearest pub.

Proctor stood the first round for them all. He was a likeable chap. On Civvy Street they might be poles apart, but on the ship they were equal, Proctor conferring with him on navy protocol, but leaving the final decision with him, as skipper. He would have to make his report and Alec would get it in the neck from some bugger of rank. He knew they wouldn't keep him ashore; they needed every minesweeper they could get their hands on out on the water. The *Artemis* was another loss. One of many, and each one they witnessed shortened the odds. His lads were well and truly shook up, it was the closest they had been to disaster. Over the past months, they had got to know many of the men on the *Artemis* when they had spent time ashore. It had brought home how close they were each day to death.

They spent all night in the pub, glad of the warmth and the company. The conversation was of football and local gossip and not much of the war itself – they didn't want to hear it, not tonight. Customers came and went, but they remained where they were, not wanting to move, craving a bite of normality before they went back on board. The local lasses came round with their baskets of cockles and whelks, Becky flirting with the fellas as she always did. She came to their table, slipped her arm about Alec's shoulder, and leaned forward, giving young Henry Evans a good view of her full breasts. 'What takes yer fancy?' she asked Alec, and the lad's eyes almost popped out of his head. It made Alec smile. Henry was easy prey for a lass like Becky and the lad put his hand in his pocket and paid for cockles he wouldn't eat. When she had got what she could from them she moved on, giving Alec one last lingering look before she left.

Someone bought another round, stuck a bottle in front of him. He called out his thanks. New blokes came in, talking of the minesweeper crew at the mission, the story warped in just a few hours. It was not a mine but a torpedo, they argued over it at the bar and he didn't bother to correct them. He wanted to forget, to shake what he had seen from inside his skull, thought of the skipper, his kiddies, thought of Stella and Alfie. Of Letty and his mother living a life without him. Would he be missed? He became maudlin with the drink, tired of hearing men talk.

Someone was playing the piano and men were gathered about it, singing. He thought again of the skipper, of the moment when the wheelhouse exploded. Had the skipper felt it? Did he know? Or was it instantaneous – that one minute you were living and breathing and then you weren't. Life was over.

Alec felt bilious and went outside, wanting air, wanting to fill his lungs with fresh, sharp, air. He pulled his coat about him, gulping in large breaths, expanding his lungs as far as he could. He belched, slapped his chest, swayed a little and headed for the Grit, staggering down the score and into the beach village.

The moon was big and round, lighting a path before him, and he followed it down to the water's edge, stumbling here and there as he went, losing his footing and righting himself. From time to time, he took swigs from his hip flask, feeling the bite of brandy in his throat. The air was sharp and cold on his face, and he was glad to feel it, to feel alive, to taste, to smell, to breathe. He walked unsteadily along the shore and sank down on the sand, watched the water lap the shore.

There was little movement in the harbour, and he laid back on the sand and looked up at the night sky, the stars so far away. It was sometime before he was aware someone had lain beside him, was naming the constellations. 'The Great Bear, the Plough, Orion...' A hand pointing. He recognised Becky's voice, and was glad to have something familiar, a sound, another human, a living thing. She took her hand in his. 'The Milky Way...' She leaned over him and kissed his mouth, and he didn't resist. Her lips were warm and full, and he wanted warmth, longed for it. To *feel* something.

He put his hand to the back of her head, feeling her breasts hard against him, enjoying it, and though he knew he should stop, he didn't want to. She unbuttoned her blouse, put his hand to her breast and he, overcome with lust, rolled her onto her back. She unfastened his trousers, her fingers nimble, and he pulled them about his waist, pushed up her skirts and forced himself inside her, thrusting hard, with not a care for her until he was spent. Then he rolled onto his back and lay on the sand, breathless and empty. And the emptiness was like nothing he had felt before, not when his father died, nor Robbie. A great hole had opened up inside him, filled with echoing darkness.

Alec lay very still, watching his chest rise and fall as his breathing returned to normal, and felt warm salty tears run down the side of his face, glad that it was dark. Becky reached for his hand, but he could not take it. He closed his eyes and a tremendous wave of shame rushed into the hole and sealed itself shut.

31

In the months of October and November, many letters arrived at the Grimsby Mission addressed to Ruth Evans. Her work had been fruitful, and postal orders had been sent from as far away as Portsmouth and Aberdeen. She had written to people with whom she possessed only the most tenuous of links, and amounts had arrived, large and small. It had given her great satisfaction to elicit such contributions and she felt her time at the mission fruitful. There had not been further occasion to scrub floors, but she had changed linen when required and served a time in the dining room. For once in her life, she felt useful, not used. She had written one more time to Colin Wilson but received an almost identical letter to the one he had sent previously. There had been no point in writing any more.

She had spent most of the day at the desk in the small windowless room that had become most familiar to her, and her body ached with lack of movement. The mission for once was quiet, the men in need of nothing more than a warm bed and hot food, and there were many other people to do that.

She picked up the envelopes and went into the lobby. Raindrops spattered the glass of the doors and windows. 'How long has it been like this?' she asked the man on the desk as she buttoned her coat, cursing that she had not thought to bring an umbrella.

'The last few hours. I think it's in for the evening.' He smoothed his hand over the counter. 'The forecast isn't good.'

She thought to try her father's office. He might still be there, and she could wait, go home in the car. But why wait? She could catch a tram.

'Do you have an umbrella I may borrow?'

He checked under the counter, shook his head.

Miss Sheldon came from her office and stood beside her. 'It's going to be a filthy night. Better on land than at sea.'

Her words made Ruth shudder. She had heard from Philip Proctor that the *Black Prince* been involved in a rescue. That it had been a close shave. He'd told her of the men rescued, that they were made welcome at the Lowestoft mission. There was a page from Henry, letting her know he was well and not to worry, that his shipmates were good fellows. That he had met with Colin Wilson, who sent his kindest regards. She had read that line twice over, her heart pinching with disappointment before she could read on. Her brother had asked her to give his best wishes to Father. Told her that he missed her. That he was glad she was doing something that had meaning to her. He had signed it, *Your loving brother, Henry*.

She watched the rain batter at the window. Would the *Prince* be out in this filthy weather as Miss Sheldon had called it, or had they dropped anchor to sit it out until first light? She said a prayer in her head for the Lord to keep them safe, for Charles, and for Daphne, and all those fighting for a just cause.

She pulled on her gloves, ready to leave.

Miss Sheldon put a hand to her shoulder. 'Why don't you wait, Miss Evans? It might ease off a bit.'

'I think it might not, and I am fortunate. There will be a good fire waiting for me.' And a warm bath if she wanted it. Working at the mission had brought the luxuries of her life to the fore, the things she had previously taken for granted. She was far more appreciative of the life her father had worked so hard for, for the comforts of it. He had looked aged of late, his worry for his business and his sons taking a heavy toll. She had asked many times how she could assist, but he had not wanted her help. In a way, it had released her, for with nothing else to occupy her, she had spent more time at the mission. The house had never felt so empty as it had these past months. But her father was there most evenings and she liked to sit with him, even if they did not converse.

Out on the street, the rain was not as bad as she'd thought, but the wind was bitter and she was glad of her warm coat, and that she did not have far to walk. The lights were on at the *Herald* offices, and it crossed her mind that she could take a lift home with her aunt or uncle. One of them would be there – if not both – but she decided against it, too tired for their probing, and no energy to defend her choices – for she knew that was what she would be expected to do.

There was a queue at the tram stop and Ruth decided not to wait, to walk to the next, and crossed over the main road and made her way onto Freeman Street. Even though the weather was dire, there were still many people about, the lads with the newspapers, caps down and collars up. Lights shone from the pubs that were on almost every corner and as she passed the Red Lion, she saw two tiny figures, huddled against the wall. Light from the lamps illuminated their small, bedraggled forms and she recognised Mary Owen's girls, their clothes soaked and dripping with only an assemblage of thin clothing, nothing that was any defence against the weather. There was no need to ask where their mother was. Daphne had been right. Her shillings had been wasted, and the thought of their mother's neglect filled her with rage.

Ruth pushed her way into the pub, the smoke catching in her throat. It was noisy, but the sound softened as she searched for Mary Owen and found her asleep on the banquette seating. Ruth felt no pity in her, just an enormous swell of anger rising.

A middle-aged man touched her shoulder. 'Miss Evans, this is no place for a young lady like yourself.' She recognised him as being in the mission a day or two ago.

'Mrs Owen's children are outside. She needs to take them home.'

The two of them looked at the woman slumped on the seating, her face red and bloated. Mary Owen had dribbled down her chin and her dress was marked with stains where she had spilled her drink. Ruth wanted to shake her. Her own mother had tried so hard to live, had fought her illness until the last, to smile, to comfort her children, knowing that she would leave them.

'When she bothers to wake,' she told the man next to her, 'tell her I have taken her children to the mission.'

She pushed through the men to the entrance and scooped up the smallest child, took the hand of the other. Her little fingers were like ice and Ruth was enraged. 'My name is Ruth,' she said to the girl. 'We are going to get warm and dry and get something to eat.'

The child did not argue, was happy for her to lead her away, and Ruth thought of the dangers that could befall them. Anyone could have taken them.

She marched down towards the mission with renewed vigour, her coat sodden, her hat collapsed with the weight of the rain and drops running down her face and into her eyes.

A car pulled up beside her and the window was wound down. From the back seat, Arthur Marshall leaned forward. 'Ruth! I thought my eyes had deceived me. What on earth are you doing? For heaven's sake, put those children down and get in.'

Ruth pushed the child forward, but he put out his hand.

'Not them. They might well have lice.'

Ruth held the child firm. At that moment, she despised Arthur Marshall, that he cared more for his car than for two vulnerable children. 'Then we'll walk.' She turned away from the car, heard it pull away and headed for the mission. She would get them settled, then work out what to do next.

Once there, she did not wait for permission, but took the children down to the baths, requesting one of the attendants find her towels and old shirts to wrap them in while their clothing was dried. She was on her knees soaping the children when Miss Sheldon entered.

'Miss Evans, could you kindly explain what is going on.'

Ruth got up, dried her hands on the towel. 'The children had been left outside a public house. I have no idea how long they had been there. Their mother was asleep inside. Warm and dry.' Ruth could not keep the anger from her voice.

Miss Sheldon spoke quietly. 'May I remind you, Miss Evans, that we are here for the men, not for waifs. If you had to take them anywhere, you should have taken them to the orphanage on Victor Street.'

'They are not orphans. Their mother—'

'Has neglected them,' she replied firmly.

Ruth felt her throat thicken. The two little girls sat in the bath, watching the women discuss their future.

'This is not our work, Miss Evans.'

'I couldn't walk by.' Ruth felt her voice waver. She looked at the two little scraps of humanity, large eyes in such tiny faces. 'Their father was a fisherman, Miss Sheldon. Lost at sea. These are his children. Are we not here for them too?'

The port missioner capitulated. 'I will arrange for them to have something to eat. Bring them to my quarters when they are done.'

With the help of one of the attendants, Ruth carried the children to the house next door to the mission. At the door, Miss Sheldon took hold of one of the children and invited Ruth to follow her.

She was surprised how comfortable it was. She had not thought for Miss Sheldon to have a mind for pretty things, but her walls were adorned with prints and paintings that softened the darkness of the plain and practical wood panelling below the dado rail.

She was taken through to a small sitting room and the children were set down on the floor in front of the hearth, where a small fire burned in the grate, the guard in front of it. Heavy drapes were drawn at the window that faced the street. Before she had been disturbed, it looked as if Miss Sheldon had been writing her report for the magazine, for upon a table in the bay was a large notebook and sheets of vellum. She invited Ruth to sit in one of the armchairs that faced the fire and disappeared, shortly reappearing with a tray upon which was a plate of bread and jam and two mugs of milk. When it was placed in front of them, the children did not move, so Ruth handed them a slice of bread and jam. They ate so hungrily that Ruth wanted to weep. Miss Sheldon watched silently, then asked Ruth if she would like a hot drink.

She returned moments later with another tray bearing a teapot, two china cups and saucers and matching jug and sugar bowl. It was all so far removed from her work, and it was odd to sit in companionship with this woman who appeared so fearsome, so invincible.

Ruth watched the children, and when they had eaten, removed the tray. Miss Sheldon fetched a blanket and a pillow and settled the children by the fire. Ruth saw their eyes grow heavy, then close. 'At least for one night they are warm, and their bellies are full.'

Miss Sheldon sank back into her chair. 'One night is not enough, but it is better than nothing.'

Ruth could not answer her, too full of anger and bitterness. For a time, they sat without speaking until Ruth broke the silence between them.

'Had you always wanted to do this work, Miss Sheldon?'

'Not to begin with, but I was always involved in one way or another. I was born in Portsmouth. Two of my three brothers joined the navy, as did my intended.' She gazed down at her hands. 'He was taken ill with yellow fever. Strangers tended him in his last days, made him more comfortable. It seemed right that I might do the same.' She checked her watch, looked steadily at Ruth. 'Sometimes we have to hand these things over to others, when we cannot care for those we love. We can only hope they are met with kindness at every turn.'

Oh, how Ruth agreed with her. She hoped that people were caring for Charles and Henry and men like them. She thought of Daphne and the other women who had gone to do that very thing. She talked of Daphne, of the VADs, of her not being brave enough to go herself.

'Bravery is not always the fight, Miss Evans, many times it is simply holding the ground.'

There was a sharp knock on the door, and Miss Sheldon got up to answer it. Ruth gazed at the children, cosy and content, and wished for all the world she could do more. Thoughts zipped about her head. She closed her eyes, recalling Daphne's words the day Lord Wolsely's death had been reported in the *Herald*, the day she had seen the two children outside a public house, had wondered what had happened to the baby. 'You can't help them all,' that she would 'have every beggar in the street after her'.

Miss Sheldon returned, followed by a nun in her black robes and white wimple. Her face was round, her plump cheeks shiny, and as she stared down at the children, Ruth suddenly realised why she was there. She looked quickly to Miss Sheldon.

'I left a message with their mother that they had been taken to the mission.'

'And so they have,' Miss Sheldon said, kindly. 'But we cannot look after them here. And you cannot take them home with you. Until such time as their mother can care for them, they will be better off with the sisters of St Anthony's.'

'But what shall I tell her?'

'You won't be here,' the port missioner told her.

'It's my responsibility—'

The nun bent down, gently shaking the children awake.

Miss Sheldon touched Ruth's hands. 'They are their mother's responsibility, not yours. You did the right thing. You brought them to safety. You must leave the rest to me.'

The sister took the toddler in her arms, the child by the hand. Ruth had dressed them in men's shirts, the sleeves rolled up many times, but their feet were bare and at the sight of them, a stone lodged in her throat and she had to look away.

Miss Sheldon pressed Ruth down into the chair and left the room. She could hear them in the hall, the missioner speaking with the nun, talking gently to the children, the cold blast of air as the door was opened, and she picked up the blanket and ran to them, handed it to Miss Sheldon. 'They'll get cold.'

She watched as the children were handed up into a wagon, the blankets tucked about them, at the horses braying, breath flaring from their nostrils and swirling in the night air. Helpless, she turned away and went back into the house to her chair by the fire, and let the tears fall.

Miss Sheldon returned, pulled a clean handkerchief from her pocket and gave it to Ruth, who dabbed it at her eyes.

'I'm sorry, I've interrupted your evening.'

'I'm pleased you did.' She removed the guard from the fire and returned to her chair. 'Those children would have caught their deaths in this weather.' Her words caused Ruth to press down on her own lips, with misery and with rage, her feelings for Mary Owen so conflicted.

'I can't imagine what their mother was thinking of.'

'She wasn't thinking. Not of her children anyway.' Miss Sheldon made herself more comfortable. 'Tell me, Miss Evans. What connects you to this woman and her children?'

Ruth told her of the day on the wharf, of Mary Owen's loss, of her husband, her child, of first seeing the children outside a public house. 'I feel I contributed to Mary's drunkenness.'

Miss Sheldon furrowed her brow.

'I gave her two shillings. My friend rebuked me and said it would not go to feeding the children, that the mother would take it for herself. She was correct.'

Miss Sheldon considered her answer. 'You acted with compassion. You saw need – and it is in your habit to be generous. However, giving money in such circumstances was perhaps unwise. The woman was not in the correct frame of mind to use your money well, she was intoxicated and grieving. But your heart was in the right place. You can't help Mary Owen if she is not ready to help herself.' The words eased her guilt a little and Miss Sheldon smiled kindly at her. 'You have had a good response to your petitions for donations. You must be delighted with your success.'

It was a gentle turning of the conversation. 'People have been very generous.' Her father had donated, as had her uncle, and almost all of the great worthies of the town. On learning of her task, Henry had had a whip-round on the *Black Prince* and had sent a postal order.

'I find most people are generous in times of great need.'

A sudden gust rattled the window and lifted the bottom of the curtain, making the papers flutter on the table in front of it. Ruth had taken up far too much of Miss Sheldon's time. She got up.

'I ought to leave you to what's left of your evening.'

Miss Sheldon walked with her to the door, paused before opening it. 'We have more than enough to cover the parcels. I thought the residue could be used for some other benefit. I was thinking to set some aside for a small Christmas party for the families whose men are POW.'

Ruth agreed. 'It will perhaps bring a little extra cheer. At least those women know their husbands and fathers will come home when this is all over.'

Miss Sheldon was quick to agree. 'One would like to hope so.'

32

Ruth drifted in and out of a fitful sleep. The wind howled all night and the branch of the tree outside her widow tapped as if a child trying to get in. At one point, she got up and drew back the curtain, knowing it was only the branches – but wanting to make sure. She thought of Henry being tossed about in the storm, of Charles now somewhere in France. Of Daphne who was working in Portsmouth and hoping to follow him. She'd been disgusted by Arthur's actions, but not surprised, grateful for her lucky escape. If it hadn't been for Henry and Proctor, she might have committed herself to marriage, but she could not marry an unkind man. Her thoughts turned to Colin Wilson. Had he given her the slightest indication that he had feelings for her, she might have followed him to Lowestoft. Oh, what a fool she had been.

She thumped at her pillows to plump them and sat watching the hypnotic sway of the shadows outside. Here, she was protected and warm. Father loved her, she was secure in that. It was the one thing she was sure of. At least they had each other, and she considered now whether she really could have left him to be with the port missioner. That perhaps she did not have feelings for Colin Wilson after all. Admiring him from afar had rendered him faultless. His curt letter had hurt her more than she realised, but so much had been going on – her brothers' departures, Daphne, the upset over Arthur. There hadn't been anyone to confide in, Letty being perhaps the closest she had to a friend, but there were still things she felt unable to share. She'd been worried about the immense pressures on her father and had only caused him more. She longed to run to him now, to climb beside him, a child, and feel his arms about her as she did when she was young, when Mother was alive. Meadowvale was a different house then.

As dawn broke, Ruth thought of the Owen children, waking up in the dormitories. She had visited the orphanage with her father when he had attended a meeting of the governors. Unlike Arthur, he was kind, he cared, he did what he could. And she thought of Miss Sheldon's words, the day she had scrubbed floors, to use her skills more wisely. In her stubbornness, she had not been thinking – as she had not been thinking when she'd given the money to Mary. Though she was loath to admit it, her aunt had been right. Scrubbing floors would not bring the benefit her fundraising had done. Ruth promised herself that from now on she would use her head as well as her heart. For one was no good without the other.

* * *

Father looked weary at breakfast, and Ruth took more time to stay with him. 'Can I not come to the office with you, Father, or at least help you in your study? I would be a willing assistant.'

He clasped her hand on the table. 'I have Tate and Swift and have taken on some older men. We will get things shipshape, bring order.' He squeezed at her hand, then released it. 'I do not want you to follow your aunt's, or my mother's example, and become hard-nosed and business-minded. You are gentle, as was your mother, and the things you do are far more important that sorting documents for me.'

Knowing she could not persuade him otherwise, she waited until he left for the office and went direct to Hardy's Café to find Letty.

'Where does Mary Owen live?'

Letty finished an order and came to one side. 'The back of King Edward Street, why?'

Ruth told her of the events of the previous night.

Letty shook her head. 'I'd hoped she would have got herself together by now. She had those girls of hers to keep her on the straight and narrow.'

'She lost her baby.'

'Ruth, there are many women about this town who have lost husbands, children. My own mother-in-law is one of them. But she did not give in to drink.' Letty was irritated. 'It's not as if she didn't have help for the asking. She just never bothered to ask. And people have their own worries and problems to be getting on with.'

'I'd still like to tell her myself why I took her children. I feel I owe it to her.'

'You owe her nothing.' Letty shook her head. 'Be careful, Ruth. I'd come with you, but we're rushed off our feet.'

'I don't have need of a chaperone.'

Letty raised one eyebrow.

'I'll not be there more than ten minutes at the most.'

Letty told her the address and Ruth hurried towards it. There were shortcuts down side streets and alleyways, but Letty would not tell her of them, advising her to keep to the main road where she would be more conspicuous and thereby safer. She could see

Letty's reasoning when she approached the small courtyard of Victoria Buildings, but she was not afraid. Women and children gawped at her, but she was not approached, striding down the street with an air of purpose.

Ruth knocked on number 3, waited. Knocked again.

Someone called out, 'It's open.'

She hesitated, her hand hovering gingerly on the latch before taking it with a firm grip and entering.

Mary was not alone in the small, dank room with its drab interior and few sticks of furniture. She was slumped in a chair, an older woman Ruth took to be her mother bustling in and out of the scullery, rubbing briskly at a pan with a cloth. She stopped when she saw Ruth, and Mary struggled to her feet.

'Are ya lost?' the older woman challenged.

Ruth remained on the doorstep. 'I came to see Mary.'

The two women exchanged glances.

'How do you know my name?'

Ruth closed the door behind her, less fearful. 'Mrs Hardy told me. I was on the wharf when you learned of your husband's... loss.'

The older woman pulled out a chair. 'Would you care to take a seat, Miss...'

'Evans,' Ruth told her.

'What, as in Excel Evans?'

She nodded.

'Well, her Lenny weren't on one of yer father's ships. He was on a Hammond ship. It's nowt to do with you.'

Ruth hadn't expected such questioning. 'No, but Mary and her girls have remained in my mind ever since.' She leaned over to Mary and touched her hands. The woman was a shadow of what she was, and in such a short time, every line on her face marked by grief. 'I was sorry to hear of the loss of your child.'

The old woman put her cloth and pan on the side and came forward, put her hand on Mary's shoulder. 'She's had a rough ol' time of it. And now 'er kiddies are gone, took off to the mission by some busybo—' The woman nodded. 'Ah, that's why yer 'ere.' She folded her arms, stared accusingly at Ruth, but Ruth was not intimidated. She had thought long and hard over what she had done, not just last night, but the last few years of her life, when she had come to womanhood. Her hopes, her dreams, her duties, her responsibilities – not only to her family but to herself.

'A few weeks ago, I saw your girls standing outside the Saracen's Head. I was with my friend. I gave you two shillings.'

Mary furrowed her brow, it softening as she remembered.

'I had thought you would use it to the care of your children.'

Mary's mother turned her threatening look to her daughter. 'Well, that was a daft thing to do. If she was pittled up.'

'It was. I didn't think it through. But last night when I saw the children in the cold and the rain... I went into the pub and you were asleep inside, warm and dry. I couldn't bear to see them suffer.'

Mary hung her head in shame.

'Oh, Mary, Mary. What have ya com' to, lass.' Her mother looked to Ruth. 'She was always a good gentle lass, kindest and sweetest of all my girls. I've tried me best, but I can't be with her all the time. There's not enough room to have 'em all at mine. Me husband's ill and off work, an' I have to keep an eye on 'im as well as his father.' She clasped her hands on her lap.

Ruth was sympathetic, but she must not get sidetracked.

'The children are at St Anthony's. Temporarily,' she informed them. 'I didn't come to criticise, Mary. I came to help.'

Tears streamed down the woman's face, and she wiped them from her cheeks and from under her chin with the back of her hand. Her mother passed her the cloth she had been wiping the pots with and Mary blew her nose.

'I thought about why you put money over the bar when you could have bought it cheaper from the off licence. I came to the conclusion that you needed company. That you were lonely.'

Mary nodded. Her nose was red and bulbous, and she rubbed at it again.

'I know Mrs Hardy has been here on occasion.'

'She 'as. Lots 'as been to help, neighbours and the like, but she can't seem to help herself.' The echo of Miss Sheldon's words were never truer.

'I have come to remedy that. If I can – and if Mary will meet me halfway? Can you knit, Mary?' Ruth had given her idea great consideration before she offered it. For some reason, she was hell-bent on rescuing Mary Owen.

The young woman nodded, she had stopped crying and had managed to lift her head. Ruth could see the emptiness in her eyes, and it firmed her resolve to help.

'Miss Sheldon, the new port missioner, has need of knitters. It is paid work – jumpers, socks and so forth, for the comfort of our troops. It can be done at home.'

'Well, that's good, in't it, Mary. You could do that.'

'You could also come to the mission to do it. There are various gatherings but... I help at the mission, in a small room set aside for me. You are welcome to come along at any time and sit with me, all day if you so wish.' Anything to keep her away from the public houses. 'In time, I have every hope that you will create a different habit, that of sitting with me to fight out loneliness. Until you can do so by yourself.'

Mary looked to her.

'I lost my mother when I was eleven. I would not want your

children to lose theirs. My father is everything to me and I couldn't bear to lose him too. Be strong for your daughters, Mary, even if you cannot be strong for yourself.' Ruth reached for her hand and gripped it tightly. 'And then we will work on getting your children back home.'

33

In November, Letty's mother wrote of the goings-on at the farm, and recent news of her brothers at training in Wiltshire. One of her sisters was pregnant, the other had broken her foot. She supposed Letty had heard of the naval raid? German ships had been laying mines offshore of Yarmouth and Lowestoft and had been interrupted by Navy destroyers and patrol ships. Shells had been fired, landing on the beach but causing little damage. It had made them all realise how close they were to war.

It left Letty restless with worry. Alec was working the east coast and she wondered if the *Black Prince* was in the area when the battle happened. On the first of the month, HMS *Good Hope* had been sunk, and a Grimsby man, James Sutton, had been on it. Another widow made.

She heard Alfie cry out for her and pushed on her slippers, picked up her shawl and went to him. Her breath curled in front of her. The nights were bitter now and she had not built the fire in her room, wanting to save pennies where she could.

'What's the matter, Alfie?'

He was curled up like a field mouse in his bed. 'I heard a noise, Mam. I was scared.'

Letty went to the window and lifted the sash. A cold blast filled the room and Alfie tucked his head under the sheet. Letty pulled her shawl about her and leaned out. The hens were restless tonight, and she wasn't certain, but it sounded like something knocking against a dustbin. A cat?

She sat beside him, rubbed at his back, peeling the sheet from his face. He looked at her, eyes wide. 'It was a cat. The hens saw it off with their cackling.' She kissed his nose. 'Go back to sleep.'

To reassure herself, she went downstairs. The fire had been backed up before she and Dorcas went to bed and was molten red about the edges. Dorcas's knitting had been left on her chair, as if she'd take it up any moment. Letty picked up a lamp and went out into the yard. The air held a hint of frost and she drew her shawl tighter as she walked to the coop. It was secure, but the back gate had not been fastened properly. She lifted the latch and clicked it into place. She should have got a goose for Christmas. They were always the best alarm.

The moon was a crescent, the stars bright and she said a little prayer for her family in Lowestoft, for Alec and her brothers, for the men looking at the same stars somewhere out on the sea or land. Alec would not be home for Christmas, which was not unusual, for many of the fishermen spent the period out fishing. Christmas could be held any time in the weeks following the twenty-fifth, whatever time the men landed their catch. Then they would celebrate.

Letty went back into the house. There was no sign of anything being over by Christmas as many had hoped at the start of hostilities, maybe not the next, or the one thereafter. The children would not know that, and she was determined to make things as cheerful as she could.

* * *

School had broken for the holidays and Letty had set Alfie and Stella making paper chains and snowflakes to hang about the café. Or rather Alfie was doing the best he could. Stella enjoyed ripping things, the men enjoyed watching them, and one or two would sit with the kiddies and join in. It was a slow process, but what was the rush? The enjoyment and expectation was half the fun. She had taken a few moments to sit with them herself. It was easier to do so since they'd taken on two more staff. Hilda Kettle's husband was one of the men taken POW and she and her twelve-year-old daughter, Poll, had been a godsend. They were also a buffer against Dorcas's negativity.

'Eeh, I don't know why you're bothering,' she said as she bustled past, a fistful of dirty mugs in her hand. 'These men won't notice. They don't come here for pretty.'

Letty rarely rose to her mother-in-law's baiting these days. She gave Alfie a gentle nudge to keep going.

'It's coming up to Christmas, Dorcas. And we need to make it as cheerful as we can. For everyone. Whether they notice or not doesn't matter. We're having fun.'

When they'd finished, she threaded cotton through the snowflakes and hung them from the window latches, and when Wolfie arrived, she got out the steps and they strung the paper chains across the ceiling. She had already bought a small tree and decorated it with tinsel and bits of cotton wool to give the effect of snow. She had been delighted by the result, more so when a group of men came in from Doig's, their faces and hands black with dirt. One of them put his arms out to halt his colleagues, then put his hands on his hips.

'Na, that looks a treat. Don't it, boys. You've done a grand job these past days, Alfie and Stella.' The men came forward to the counter, gave their orders. 'Thanks for making the effort, Mrs Hardy. Sometimes we gets forgotten. Not the heroes the men are who are on the front line.'

'No, but without the ships or the armaments, they would have nothing to fight with. We are all important in our own way. All doing our bit.'

And they were, the men in the factories and fitting rooms, working long shifts and through the night.

When the dinnertime rush was over, Letty took Alfie and Stella to the Parkers. She led them down Henderson Street, Alfie charging ahead and waiting on the pavement for her, snowflakes dangling from his hand. She had already dressed the window, as she had done each year since that first Christmas. It had been easy enough to put together, Milly helping her to get the boxes out of storage. Letty glanced at the empty shop next door. How it rankled – how much easier her life would have been had she been able to pop in and out.

Milly was serving with Norah, and Letty mouthed a quick hello and went through to the back. Stella climbed on Percy's knee.

'Nah then, trouble. What've you been up too?'

Stella giggled, pulled at Percy's glasses. He put up his hands and patted the air, making her laugh even more.

'Can I leave her with you a minute or two? Alfie wants to put his snowflakes in the window.'

'Course. She'll keep an eye on me, won't you, Stella the star.'

Letty lifted Alfie onto the platform of the window display and got beside him. She had already prepared the thread, so all Alfie had to do was attach them – and he was now expert at fastening knots.

'What knot should I do, Mam?'

'Just a simple one, Alfie. One that will hold it in place.' She glanced out of the window to catch Gilbert Crowe staring at her, his arms folded, that irritating smirk on his face. She ignored him, her attention on Alfie.

When they were done, she waited while he jumped to the floor, then stepped down behind him. He ran through to join his sister and Letty waited for Norah to be free.

'He gets my goat, that man!'

'No need to ask which one,' Norah said, writing the sale in the ledger.

'I'd dearly love to wipe that smile off his face. One day I will.'

'Don't let him spoil things for you, lass. You've made a success of the café despite his games.'

'Has he said anything?'

'Not to speak of. Like you, I avoid him. I've heard noises, stuff moved about next door, but it's not every day – or night, come to think of it.'

'Night?'

'Oh, aye. I wondered what it was at first. I thought there was somebody downstairs. I went into the shop, a poker in my hand, then realised it was from Websters.'

Letty shook her head. 'You can't tell me that "storage" is his legitimate business.'

Norah eyed her. 'Don't you go poking about, Letty. Leave him to it. He'll get his comeuppance one of these days.'

'Let's hope it's soon.' She put her arm around Norah's shoulders. 'Best go see what Stella has done to poor Percy.'

'Poor Percy, my eye. He loves her to bits.'

34

Ruth picked at her breakfast, unable to eat after her father read out reports of the raid along the east coast – this time successfully. The Imperial Navy had bombarded Scarborough, Hartlepool and Whitby two days ago, on the sixteenth of December. There had been 137 civilian deaths and many casualties, among them women and children. 'It must have been terrifying.' Ruth imagined people running for cover – but where would they run? Where would she run if the same happened here and she were at the mission, or walking the streets?

'The docks and factories will have been the primary targets.' Her father threw the newspaper onto the table and removed his glasses, rubbed at them with the corner of the tablecloth. 'What a fiasco! Where the blazes was our navy?'

Although the British and French had been victorious at Ypres, the news worsened as each week passed. The number of men lost, at sea and on land, was already in the thousands, each one a brother, a son. Henry wrote a little of his experience on the *Black Prince*, but it heartened her that he was with Alec Hardy and Philip Proctor. If anything should happen...

Her father returned his glasses to his nose. 'Everything in order for the party this afternoon?'

She took a sip of her tea. 'I believe so. I hope you can find time to call in. I should like you to meet some of the people who have been able to benefit from your donation.'

'I will do my utmost.' He got up. 'I need to get into the office and to the Board of Trade. Discover what is being done. In the light of this morning's news, Grimsby and Hull will be prime targets for attack.'

Ruth tensed.

'I don't mean to frighten you, my dear, but it as well we are prepared.' He kissed the top of her head. 'I hope it all goes well. I know how hard you have worked for this. At least the men in Ruhleben and other camps will receive a little joy this Christmas. It can't be pleasant.' He looked about the room. 'Makes one appreciate one's home all the more.'

Ruth got up and went with him to the door, handed him his hat and coat. 'I'll see you for dinner?'

'You will.'

After much debate, she and Mrs Murray had decided to decorate the house for Christmas. It seemed more important than ever to keep the home fires burning. The popular song by Ivor Novello had taken the country by storm, and people wanted to do their best till the boys came home. Charles had hoped to get leave, but it would not be for Christmas. He had two days, and he and Daphne had chosen to meet halfway. Ruth would have liked to have seen him, as would her father, but they totally understood his choice. Henry's leave was unlikely, especially since this last raid. Any hopes of that would surely be dashed. While there was threat, the men would be there to defend it.

When Mrs Murray began clearing the breakfast table, Ruth went to her room and wrapped the remaining presents for her father. She had bought a headscarf for Mrs Murray and a collection of poetry for Miss Sheldon. She had much to thank her for. Through her, Ruth had learned to stop and consider the best use of her time, let alone her money. She'd told Arthur Marshall that there was no point waiting. The night he had stopped his car and refused to help had fixed her opinion of him, and no amount of persuasion from her aunt had made the slightest difference.

There was no man in her life at the moment, she had no need of one, for her work with the mission and other charitable commitments filled her days. She was no longer the lonely and indecisive young woman she once was.

Ruth changed into a plain frock, dithered, changed her mind again. Would the children want to see something pretty? Would it make the other women feel drab? Was she flaunting her wealth? Was it over the top for a Christmas party at the mission? Had it been Saxon Hall, she would have had no qualms in choosing the correct dress for the occasion. She looked at the array of dresses laid across the bed and laughed. Perhaps her indecisiveness hadn't been completely cured.

In the end she chose a blush rose, with lace cuff and neck. It fitted the in-betweenness of the occasion and the in-betweenness of her life.

Downstairs, Mrs Murray was already waiting in her hat and coat. Ruth had been delighted when the housekeeper had offered to come along and help and looked forward to working alongside her. It was in these small but not insignificant ways that Ruth felt life at Meadowvale House was gradually becoming the home it might have been had her mother lived.

* * *

The meeting room had been set aside for the occasion and there were already a few assembled when the two of them arrived, foremost of them the Hewitt sisters and Mrs Barton. Letty Hardy was counting knives and forks, Alfie keeping Stella occupied playing cat's cradle. Mrs Murray removed her outdoor clothes and rolled up her sleeves. Miss Sheldon had spared some of the attendants to do the heavy lifting of tables and chairs, but the women were more than capable of setting them out and laying out the cutlery. Some of them had brought plates of sandwiches and bowls of jelly, cakes small and large. Aunt Helen had sent her car, laden with trays of sausages and small savouries, and had managed not to interfere. Ruth had reason to believe Miss Sheldon had put her foot down, and she was relieved not to have her aunt commandeering the situation.

With fifteen minutes to go, the tables were ready and Ruth prided herself that it looked so wonderful. The tables had been decorated with holly, ivy and small trinkets. A large tree, decorated with baubles and beads, stood proudly in one corner. Underneath it was an array of gaily wrapped presents, and a throne for Santa – the chair from Miss Sheldon's office. Ruth had wrapped the gifts with Mary Owen, who had come to sit with her each day, to knit and to talk, and as she formed the stitches, she created new habits and a new confidence. That made two of them.

At five to two, Ruth joined Miss Sheldon at the entrance and greeted each guest as they came into the mission, directed them to the room where the party was to be held. It was good to see small eyes shine bright, to hear the excited chatter, and it warmed her to think she was a small part of it all. Happiest of all was the sight of Mary Owen coming towards her, Emily and Kitty beside her. Their clothes were clean, and their hair shone, and Ruth could not have wished for a finer gift.

When the guests were all accounted for, Ruth followed Miss

Sheldon to the meeting room. Miss Sheldon led Grace and, small hands clasped together, eyes closed, the children said Amen. Miss Sheldon looked to Ruth, who took it as her cue to speak.

'Thank you all for joining us here today. Each and every one of you.' She felt a little flustered and her voice was thin to begin with until Letty caught her eye and smiled warmly. It gave her courage and she said, more loudly, 'We wish you all a merry and heartfelt Christmas.'

Faces looked at her expectantly and she wondered why they didn't move until Letty mouthed: 'Tell them to start.'

She smiled out to the children, all hanging on to her every word except for an impatient little one who reached out to take a sandwich and received a gentle tap on the hand from their mother. 'Please begin – and enjoy the party.'

The noise was like a train as excitedly the children helped themselves, cautioned by many a mother not to be too greedy but the sight of so much food was beyond temptation and all too soon the plates were empty, tummies full.

Afterwards, the tables were quickly cleared and removed and the children settled on the floor facing the tree. Rosa Hewitt played Christmas carols and everyone sang along, the adults joining in as they worked around them, and Ruth thought she had never spent such a joyous afternoon. There was much excitement as Father Christmas, one of the rotund attendants who rather resembled the man himself with his white hair and beard, came to deliver his gifts, a sack on his back. Ruth thought he didn't look unlike the mission founder, Ebenezer Mather.

'This was a marvellous idea of yours, Miss Evans,' Miss Sheldon told her as Father Christmas handed out presents.

'Was it my idea?' She couldn't remember.

Miss Sheldon pressed her arm. 'You take so little credit for all you do, but it doesn't go unnoticed.'

Ruth was filled with something she had never felt before, a sense of purpose, of satisfaction that she had used her days wisely.

Someone came to stand behind her. 'It has been a success?'

She turned, grasped her father's hand. 'It has. We managed to make something of Christmas after all.'

35

Letty and Dorcas waited on Grimsby station for the early-evening train. Stella was asleep in her pram and Alfie had gone up onto the bridge, watching the trains come and go from the station. Letty waved to her boy as Alec's train pulled in and he ran down the stairs as quickly as his little legs would carry him, squeezing through gaps to get to her, his face shining with excitement. Alec had been away for almost six months and though she ached to be in his arms, a part of her was nervous at seeing him. Would he be disappointed? Would she? Since they'd wed, they'd spent more time apart than together, and she felt like a young lass going a-courting than a married woman waiting for her husband, such were the butterflies in her stomach.

Dorcas had been sitting on the bench and she got up and came forward as the train drew to a stop, the brakes screaming on the bare metal, smoke escaping from beneath them and billowing onto the platform. Further along, she could see Ruth Evans and her father. Ruth had smiled and waved, but they had not spoken. They had seen little of each other since Christmas, each of them busy with their own endeavours. There was little time for anything these days – the shop was ticking along, and the café was busy from the moment they opened the doors. In January, she had taken on extra staff, two sisters who would help Hilda and Poll and cover for her and Dorcas while Alec was home. He and his crew had four days' leave and Letty planned to make the most of every precious minute.

Letty was shocked when she saw Alec step down from the carriage, and fought not to show it, though he had not yet seen her. His face was lit by the biggest smile as he caught sight of her. Leaving the children, she ran to him and felt his arms come about her, and looked up at him, her dearest Alec. He was so changed, his face thinner, more drawn. That he was tired was obvious, but his eyes told her it was more than fatigue.

'What a sight for sore eyes.' He clasped her hand in his, squeezed it so that it almost hurt, and she took it as a measure of his longing, for she could not hold him tight enough or long enough, and she didn't want to let go, not yet.

For all his excitement, Alfie clung to Dorcas's skirts, suddenly shy, and Alec dropped his kitbag and squatted on his haunches, pushed his cap back from his forehead. 'Nah, then, is that my boy, Alfie Hardy. Have you not got a big hug for your Dad?'

Alfie came forward, grinning, and Alec rubbed at his hair, then pulled him close. He got up, embraced his mother, then looked about for Stella, saw her pram and went over. The child was still asleep, and he took hold of the handle and reached over her.

'Bonny, just like her mother.'

Letty grinned, reassured.

As they left the station, he put up a hand and shouted to the Evans' party. 'See you back here on Wednesday.'

'Who was the man with Henry Evans?' Letty asked as she linked her arm in his.

'Proctor they call him, nice chap. He's navy proper, not the wavy navy like me.'

She laughed. The RNR was called such because the braid on their arms did not run smooth but had an up-and-down curve to it. 'I'll bet you've tormented the life out of him, poor chap.'

'Aye, I can't say the lads haven't pulled his leg a time or two.'

They walked home, the weather cold but dry, and he asked of the café and the shop, of how the Parkers were doing.

'You must come along and see for yourself. I think you'll be impressed.'

He asked them lots of questions but answered none and Letty, not used to him being so evasive, took it as not being the time and place. There would be chance later –for all they wanted to say, and do.

When they got to the house, he stopped outside while Dorcas went in with the children.

'What's wrong?'

He shook his head. 'Nothing's wrong. I just wanted to stand and take it all in, so I remember it when I'm away again.' He turned to her. 'I want to remember how it looks, every brick and slate. I want to imagine you going about the rooms and pottering about in the garden. This is home, Let. *You* are home.' He put his hand to the back of her neck and drew her close so forcibly that it hurt and, noticing, he frowned, apologised for his roughness. 'You are everything to me, Letty Hardy, always remember that. Everything.'

* * *

That night, she lay in his arms. It seemed she had done all the talking that evening with his mother and the children, and she wanted to hear something of how he spent his days. He told her little of what had happened at sea, only that it was boring, going up and down the same part of the ocean. He talked more of being ashore.

'I went back to my old house, where I lived with Mam and Dad. It was smaller than I remembered it. Everything seemed smaller, my uncle and aunt's house, the pubs, everything squashed in.'

'Did it make you want to go back there?'

He didn't answer straight away, and she lay with her head on his chest, listening to his steady breath, in and out.

'It held a lot of memories, good and bad. Of fishing with Father and Robbie, of life as it used to be when I were a boy.' He put his hand under her chin and tilted her face to his. 'But we can't go back to how things were, wishing we could do things different.'

He looked troubled, his words heavy with regret, and it unsettled her. The lamplight reflected in his eyes and he leaned closer, pressed his full lips to hers. He kissed her neck and her breasts, and when they made love, he was more tender than she had ever known him to be. It was as though life was more precious to him, that *she* was more precious to him, and for all her longing that the war would end, it had made her man more thoughtful, and she was glad of the change in him.

* * *

It had been a bad night, Alec thrashing about, his body soaked with sweat. At one point, he had called out and Alfie had come into them, afraid. Letty had seen him back to bed, then climbed into her own. Alec had laid his head on her breast and she had held him, the way, hours ago, he had held her, holding her hand against his forehead, feeling the dampness of his hair.

In the morning, she left him sleeping, keeping the children quiet while she pressed Alec's uniform and made sure he had a clean shirt. It was almost noon when he came down to them, his hair sticking up, his eyes bleary.

'You should have woken me.'

'You were tired.'

'I've time enough to sleep back on ship. I don't want to be wasting time with you.'

She handed him his shirt. 'Get yourself washed and tidied. I've booked George Eustace for one o'clock. It's about time we had a family photo to go on the mantelpiece.'

* * *

The five of them set off in their best clothes, and Dorcas pushed the pram while Letty and Alec walked arm in arm. The sitting had been on her mind since he'd left, with no time to take a photo, to capture their growing family. All Dorcas had left of her husband and young son was a few photographs and Letty knew how precious they were. She wanted to catch them all now, just in case.

They posed as a family: Dorcas and Letty seated on chairs, Alec standing behind his wife, a hand to her shoulder, Stella on Letty's knee and Alfie in the middle of the two women. Dorcas posed for a photograph alone, and with her son, and Letty and Alec had one taken together. Stella cried and Alfie soothed her and made her laugh. A family. It had been a brief interlude in their day, but a precious one.

'I don't know if the photographs will be ready before you leave, but I'll send them on.'

He reached into his inside pocket and pulled out a piece of crumpled paper, showed it to her. It had been taken on their wedding day, Letty wearing a simple white dress with lace about the collar and cuffs.

'I look so young.'

'You were. You are.'

She fussed at her hair. Since she'd had Stella, her waist had thickened and she'd lost that fresh-faced look. But seeing the way he looked at her now, the love in his eyes, somehow it didn't seem to matter at all.

* * *

When they left, they carried on into Cleethorpes for a stroll along the promenade. It was cold and the wind had a sharpness to it, but they were well wrapped up and the walking kept them warm. They stopped for a bite to eat at one of the tearooms on Alexandra Road and Alec bought the kiddies a half-pound of dolly mixture, telling Alfie to 'make 'em last.' The delight on the boy's face as he handed over the bulging paper bag was a picture.

'They'll be sick, the pair of 'em,' Dorcas clucked.

'Ah, go away with yer, Mam,' he told her, laughing. 'They've got some catching up to do, and so have I.'

Some things he could never catch up with, some things he could never undo, although he wished with all his heart he might. It was good to be with his family. To have a day when he was wasn't continually watching the horizon and now he would be forever looking over his shoulder, wondering what mischief Becky might cause. He had been out of his mind and half drunk when he'd his way with her on the beach that night – or had it been the other way around? He had taken no precaution and it crossed his mind that she could have caught for a nipper. He had not seen her since and hoped he never would. Now, he looked to Letty, the love of his heart. A bitter taste came into his mouth, and he swallowed it down, slipped his arm about Letty's shoulder and pulled her close.

* * *

Henry had invited Proctor to stay for the four days of their leave and his father had been delighted to have their company, as was Ruth. Mrs Murray had already aired the extra bed and it was wonderful for the house to possess life and movement again. For once, her father did not leave early for the office, but lingered at the breakfast table and at supper, enjoying the company of both his son and Lieutenant Proctor. Henry had matured, was less combative with his father, but he had lost some of his light too. Ruth thought of all the young men she knew, some already lost, others returned injured. It was not the adventure he had thought it was.

'Any plans for these few days, Henry, Philip? Anything you'd like me to arrange for you?' Richard asked.

'Sleep,' Henry said, 'and more sleep. Just to be in my own bed is the most wonderful thing. And to have Mrs Murray's excellent cooking. All a man can ask for. It's good to be home.'

Her father was bright, but he couldn't have failed to notice the change in his son. Ruth sensed regret, that they were trying to build bridges. He turned to Proctor.

'I'd like some time to sketch, something other than seascapes and fighting men.'

'Ruth will perhaps sit with you,' her father suggested. 'Unless you'd rather be alone?'

He shook his head.

'You might like to sit in the garden,' Ruth offered. 'It might be cold, but there is a sheltered spot, away from the wind. I have my watercolours and you're welcome to use whatever you wish.'

* * *

Henry went with his father to the office, and Ruth delighted in seeing them close for once, not sparking each other like flints.

After breakfast, she and Proctor wrapped up warmly, gathered sketchbooks and pencils, two collapsible chairs and walked out into the garden. She settled herself by the apple tree, pointing out the pond, the ivy that scrambled over the red-brick wall, the shrubs that still had colour even though spring was a way off. The first daffodils had appeared, and here and there were signs that the warmer weather would come. Hope eternal.

They spent the morning out there, their conversation light. She already knew so much about him from his letters, and they chatted easily. He was attentive, interested as well as interesting. They talked of artists they admired, of books and plays.

They were still in the garden when Henry returned. He stood behind Philip admiring his work.

'You said you were a marine artist?'

'I am not at work and free to paint whatever takes my eye.'

'And in this case, it's my sister.' Henry drew his hand about his chin. 'You have captured her perfectly, the line of her neck, her eyes. Her mouth.' He touched the paper. 'You must have been paying such deep attention.' He raised his eyebrows at Proctor.

'Honestly, Henry,' Ruth interrupted. 'You'll make Philip feel uncomfortable, and he is our guest.'

Her brother looked at her for a long time, then down at the drawing. 'You have captured the essence of my sister that she is careful not to reveal.'

'What essence, Henry?' Curious, Ruth got up, came to look for herself. The detail was incredible.

'Your gentleness, but also your strength.'

'I have strength?' She peered at the representation of herself. Did she really look so serene? 'I was relaxed, I wasn't paying attention.'

'Not thinking too hard,' Henry affirmed. 'It shows. You should do more of it.'

'Sketching?'

'No, not thinking. It stops you doing things.'

'I'm not like you. I can't be spontaneous.'

'And on that note.' He put his arms about her waist, lifted her off her feet. 'Enough of sitting, you two. Time is brief and we shall all be spontaneous. I have five tickets for the Prince of Wales.'

'Five.' Had he met a girl?

'I thought we'd take Mrs Murray. She deserves a treat.'

She leaned to him. 'What will Father think?'

'We're not thinking, remember. We don't have time enough for that.'

* * *

In the end, her father had not made the fuss she'd expected and even seemed delighted that Henry had been so thoughtful. For the first time in months, Ruth actually felt happy. Father drove them there and they got out of the car and waited on the steps of the theatre. A gaggle of children were moving along the queue, singing for coppers, and generally making a nuisance of themselves until they were given pennies to go away. The line moved, and in no time at all they were in the auditorium and taking their seats, waiting for the show to begin.

The evening had been the perfect escape. There had been no time for thought, only laughter and song and dance, and for a few brief hours, Ruth forgot about everything outside of the building and was sorry when the curtain came down. Philip helped her on with her coat and Henry did the same for Mrs Murray. Their housekeeper, who had looked uncomfortable to begin with, was now relaxed and chatting to Philip Proctor as if he were an old friend. Ruth had enjoyed his company and the hours and minutes they spent together had skipped by. He was kind and he was considerate. It was such a shame he had not found the right woman to share his life with.

* * *

Back at the house, Mrs Murray resumed her role and got them all drinks before retiring to her bed. Henry joined their father in his study and Ruth sat with Philip in the drawing room.

'How are things at the mission? Do you still enjoy it?'

'I do. I admire Miss Sheldon so much.'

'It comes through in your letters.' It pleased her.

'When Mr Wilson left so suddenly, I didn't care to go back, but I am so glad I did. I enjoy being of use and Miss Sheldon uses me well.'

He laughed. 'No more scrubbing floors.'

She shook her head. 'She taught me a valuable lesson. That I can do more than I believed I could.'

'Believed? Or were allowed? They are two different things.'

She considered his question. 'Both,' she said after some thought. 'Henry says I think too much about things, and he is right.' She gave a small laugh. 'And sometimes he does not think enough. I suppose being allowed to do more has made me believe I can do more. I suppose we can all stretch ourselves beyond our limits.'

'You are different,' he told her.

'In what way?'

He smiled. 'Your brother said I had captured it in my sketch today. Your strength, I suppose. But it's not just strength.' He took in every freckle, her hair, every eyelash. When he was sketching her, it would have gone unnoticed, but now he fought the impulse to stare at her so intently.

'Capable? Confident?' she suggested. 'They are different qualities.'

'Subtly so, but then most things are subtle and go undetected.'

It was clear she had no idea of the meaning his words implied, that she had not the slightest notion of his feelings for her. If he were a few years younger, he might have spoken of them. Instead, he held his tongue, happy to be in her company. There was something very still about her, and perhaps that was where her strength lay.

36

Relations between Ruth and her aunt had cooled since Colin Wilson's abrupt departure, and in the months that had followed, neither woman had spoken of it. Ruth had not been brave enough, and her aunt obviously deemed it not worth comment. As time passed, Ruth was inclined to agree. She was much changed since that afternoon when she had discovered Colin Wilson's impending departure. Back then, she had been more passive, more accepting – wanting to please her father, her aunt, to do her duty to her family by marrying Arthur Marshall. She had thought she could learn to love Arthur, had thought she loved Colin – but that's all they were – thoughts. Miss Sheldon had encouraged her to take a moment to step back and take an overview of each situation, of how her energies and time would be best spent. It had given her a growing confidence, in herself, and in her abilities. Proctor was right, she did have a quiet strength – she had simply not appreciated its worth before.

The meeting room at the mission that late February afternoon was well attended. Ruth was once again seated at a desk behind her aunt, taking the minutes, and Aunt Helen stood where she always stood, facing rows of ladies, young and old, who had contributed to the work of the Guild.

Her aunt looked to the clock, the minute hand just about to reach the hour, when the door opened, and Miss Sheldon quietly took a seat on the back row. Ruth was curious. Miss Sheldon had never attended a meeting, leaving them to their own devices, only too grateful for their contribution and support of the mission.

'Ladies, first of all, may I extend a welcome to the new faces I see among us, and a thank you to those of you who have long supported the Guild, most especially in these last six months.' Women smiled with satisfaction at the appreciation of their work. 'Although we have achieved tremendous things, there is more call on our services than ever before. And, as Miss Sheldon will vouch...' Aunt Helen paused, allowing heads to turn to peer at Miss Sheldon, who was resolutely still.

Ruth looked down at her ledger and bit back a smile. The port missioner was immune to flattery and, try as she might, her aunt had found her difficult to work alongside. She might also regret Mr Wilson's leaving in time.

'We must keep up our efforts to provide comfort and assistance to those poor souls.'

There was a collective nod of heads, which carried on as Aunt Helen reeled off the sums raised, and good deeds done. The ladies who had provided assistance, knitting items, altering clothing, cooking meals, cleaning homes and caring for children. No small action had gone unmentioned, and Ruth watched the women as the list of their commitment and dedication was spoken of. It amounted to a huge effort from so few women, and she felt privileged to be a part of it.

When the list came to an end, there was a round of applause and Miss Sheldon got to her feet, waited until it had died down.

'Yes?' her aunt asked.

'I'd like to say a few words.' It was not a request but a statement.

'Would you like to come to the front?'

'No, thank you. I can say what I've come to say where I am.'

Women twisted in their chairs to look at her.

Miss Sheldon smiled. 'Ladies, I'd rather you face forward, and save your necks. I only need to be listened too, not to be seen.'

Ruth saw her aunt stiffen. If it was meant as a slight, it was taken as such, not that it would bother Miss Sheldon.

'We are all, at the mission, grateful for the work of the ladies of the Guild. Your help has been most welcome in a time of great hardship.'

Ruth wished she could see her aunt's face. She imagined her trying to keep smiling as Miss Sheldon said her piece.

The superintendent looked directly to Ruth. 'I came today to thank Miss Evans.' Ruth felt the heat rise in her neck. 'You all give of your time – and of yourselves – so graciously, and I thank you for that, we could not carry on as we do without you. But this young woman has excelled in her service to the mission. I had set her a challenge, which she met with great dignity and diligence. She single-handedly raised the sum of five hundred and twenty-four pounds, eight shillings and sixpence.'

There were gasps and a spontaneous round of applause and Miss Sheldon waited for it to abate before carrying on.

'This money has enabled the mission to do numerous things, but its main purpose was to send Christmas parcels to the many Grimsby men who are prisoners of war in Ruhleben.' She held up a wad of papers. 'These are letters I have received today from the men, giving thanks for the most welcome gifts.' She walked to the front, ignoring Aunt Helen, and placed them before Ruth, saying quietly, 'I thought you might like to read them.' Ruth pulled them towards her, quite overcome as Miss Sheldon said, more loudly, this time, 'Thank you, Miss Evans. Your tenacity has made a great deal of difference.' She looked kindly at Ruth, and when she smiled, Ruth felt her heart swell with gratitude, not that she felt she deserved the recognition, but that praise came from Miss Sheldon meant so much more than if it came from elsewhere. It had not been for show on the superintendent's part, she had not craved the glory as her aunt did, but she had wanted Ruth's endeavours to be recognised.

The superintendent gave a brief nod to Helen Frampton and went to leave, her aunt momentarily nonplussed until she began to clap to regain command. The women followed suit as Miss Sheldon left the room and closed the door behind her.

The meeting carried on as if there had been no interruption, and when it came to an end, and the tea and biscuits were produced, Letty was the first to come over to congratulate Ruth. 'Well done. What a marvellous achievement.'

Ruth placed her fingers on the letters. 'I had a purpose, it made it somewhat easier – and Miss Sheldon challenged me.' The thought had only just dawned on her, and she realised how little was expected of her, how much she had drifted along fulfilling everyone's expectations, instead of having any of her own.

'And you rose to it,' Letty replied. 'Not everyone does.'

Her aunt joined them, and after a little polite chit-chat, Letty moved on.

'Well, that was rather rude.'

'Rude?' Ruth knew very well what her aunt was talking about, but for once she preferred to be obtuse.

'Miss Sheldon. I thought she might have come to stand by me to make her announcement. *And* I thought she might have notified me first?'

'Why?' Ruth asked her. There had been no congratulations or commendations from her aunt, not that she'd expected it, she had been too wrapped up in Miss Sheldon stealing her thunder.

Her aunt narrowed her eyes. 'Because I am the president of the Guild.'

'And she is in charge of the mission.' Ruth wanted to laugh at her aunt's punctured ego. 'Perhaps you found it easier to deal with Mr Wilson. What a pity you got him moved.'

'I did no such thing,' her aunt whispered. 'What a foolish thing to say.'

'Is it?' Ruth was quite enjoying seeing her aunt so ruffled, it had never happened before, not to her knowledge anyway, and she suddenly felt less diminished by her. Miss Sheldon had not been cowed by anyone, nor deferential. As she had told Ruth not so long ago, respect had to be earned. 'How strange that you came that day and interrupted myself and Mr Wilson. That you went back in to have a word with him and days later he was moved on.'

'I did not get him *moved on*.' Aunt Helen looked about her to check the women closest to them, smiled and guided her niece to the corner. 'I might have had a quiet word, warned him off.'

'Warned him off!' Ruth was incredulous at her aunt's admission. It threw an entirely new light on the situation. Was it the reason for Colin Wilson's reticence?

'Shh. Don't draw attention to yourself.'

'I'm not the one who likes attention, Aunt Helen.' Ruth gritted her teeth. Warned him off indeed. How different things might have been had her aunt not interfered.

'I reminded him of his position. He could never provide for you in the way your father has. You were courting Arthur at the time.' She briefly closed her eyes and gave a small shake of her head. 'And what a mess that turned out to be.' She held up her head, sniffed. 'Can you think what a scandal it would have caused. A young woman of your position and the port missioner!'

'What!' Ruth thought of Letty, who had followed Alec to

Grimsby, taken up a life she knew nothing of, for the love of him. 'If we loved each other, we would be happy.'

'Love does not last, nor does happiness. It is fleeting. Love soon goes when the debt mounts and the workhouse beckons. Mr Wilson left because he thought more of his job than he thought of you. It's as simple as that.' Her sharp words pierced Ruth, as she no doubt knew they would, taking her own irritation out on her – just because she could. Because for so long Ruth had allowed her to.

'How do you know?'

'Because if he had any strong feelings for you, he would have spoken of them. He wouldn't have paid any attention to the slightest thing I said, but he did. And he left accordingly.' She altered her tone, softer now, but Ruth didn't want her sympathy. 'You need a man who will stand by you when times are tough, not one who runs away.'

Ruth couldn't bear to hear anymore, and she gathered the letters and left, went to the room where she had worked the past few months. She had looked forward to reading the replies, but now tears threatened and the words blurred before her.

A gentle knock on the open door made her look up.

'Oh, I have disturbed you.'

Ruth took out her handkerchief and dabbed at her eyes. 'No, not at all.'

Letty came and sat in the chair opposite. 'The letters have moved you?'

'I haven't read them.' She looked to Letty, who was always so supportive, glanced to the open door. Letty got up and closed it.

'Has something happened?'

Ruth hesitated. She could trust Letty, and Letty knew how she felt about Colin. She told her of her aunt's interference. Letty reached across the table and touched her hand. It was such a simple gesture but so powerful. Ruth felt connected to Letty in a way she did not with anyone else.

'Your aunt put Mr Wilson in a difficult position. His concern would be for his job. Without it, he would have nothing – nowhere to live, no income. He wouldn't have made his decision lightly. Perhaps your aunt forced his hand.'

She considered Letty's explanation. Aunt Helen wielded a huge amount of influence in the town. If she withdrew her support, it could spell disaster for any number of businesses. Miss Sheldon had stood up to her, but not everyone felt comfortable doing so.

Ruth looked down at the letters on the desk. There was power in the written word. She would write to Colin and ask him herself. Knowledge of what her aunt had done changed everything. Perhaps he had loved her all along.

37

Dorcas had known something was wrong when Letty got up that morning. She had been in the kitchen getting the kiddies something to eat and Letty had come downstairs all of a dither, pinning up her hair, her clothes awry. It wasn't like her, the lass was always so together, but it was clear to a blind man that she was running out of steam – not that she'd ever admit it. Since Alec had gone back to sea, she had worked herself into a frazzle, cramming more into a day than was healthy.

'I didn't hear the kiddies. I can't believe I didn't wake up.' Letty glanced to the clock. 'Oh, Lord, I should have left half an hour ago.'

Dorcas rubbed a damp cloth round Stella's mouth and over her hands, did the same to Alfie, who wriggled himself free as soon as he was able. 'Sit down, get something to eat. It won't hurt the men to wait half an hour.'

'That's not the point. I can't afford to be sloppy. They'll go elsewhere. There's plenty of other cafés.'

'There is, but the men prefer yours.' Dorcas pushed a mug of milk into her daughter-in-law's hand. 'I keep telling you, you're doing too much. Working all hours, and the kiddies to look after. Let alone popping over to Parkers in the middle of it. It'll all come tumbling down about you if you don't take a step back.' She pushed Letty down into a chair. The lass had lost weight and her skin no longer had its healthy shine. 'Five minutes. Don't mither about the kiddies, I'll bring them along. Hilda can get on with the food and Poll knows well enough how to serve.'

It had been an education watching Letty build the café into the success it now was. In a few months, she had made it turn a profit. Business was constant from early in the morning until ten at night when they closed the doors. Letty had extended the opening hours when she realised there was a call for it. In no time at all, she had taken a woman and her daughter to help. Hilda's husband had been captured in the first weeks of the war. She had thought him drowned but then discovered he was in one of the internment camps. Things were difficult and Letty had thrown a lifeline to her and her twelve-year-old daughter. She'd probably thrown a lifeline to many more. There were any number of women at their disposal who came in part-time when needed. Dorcas figured there was nowt the lass couldn't do if she had a mind to it. That was the trouble: Letty wanted to do it all, but no one could keep up that pace. They were paying for this lovely house and none of them spent more than a few hours in it.

'I feel like I've put on you too much already?'

Dorcas shook her head. 'Isn't that what family's for?'

Letty drank the milk but wouldn't stop to eat, saying she would get something at the café.

'If you stand still long enough,' Dorcas called after her as she dashed out of the door.

Dorcas walked with Alfie to Sally Penny's and stopped awhile to chat with her while Alfie went off with the other kiddies to school. Her old neighbour, Bet Chapman, was waiting for her nets to be collected. The man from the braiding lofts would collect the finished nets and leave the twine for more to be made. It was what she had done herself when she had lived here. It seemed a world away now and her life in Lowestoft a distant memory. They exchanged a few words but Dorcas was anxious to get off and didn't linger as she once would have done, and made her way back to the docks.

She enjoyed pushing Stella along in her pram. She was a curious child and took in everything about her, just like her boy. Sometimes she saw glimpses of Robbie – in her eyes, in the way she chuckled – but she had her mother's will, and Dorcas didn't know if that was a good thing or bad.

When she arrived at the café there was a line of men waiting about the doors, there being no more room inside, and they parted to allow her to get the pram down to the back of the building. Poll was at the counter taking orders, making drinks and rushing about like a blue-arsed fly, and her mother looked like she didn't know whether she was coming or going, as she cracked eggs into a frying pan, then began slicing into a pile of bread cakes. 'Am I glad to see you,' she muttered as Dorcas pulled off her coat and fastened her apron.

'Where's Letty?' She took the knife from Hilda and dealt with the buns, leaving Hilda to see to the eggs that were spitting in the layer of fat.

'She had to go off and fetch more milk, more bacon – more of everything. She forgot to put the order in.'

Dorcas rolled her eyes. 'Never mind. The lass will sort it out.' She finished the last of the bread cakes and turned to face the sea of men at the counter. 'Now, then, who's next?'

* * *

Letty returned looking far worse than she had done that morning, four great bags in her hands, her shoulders sagging with the weight of them. One of the men, who Dorcas knew to be Oskar, took them from her and brought them up to the counter. 'Looks like the young woman needs carrying too,' he said, as Dorcas thanked him.

Letty was full of apologies to Hilda and Poll, to Dorcas, as she emptied the bags and stored the food. Stella began to whinge for her mother and one of the men in the queue bounced the pram by the handle to settle her, another tweaking his ears to distract her.

In less than half an hour, order was restored, and there was time for Poll to go out and clear the tables and get the mugs washed ready for the next rush.

Letty leant at the sink and stared down into the water. Dorcas had two fistfuls of mugs and she put them on the draining board and pushed her daughter-in-law out of the way, shoved a tea towel into Letty's hand and put her hands in the water. 'Did you get anything to eat when you got here?'

Letty shook her head. 'There wasn't time. Men were waiting. And I realised I had forgotten to order the milk, more bacon. We were short of onions.' She let out a deep sigh. 'I was on to a hiding from the off.'

Dorcas shook the water from a mug and handed it over. 'How long do you think you can keep this game up?'

'Game?'

'Don't be coy with me, Letty Hardy. Stop trying to control the ruddy world. Even God had a day off – and you're not God.'

Letty was just about to argue back when there was a clatter, then a sickening thud and Stella began to wail. Letty dropped the mug, which smashed on the floor, and ran over to the pram, but Poll had got their first and was picking Stella up from the floor. The child held out her arms for her mother, and Dorcas saw the angry red mark on her head. Letty took her from Poll and hushed her, kissing her cheek and jiggling her up and down, pacing about the floor as men looked on.

Dorcas dunked a cloth in cold water, wrung it out and pressed it to the child's head. Letty stood with her face to the wall, soothing the child and when Dorcas put a hand on her shoulder, she saw Letty was crying too. She pulled out a chair and guided her to it, made her sit down. Stella was gradually settled, and Dorcas handed her to Poll, who sat her on her knee and played 'Pop Goes the Weasel' with her. In no time at all, she was chuckling, her little disaster forgotten.

Letty sat with her hands between her knees, and even though Dorcas had seen it coming, she felt for the lass. She should have spoken sooner.

'Right, miss. I'm putting my foot down. Get yourself off to Lowestoft for a few days. Your mother will be pleased to see you.'

'But I can't. I—'

Dorcas put up her hand. 'Even the troops get leave. Everyone needs a break. Take the kiddies. I can look after this place with Hilda and Poll. You've got the new lass starting next week. Norah can manage with that lass you've got over there, and I can manage here.'

Letty chewed on her lip, but the tears fell regardless, and Dorcas handed her a tea towel to dry them. The lass gave her a small smile. 'I can't expect—'

'Ah, ah,' Dorcas interrupted her. 'What does it say outside? Hardy's Café or Letty's?'

Letty gave a tearful laugh. 'Hardy's.'

'Right, so off you go to your mother's. It'll do you better than anything the doctor can give you.'

It took no more persuasion, not that Dorcas would have given in, not this time. She couldn't bear anything to happen to the lass. In the early days, she had thought her the wrong one for Alec, but the lass was good for the pair of them. Letty had given her a family again, given her something to live for.

38

Ruth happened to be in the hall when the postman arrived late morning. She had long ago ceased to rush for each delivery, hoping for a reply from Colin, but this time, taking the letters and going through them, she saw a letter she did not want. It was addressed to her father, but she knew the contents would contain bad news. She sank down onto the bottom stair and was still there when Mrs Murray came through.

'Was that the door? Oh, Miss Ruth, is everything all right?'

Ruth lifted her head, showed the official envelope.

'Oh, dear God.' Mrs Murray put her hand to her throat.

'I must tell Father.'

'Let me call a cab for you. I'll go out onto the street.'

Ruth hauled herself from the stair, holding on to the newel post to steady herself. 'No, please. I'd rather walk. I need the air.' She needed to delay the opening of the letter, dreading its contents.

She walked the length of Freeman Street, the dock tower in her sights. The streets were busy with men in uniform and people going about their business. At one point, it crossed her mind that she was dreaming, sleepwalking down the street, and that she might wake, until a man, not looking where he was going, barged into her and apologised. The jolt had shaken her but did not stop her.

She kept to Fish Dock Road, still busy with men and women, carts and wagons, the trains taking what fish there was to market. Father still had eight trawlers, albeit not his finest, but fish was landed, and he had a modicum of income that was keeping Excel Trawlers in business when many had already failed. The overheads were less, he had cut his cloth to suit, as they had at the house, making adjustments, large and small. If he managed to get the business through the war, he could rebuild it. With his sons.

Ruth clutched her bag, praying it would not be the worst news. There had been a shift when the war began, when the men went off to fight, a shift she had felt herself, readjusting, stepping to find firmer ground. Now, as she walked, she felt it shifting again, and the sickening in her stomach increased, rising in her throat the nearer she came to Wharncliffe Road.

She quickened her pace, then slowed again, wanting to know, not wanting to know. Was it better to have the news and deal with it, or delay it as long as was possible? She stood for a moment outside the offices, stared at the sign above the entrance door in gilded letters, then pushed on the door and went inside.

Mr Tate was not at his desk and Mr Swift made to get up as she came in, but she indicated for him to remain at his work and made her way up the dark staircase. Her father was sitting back in his leather chair, eyes closed, his hands clasped across his stomach, as if in prayer, which might be the case. He had changed these past few weeks, his face more lined, his cheeks more sunken and she worried for him. 'Father.'

He opened his eyes, sat up. 'I nodded off.' He cleared his throat and moved his blotter, picked up the papers he had been working on. There was a pile to his left and more on the cabinet behind him.

Ruth hesitated, not knowing whether to sit or stand. She opened her bag and handed over the letter. Her father took it and held it for some moments before opening it. Ruth sank into the chair facing him and watched as he began to read. His expression did not change, though she searched it for every small movement and in the end, she said again. 'Father?'

He looked up, startled, as if he had forgotten she was there. 'Charles is missing, believed killed.'

He handed it over for her to read, got up and went to the window that overlooked the dock.

'Missing? *Believed.* What does that mean?' The words were simple enough.

Her father did not turn to her, and it took some time for him to answer. 'That he has not been found.'

'So, he's... he's... still alive?' It was not the worst news.

Her father clutched at the windowsill, his head against the glass. 'It means they can't be sure, I suppose.'

There was hope then?

She got up and went to him, clasped his hand in hers. 'He could be badly injured, unable to speak, he might have lost his memory. Some kind soul might have taken him in, be hiding him.' She thought of the men in Ruhleben. 'He could have been taken prisoner of war. Any number of things might have happened.'

'They might.' He faced her. 'And they might not.'

She didn't want to feel this afraid, she wanted her father to tell her it would all be all right, but he had no words, and the sickening she had felt earlier sharpened, the acid rising in her mouth. 'Come home, Father. You spend far too many hours here. I'll get Mrs Murray to make lunch.'

'I can't just up and leave,' he snapped. 'There is work to be done.' He immediately apologised for his outburst, and was instantly forgiven.

He let go of her hand and went to his desk, drew the papers in front of him and put on his reading glasses, removed them, sat back in his chair. She watched him, not knowing what to do until he managed to look up at her, gave her a sad smile.

'Tell Mrs Murray I'll be home within the hour.'

Ruth chose to walk back towards the town, calling in at the mission, for want of something to do, for distraction, but Miss Sheldon was out on calls and she knew that meant more men had been lost. Henry swam into her thoughts, and she forced herself to imagine him right here, next to her, as he had been the day when he came for her only a few months ago. She brought Charles to her mind in his uniform, and Daphne in hers, and while she could conjure them before her, she knew they were safe. Charles was missing, not lost. Missing, like a pair of spectacles that had been mislaid, that was all.

39

Letty's mother was waiting for her at the station, along with Letty's younger sister, Jenny, who held Alfie's hand and helped him step down onto the platform, then took Stella as Letty turned for her bags. Her mother reached for them, Letty chaffing that she could manage, Maggie Palmer ignoring her. At the other side of the picket fence, her father waved to them as he waited with the horse and cart. Alfie and Stella were delighted when he lifted them up onto it. Letty climbed beside them, taking Stella's hand. She had never visited with the children before, there hadn't been time with everything else she had been doing, and now she regretted it. For to see the delight on their faces was worth more than any riches. She only wished Alec were here to enjoy it with them.

The fields were tilled and the grass thick along the verges. All about were signs of growth and fertility, the hint of leaf on the oak and ash, the hawthorn already green. Most of all, it was the air, the clean fresh air, that smelled of animals and crops and sweet things – nothing but goodness. It was balm to her mind and her heart.

Her mother climbed up beside her father and they trotted along the lanes, Jenny pointing out the animals and birds to the children, who were enjoying the measured step of the horse. It was a world away from the dirt and smoke of the town; the light was different, it was quieter, calmer, and Letty felt the tension fall away the closer they came to Honey Farm.

Her father stopped at the gate and Jenny got up to open it, but Letty put out an arm to stop her and climbed down herself. It gave her great pleasure to push on the old five-bar gate and allow the cart to pass, and she stood for a moment, leaning against it, taking in the fields and the trees, the cows and sheep grazing, and realised just how much she had missed it. Her small patch of garden and the nearby park were no substitute. And never would be.

While her father unloaded their things, Jenny took the children to explore the barns and outbuildings to allow Letty a bit of time with their mother. As Letty removed her hat and coat, her mother made herself busy at the range. 'My goodness, our Letty, what on earth have you been doing to yourself. You look like a sparrow.'

She passed her a mug of hot sweet tea. It was refreshing after the long and trying train journey and Letty took a sip, closing her eyes to savour it. Her mother didn't expect her to answer, had already turned away and was slicing a large loaf of bread and spreading it thick with butter.

Her father came in and hung his cap on the nail at the back of the door, kissed her forehead, and she forgot her tea, got up and put her arms about him. He smelled of the fields and tobacco, of cattle and hay, and each familiar scent delighted her.

'Good to see you, my darling girl.' He held her a long time and she didn't want to pull away from him, feeling like a child again, safe in his arms. When he released her, he took her hands in his. 'By the looks of you, you need fattening up.'

'You make me sound like one of the pigs, getting ready for market.'

'Nothing that a bit of good food and fresh air can't put right,' her mother said, placing large plates of bread and bowls of jam on the table. There was ham and hard-boiled eggs, a great hunk of cheese and her mother's home-made piccalilli, enough to feed the five thousand, and when Alfie came in, he could only stare at the feast.

'Git yerself at the table, boy Alfie. Yer can sit next to yer mother.' Her father put his hands under Alfie's armpits and lifted him up onto the chair.

Jenny brought out the old high chair. They had all used it over the years, the seat worn smooth with many a little bottom. Letty lifted Stella into it and pushed her close to the table, while her mother lathered honey on a slice of bread and butter and handed it to Jenny. Her sister promptly cut it into fingers and gave one to Stella.

'The boys will eat when they come in from the fields. Your sister will be along with her kiddies by and by.' Her mother stopped, looked at Letty, her eyes shining. 'By, our Letty, but it's good to have you home.'

'It's good to be back, Mam.' For the first time in many months, Letty felt she could finally let go, there being no need to watch every word she said. Her mother's ways were her ways and there would be no cause for conflict in the kitchen – or anywhere else.

* * *

That evening, they sat in front of the fire and her mother gave her the more recent news on her two eldest brothers who had enlisted and were attached to the Norfolk regiment, the younger two remaining at home to help her father run the farm. Ben had been talking of enlisting, but he was too young at sixteen. It had all added strain on her father's shoulders. The horses had been taken in September and the lads had been ploughing the fields with the hand plough. Everything took longer, but there was no alternative other than to dig in their heels and get on with it.

Letty slept that night in her old bed, Alfie beside her and Stella in the crib her father had made for his firstborn. She woke the next morning to find them both gone. She lay for a while, listening to their laughter and giggles as her mother chatted to them downstairs, heard Jenny telling them they were going outside to see the pigs. It was as if she'd been living the wrong life and all of a sudden had snapped back to where she belonged.

Her mother came up with a pitcher of warm water and set it in the porcelain bowl on the dresser.

'Mam, you shouldn't have done that.'

'Will you stop telling me what I can and cannot do in my own home. You were always the bossy one of my children.'

Letty pushed herself up on her elbows as her mother sat down on the side of the bed.

'I don't know what you've been doing with yourself, my girl, but these few days are for you to rest. Before you go back and do it all over again.' The very thought of doing so made Letty lie back on her pillow. She had hardly given the café a thought, knowing it was in her mother-in-law's capable hands. It seemed she had much to thank Dorcas for – mostly for insisting she come home to her family. It was exactly the medicine she needed.

After Letty had washed and dressed, she opened the casement window, saw Alfie with his feet on the fence feeding grass to the goat, Jenny instructing him to keep his hand flat, hearing giggles as the goat slobbered away at it. It made her heart lighter, and although she was still exhausted, she felt at ease, comfortable in her skin.

When she went downstairs, her mother was at the range, she was always at the range – or so it had seemed to Letty when she was a child; if she wasn't cooking at it, she was sitting by it, bottle-feeding lambs that weren't thriving. 'What can I do, Mam?'

'You can make a brew.' She glanced at the clock. 'Then we'll have five minutes' sit-down, you and me, and you can tell me all the things you haven't bothered to put in your letters.' Her mother gave her that look which meant she wanted the bad as well as the good.

As they sat down at the kitchen table together, Letty realised it was these simple pleasures she missed most of all.

'It sounds like Dorcas has softened towards you.'

'I suppose she has. She was very good about taking things on while I came away. She insisted.'

Her mother smiled. 'You won her over in the end.' It was obvious at her wedding that Dorcas did not approve of the match. She took hold of Letty's hand. 'I know you wanted to prove her wrong, my girl, but don't turn yourself inside out trying to do that for other people's benefit.'

* * *

On Friday, they rose early and filled the cart with eggs and honey, a variety of vegetables and set off for Lowestoft market as they had done when she was a single woman. Jenny had been wonderful, taking care of the children to give Letty a rest but, more importantly, time with her mother. 'Like old times, my lovely girl,' her mother said as she guided the cart along the lanes. There was a chill to the air, and Letty pulled her shawl about her and huddled close to her mother.

'It's seems five minutes and five years, Mam. And yet it's neither.'

They pulled the cart to its usual place, the pitch the family had had for years, and set out the stall, piling the vegetables to look their most temping, the eggs and honey to one side. Proceeds from these were her mother's, which would be saved for treats. Her egg money.

The work of it soon warmed them and it wasn't long before customers came. Many of them were regulars and glad to see Letty again. She chatted while she served, the routine of it coming back to her, as if she'd never left, and she enjoyed bantering with all who came along and calling out 'fresh eggs' and 'golden honey' to passers-by.

She had turned to get another tray of eggs when someone spoke her name.

'Letty Palmer. Hardy,' she corrected, giving Letty a sly smile as she turned to face her.

'Becky Drew. It's good to see you.' It wasn't – and seeing her fresh complexion and her lustrous hair framing the perfect oval of her face, Letty suddenly felt awkward. Although Alec's jilted sweetheart was only a year younger, Letty felt old and frumpy in comparison. She touched her own hair, pushing at the strands that had worked their way free. Her hands were grubby with soil, her nails too, and she tried to conceal them.

'You back home for good?'

'No, just a few days with Mam and Dad. I brought the kiddies.'

'You have more than one?'

'I do.' Letty was still serving, handing over honey, weighing vegetables, tipping them into shopping baskets. A woman asked for six eggs and Letty quickly picked them, put them into a paper bag.

'Alec didn't mention it.'

The woman was holding out her coins, but Letty hadn't noticed, until her mother nudged her. Letty handed over the eggs, took the money and placed it in her apron, keeping her hands there.

'You've seen him?'

Becky's smile was triumphant, as if she'd got one over on Letty at last, for stealing her man. 'Once or twice. Didn't he say?'

Letty smiled back. 'He might have mentioned it in his letters. I wouldn't have paid much attention.' Letty hoped she sounded convincing, for she knew each letter off by heart – and not once had he mentioned Becky Drew.

'Oh, well. I didn't think he would anyway. He wouldn't want to upset you now, would he? Nice to see you, Letty. Mrs Hardy.' She sashayed off, her hips swaying, tossing her head so that her hair shimmered in the light, flirting with men as she passed. Letty knew it had been done for her benefit, to let her know how men lusted after her still.

She stood with her hands resting on the jars of honey, going over Becky's words, thinking on Alec's behaviour towards her when he was home on leave. Was his earnest appreciation of her covering something more than fear of losing her? He had been more loving, more attentive, taking care to let her know how much she meant to him. She had thought it was because he was more aware that each day might be his last. But was it something else, after all? She ran through every day they had spent together, at the house, at the studio posing for photographs, a family. He had delighted at her success, at the café, made such a fuss and praised her as he had never done before. He had been more protective. More careful. He had only spent two hours at the pub catching up with his pals, had returned when he said he would. '*He wouldn't want to upset you.*' She heard Becky's words over and over in her head, saw again her smile, her look. Things began slotting together like one of the wooden puzzles the children had.

Her mother patted her arm. 'All right? Not too much for you.'

'No, I'm absolutely fine.' Letty picked up a jar of honey and began tempting people to come and buy, too busy to dwell on what

Becky had said for the time being. But she was weary, and at the end of the morning, when their last bit of produce had been sold, her mother made her sit down on an empty crate as she gathered the sacking and loaded it onto the cart. It had been such a lovely day and Becky was not going to spoil it.

'Tired?' her mother asked when they were up on the cart and on their way home. Here was a woman, more than twenty years older, still full of energy. Letty felt like a limp rag.

'A little,' she lied.

'What did Becky say to you?'

'Not much,' Letty replied.

'Well, something upset you. You were like your old self until she came along.'

Letty looked to the trees that lined the lanes. 'I suppose I looked at her and felt very old.'

Her mother clicked her tongue to drive the horse. 'Girls like her are torments, Letty, to the men and the women. She likes to flirt, and the fellas will lap it up, but she's not the kind of lass a man wants to marry. Too fickle by halves.'

Once again, Letty got down and opened the gate, told her mother to carry on without her, that she'd walk the rest of the way. She closed the gate and stood for a while, enjoying the beauty, the familiarity of her surroundings. She had given it all up to be with Alec without a second thought. Had she made a mistake? Had he?

She thought of him, somewhere out at sea, the living terror of making one wrong move, thought of his kisses and the way he held her, the life they had made for themselves – and knew that she loved him, that there would only ever be him. She pressed her belly. Too late now to turn back the clock. She had been late with her monthly bleed, too early to tell, and she had never been this tired with Stella. She would need to wait a while yet before she was sure, before she could say anything.

Alec loved her, deep down she knew that was the truth. Her mother was right, Becky liked to tease, for what she had said was nothing of consequence – but it was how it was said, the smugness as she had looked at Letty – and as she began to walk up to the farmhouse, she knew what it was. There was no longer jealousy in Becky's eyes, only laughter. And she was laughing at Letty.

* * *

They took the children into Lowestoft on the Saturday and walked along by the pier. They had borrowed a forward-facing perambulator from Letty's sister and Jenny pushed Stella, while her father took Alfie down onto the beach. Letty linked arms with her mother, and as they walked along, she tried to forget her encounter with Becky. It was easier said than done.

She called in at the mission, hoping to find Colin Wilson, just to say hello. He was busy, as she knew he would be, but glad to see her nonetheless. He asked after Ruth, but then he asked after others too, and she would have nothing of note to tell her friend, nothing of comfort.

She walked back to join her mother and father and Alfie ran up to her, holding a paper windmill that spun in the breeze.

'Look, Mam, look what Grandpa bought me.'

As he came close, she swooped him up into her arms and kissed his cheek. 'Well, then, Alfie, who's a lucky boy?'

* * *

They left on Sunday, her brothers and sisters and their families turning up to see them off, and Letty found it hard to hold back the tears. She felt she was leaving a part of her heart behind, hoping that she would always come back to claim it.

Her mother gave her one final hug. 'Don't leave it so long next time.' Letty told her she wouldn't.

As the train moved off there were tears, from Alfie and from her mother, Stella wailing and holding out her arms, Jenny sobbing into her handkerchief. Letty held her own tears back as long as she could, not wanting her mother to worry, knowing she would always worry; wasn't that what mothers did? Her father pretended to blow his nose, waving them off with his cap, and Alfie pressed his face up to the window until long after they were out of sight.

40

When Letty had written saying she was going back to Lowestoft, Alec had been ashamed that his first thought had been that she might bump into Becky, not that she would be happy to see her family. It sickened him to think what he had done, but he could not turn back time. He concentrated on steering the course, going forward. It was all he could do. He and his crew had been due a day ashore and if she had only come a few days later, they could have spent precious time together.

A rumble in the distance made him check the horizon to the east. It wasn't the weather for thunder, and he looked for the tell-tale signs of black smoke. Staffy was to the starboard side with Nobby, and the two of them glanced up, then quickly reverted to keeping watch about their own vessel. Between the *Valinda* and the *Prince*, they had cleared four mines in less than an hour, bringing them to the surface and disposing of them. It was evident they were in dangerous waters, fresh mines scattered about.

Nobby whistled, pointing east.

Alec followed the line, made out the dark spot. A conning tower? A rowboat. He was about to make contact with the *Valinda* when an explosion rocked the *Prince*'s stern and Alec fell forward onto the wheel, gasped as it pressed into his chest, taking the wind from him. He called for all men on deck, ordered the boat to be lowered, shouted down to the engine room to find out if they were okay.

Proctor shinned up the ladder. 'Mine hit us, port side stern. I'm going to ascertain damage. Evans is injured. The blast threw the warps and lashed his side. I have a man with him.' He went down the ladder, disappeared below.

At the starboard side, Nobby and Staffy were lowering the boat. The ship shifted in the water and he ordered full on with the pumps.

Nobby came up the ladder, face covered in smut. 'Lieutenant Proctor is down by the screws attempting to stem the leak, sir.'

'How is it?'

Nobby looked at him. No words were exchanged and the man shot down the ladder again and assisted the men as they kept watching for mines. They'd been hit by one, there was sure to be another out there.

Alec remained at the wheel and his stomach lurched. He couldn't bear to lose her, not the *Prince*, she had been his first ship, his first command. They had been together almost as long as him and Letty had been married. He couldn't bear to lose Letty. What the hell had he been thinking of. He had to get home, had to get back to port, to Letty, his lighthouse.

He talked to his ship. 'Don't let me down, lass. We've been together a long time, you and me. I don't want to lose you, we've a war to win. Fight, lass, fight.' He ran his hand over the wheel, the wood he had held for so long, recalling the times he had stood here with Skipper Harris, who had put a good word in for him. It might not be so bad. If they could fix a tear, she could be towed back by *Valinda*. All was not lost. He would not give up on her. 'Come on, old girl. We can make it all right, don't quit on me now.' He had seen her through storm and gale, she had kept him and his men safe, she was his home. He spent more time with her than he had on land.

The *Valinda* had released the line and was keeping steady, but he didn't want to give the order to abandon ship, not yet.

Proctor came up, soaked through, his face dripping with seawater. He swept a hand over his face, replaced his cap, the badge centre, always bloody centre, even at a time like this. 'We've been hit aside the screw. I crawled down, forced wood, anything I could, into it to stem the water.' He was gasping for breath. 'The pumps can't deal with the intake. I gave order for the chief and stoker to come up on deck.' He caught his breath. 'I tried, but it's too late, the blast ripped too big a hole.'

As he spoke, the ship listed and Alec staggered, held onto the side. His girl, his lovely girl. What had he done?

Proctor was waiting for the order, and he knew he had to give it.

'Tell the men to abandon ship.'

Proctor saluted, 'Aye, aye, sir.'

Two men were carrying Evans, one at his feet, one at his head, and they lowered him down to the small wooden boat. Alec watched from the bridge, wanting to hold her steady as long as he could, until all men were in it.

He kissed his hand, pressed it to the wheel. 'Let me live to fight another day, your work is done. Goodbye, old girl.'

Proctor was at the rail, the last of the men getting into the boat, and when he saw Alec leave the wheelhouse, he too went over the side.

Alec took one last look at the bridge of the *Black Prince* and made for the rope.

Henry Evans was laid in the boat, blood oozing from the wound at his side. A man had torn off his own shirt and Proctor had padded it into a wad, pressed it to stem the loss. 'Hold fast, Henry, old chap. Hold fast.' He had lost a lot of blood and was drifting in and out of consciousness. Proctor kept talking to him, looked to Alec. It wasn't looking good.

Alec turned back to his ship and watched as the *Prince* slowly sank below the waves.

41

On Sunday evening, Letty made her way to the mission to write letters. In three years, she had only missed a handful of Sundays. Ruth was in the dining hall when she arrived, having stood in for her while she'd been away, and Letty was glad to see her. She was alone, a pile of letters at her side, a pen in her hand, writing another. Letty took a seat opposite her.

'There was no need for you to come. I didn't expect you until next week. You must be tired.'

'I am, a little, but glad to be back.' In the corner, four men were playing cards, another reading the *Herald*. 'Did you have many to write?' Letty asked.

'Two or three. These are for my own purpose. I like to look out of the window, to feel a part of something. There is no window in the room Miss Sheldon set aside for me, which focuses the mind, but...' She looked out onto the street as a train moved past, the noise rattling the panes. 'It can be lonely.'

Letty placed her bag beside her. 'I was sorry to hear about Charles. Dorcas told me. Have you heard anything more?'

Ruth shook her head, pressed her hand to the pile of envelopes beside her. 'I am writing to every establishment that I know of, where men have been taken who have been disfigured, or burned, are confused, or have lost their memory. Some have lost the power of speech. One of them could be Charles.' She gazed out of the window again, distracted. 'His fiancé, Daphne, has been contacting the field hospitals for information. I am making a list of ones that are of interest, that Father and I may visit.' She forced a smile. 'Did you enjoy your time with your family?'

'Very much.' Letty told Ruth of how much the children had enjoyed being on the farm, being with her parents, her sister, getting used to the animals, that they had been into Lowestoft.

'And did you see anyone else?' Her coyness was telling. There was only one person Ruth was interested in her seeing.

'I saw Colin Wilson. At the mission.'

She perked up a little, a flicker of light in her eyes. 'Did he ask about me?'

'He did. But then he asked about lots of people, Ruth – Miss Sheldon, the other attendants.' Letty couldn't lie, but she didn't want to mislead her, give her false hope, knowing Ruth would hold on to each one as a drowning man would a lifeline.

'I wrote to him, you know, when Aunt Helen told me she had warned him off.'

'And he replied?'

'He did, saying I must not think badly of my aunt. That he had never intended to stay long at the mission. That the duty of the port missioner was to go where they were directed. It had been out of his hands, out of Aunt Helen's too.' Ruth stared out of the window. 'He is to serve the mission ships out of Milford Haven at the end of the month.'

Letty waited for Ruth to continue, but she no longer seemed interested in talking about Colin Wilson.

'I'm glad you had a lovely time with your family, Letty. It's so important to keep the connection tight and strong.' Letty nodded her agreement and Ruth gave her a small smile, turned her gaze to the window once more.

Letty took a sheet of paper and another pencil and wrote to Alec. She would not have time tomorrow. Dorcas was going to open the café and she would go to the Parkers. She told him how wonderful it was to be back with her parents, how the children had loved it, how she had worked on the market alongside her mother, just as she had been doing when they had first met. Did he remember?

Should she mention Becky? She looked to Ruth, quietly at her letters searching for her brother. Had she mistaken Becky's words, her smile, put two and two together and made five? Had Ruth looked for signs that weren't there? She watched her friend at her task. Anything could happen, from one day to the next, no one knew what dangers their men were in. Why trouble him now? Why give Becky the satisfaction of knowing she had upset her?

* * *

It was a wild night, the gales blowing as Letty and Ruth parted on the steps of the mission and went their separate ways. 'I'll see you at the Guild this week?'

'You will,' Letty told her. 'You will.'

42

Henry was taken to the mission, Colin Wilson having sent for the doctor to attend. Both were waiting their arrival. Henry's uniform was removed and his wound bathed, but it was obvious to those with him, it was too late. Proctor had stayed with him throughout. Henry had been drifting in and out of consciousness, but they had talked to him, keeping him alert as best they could.

He appeared to rally a little, opened his eyes.

'Proctor,' he said. 'Should've looked where I was going, eh.'

'Always your trouble, Evans. Too easily distracted.'

The boy smiled. 'My failing. One of many, my father would tell you that. Tell, Ruth. Her drawing. Tell her sometimes we can't see what is in front of us. Will you tell her, Proctor?'

He promised he would, and Henry made a small movement with his head, closed his eyes for the last time. Colin Wilson said a quiet prayer and Proctor and Hardy joined him with Amen.

Proctor found it hard to breathe.

'That poor family,' Alec said, speaking Proctor's exact thoughts. 'His father and sister will be distraught. First, Charles missing in action and now…' He shook his head. 'That's a letter I didn't ever want to write.'

'Don't write it,' the port missioner interrupted. 'I will take the night train. It is always better to deliver such tragic news face to face.' He looked to Proctor. 'The family have been very kind to me.'

They had been kind to him also, and he thought of Ruth, her stillness. Her letters had never ceased, she had told him of Charles being missing in action, that they hadn't given up hope. But this was not a letter of ambiguity, it was one of finality, and he wished with his whole heart that she would never have to hear such news.

43

When Ruth opened the door to find Colin Wilson upon the doorstep, she was confused, that after all this time he had come to pay a call, and at such an early hour. She smiled to welcome him, but his expression did not change.

He removed his cap and held it in his hands. 'Miss Evans. May I come in?' There was a warning in his brown eyes, a softness too that stirred something within her, a feeling she did not want.

She invited him over the threshold with a small nod of her head, the slow realisation of his visit beginning to dawn. She led him through to the drawing room and found herself trembling, grabbed hold of her wrists to steady herself.

'Would you care to take seat?' She was surprised how clear and steady her voice was. It sounded as if it were coming from somewhere other than her own body.

'Not for the moment. Is your father home?' His words betrayed nothing of his errand, but she suddenly felt as if she were walking into a blackened corridor.

This time, she couldn't speak, merely moved her head and left him. She crossed the hall, her shoes snapping brightly on the tiles, stopped for a moment to look up at her mother's portrait, then took a breath, knocked on her father's door and opened it.

'Mr Wilson, from the mission, is here.'

Her father frowned, was slow to stir, then got to his feet. She wanted to warn him, but what of? Colin Wilson hadn't said anything, but she knew he hadn't come for her.

Her father walked before her and, seeing the port missioner, put out his hand in greeting. 'Mr Wilson. An unexpected pleasure. Would you take a seat.'

'Mr Evans, Miss Evans...' He paused, looked down at his cap, then at them. Behind him, the clock began to strike the hour and he waited for it to end before continuing. 'I'm sorry to tell you that Henry was fatally injured yesterday. He died of his wounds last night. I wanted to give you the news personally.' He withdrew a letter from his jacket pocket and handed it to her father. 'Lieutenant Proctor has written a letter of explanation, but I can tell you that he suffered injuries when his ship was mined.' Ruth let out a small gasp, pressed her hand to her mouth. No, it must be a mistake. It had to be.

Her father studied the envelope for what seemed a long time, then placed it on the mantel alongside a gilt-edged invitation. Ruth stared at it, seeing him reflected in the mirror, hearing his words, but not understanding the meaning of them, didn't want to. Couldn't.

Her father went over to the grandfather clock and opened the case, stopped the pendulum and stood there, his back to them, and the silence in the room stretched and shrank. Ruth went beside him, put her hand to his back, held it there, not knowing what to do, how to be of comfort, knowing there was none.

Without saying a word, he closed the case and left the room.

'Would you like me to sit with you?' Colin Wilson asked.

Ruth found it hard to look upon him, to speak to this man who she had once yearned for. Was he asking her because of who she was, or did he say the same to all the women he called upon to give bad news? She did not know, and found she didn't care, remembering her aunt's words – that his work was more important than she was. But at that moment nothing was as important as her darling brother, Henry.

'No. No.' She shook her head. 'That won't be necessary. Thank you for coming, Mr Wilson. It was kind of you to make the journey.' She walked to the door, holding it open, then led the way into the hall.

He held out his hand once more and she took it in hers. She felt nothing, nothing at all, understanding too late that she loved what he did, not who he was.

* * *

When Mrs Murray found her, she took Ruth gently by the shoulders and led her into the kitchen, settled her in a chair and wrapped a shawl about her, made her drink hot sweet tea, took one for her father. Ruth heard her on the telephone in the hall, speaking to someone, and presently Aunt Helen came to the house. Ruth did not get up, she couldn't move, her body had atrophied, and she had lost all power of it, the realisation of Henry's loss taking hold.

'Oh, my darling, my darling girl,' Aunt Helen cried, taking her hand in hers, bending forward and pressing her cheek to her own.

Ruth felt her aunt's tears on her face, saw Mrs Murray leave the room and go out into the garden. She wanted to go out in the garden too, to smell the air, to hear the birdsong. To breathe. She felt her lungs would burst and, unable to bear the pressure, she let out a scream and wailed for her brothers, for her father, and for herself.

Her father buried himself in his study and would not leave. After her aunt had left, Ruth went into him. He was not at his desk but in his high-back chair facing the empty grate. She went and sat in the chair opposite, and they remained there until Mrs Murray came with another tray of coffee, which they left untouched.

'What is it all for, Ruth?' her father said eventually. 'What is the point of going on? The boys were the future.'

The pain in her heart moved across her chest. 'Because there is nothing left for us but to go on.'

He didn't answer. There were no answers, not anymore. Unable to bear the silence, eventually she got up and left.

She took her coat and went out onto the street, wanting to walk and walk and never return. It was late now, and the market stalls were closing, the shops locking their doors. Everything was as it was yesterday, and the day before, and the day before that – except it wasn't. It would never be the same again.

She went to the mission, but through the door saw Colin Wilson in the lobby and turned away. She did not want his pity. It was his job. She made her way down Fish Dock Road, towards the docks, not caring how she looked, what did it matter? Henry was gone. Charles, missing.

She came to her father's offices and looked up at the sign. There was no future. Her legs could no longer hold her, and she sank down onto her knees and sobbed. People came and someone lifted her, a crate was brought, and she was seated on it.

'It's Miss Evans,' a woman said.

She could hear voices and then a familiar one. 'Ruth. Oh, Ruth.'

She looked up, tears falling on her cheeks like a river, and Letty pulled her to her feet and held her like a child. It was all she had ever wanted. To be held. Ruth wanted her mother.

Letty took her to Parkers, settled her in one of the fireside chairs in the back room, and Norah handed her a tot of brandy and told her to drink it back in one go. Ruth did so, coughing and spluttering as the fire burned in her throat. Percy smiled at her, his mouth crooked, and she managed to smile back, then her mouth was crooked too as she let more tears fall.

'I am s-so-sorry,' she gulped, trying to stem the tide of tears and failing.

Norah took the glass. 'Never apologise for having feelings, young woman. Your poor heart must be breaking.'

Ruth nodded, catching her breath, dabbing at her eyes and nose, and yet more tears came when she thought she had none left. Letty was beside her, sitting on the arm of the chair and had never once let go of her hand. She held it now, clasped in hers, warm and strong.

When she was calmed, Letty offered to get a message to her father.

'No,' she said quickly. 'He is in his own grief. He cannot yet deal with mine. Nor I his. He has lost his sons, his future.'

'He has you, my dear,' Norah told her. 'You are his future too.'

She found strength in Norah's words, knowing she would need all of it, for her strength would have to be her father's too if they were to get through these terrible days.

Ruth got up and thanked the Parkers for their kindness. Norah gave her a hug, the old man too, and Letty walked out with her.

'I don't want to go home just yet, Letty. I want to walk some more, to breathe in the air.'

'Then I'll walk with you,' Letty told her, and she linked her arm with Ruth's and led her towards the water.

They walked awhile, Letty telling her more of her children and her plans for Parkers. She showed her the café and what she had made of it and Ruth looked up at the sign. Hardy's. The family name. The Evans name would be lost, for when, or if, she married, she would lose hers. The thought tore at her heart again and tears started afresh. This time she let them fall.

'Nothing will take the pain away,' Letty told her as they made their way along the wharf. 'We have to live our lives the best we can to honour those we have lost.'

Could she do that? Could her father? She was too tired to think, her head too full of memories. Of her bright and beautiful brother who had longed for adventure.

The sun rose over the water and Ruth held her friend's hand. Money might divide them, but sorrow had united them. Life would go on, and somehow so would she.

ACKNOWLEDGMENTS

In all, 156 trawlers of the Grimsby fishing fleet were lost or captured during the Great War of 1914–1918, 73 of these in the first year. In total 545 men were lost, leaving 255 widows and 531 orphans. In addition, there were 696 widows and 785 orphans of Grimsby fishermen who lost their lives in minesweepers and other naval service during the conflict.

Miss Sheldon was inspired in part by Rosina Ada Newnham, the true port missioner at Grimsby Mission during the Great War. At first, there was no hope of getting Government help for the wives of men who were POW, nor any compensation for those lost at sea. Miss Newnham was instrumental in rectifying this. She served as port superintendent for thirty-two years from 1904 to 1936. I am absolutely fascinated by this woman in a man's world. What a marvellous character she must have been.

To this end, I owe my grateful thanks to George E. Gilmour who worked and lived at the Grimsby mission, among others, in his work for the Royal National Mission to Deep Sea Fishermen during the 1960s and beyond. He gifted me his own leather-bound copy of the *Toilers of the Deep* magazine for 1915, which includes letters from Miss Newnham. I am overwhelmed by his generosity – perhaps I shouldn't have expected anything less of a mission man.

The book you have just read could not have been written without the help of a huge team of people. First and foremost, I'd like to thank my editor, Caroline Ridding, who waded through my muddled thoughts and helped me bring them to order.

To the wonderful folk at Boldwood who make the book shine – Amanda, Nia, Claire, Jenna, Marcella, Ben, Jade, Shirley and all the other Boldwood team members who get my books out into the world.

To the people who got me here – my Monday Buddy Helen Baggott, my mentor Margaret Graham, and agents past and present, Vivien Green and Gaia Banks.

This book involved a huge amount of research and to this end I have to thank so many people who have answered my numerous queries these past months: Adrian Wilkinson and Tracey Townsend at Grimsby Archives and Lincs Inspire. Louise Bowen, Dave Ornsby of the Fishing Heritage Museum, Dr Robb Robinson, Tony Jewitt, Martin Grant, and Tom Smith. Trevor Ekin, Dave Smith, and Paul Woolnough who have come to my aid on numerous occasions. Kevin from the Grimsby's Lost Ships of WW1 project. And to my new friends at Lowestoft Maritime Museum – thank you Kenny, Bob and Pete.

I only have to ask a question to tap into a huge wealth of information from various Facebook groups: Grimsby Memories, Cleethorpes Memories, Great Grimsby Fishing History, Grimsby Fish Docks Past and Present and Great Grimsby Retired Fishermen, most especially: Peter Pool, Peter Spillman, Steve Farrow, Michael Sparkes, Paul Fenwick, Ann Gracie, Janine Tanner, Fiona Poulton. Angie Burnett, Chair of the Grimsby Central Hall Trust.

Boldwood ran two competitions in relation to this book. Valerie Findlay named the good ship *Artemis* and Louise Hugill's grandfather inspired the character of Nobby Clarke. William (Nobby) Clarke didn't serve on the minesweepers but in the army in the Great War – but he did vow to save five hundred pounds before he would marry his sweetheart, Ethel, and became a successful skipper to do so.

I am grateful for the support of the fabulous team at Grimsby

Waterstones, Jess, Jane and Caitlyn and Big Sharon and Little Sharon at Williams, Cleethorpes.

To the bloggers, reviewers, and fellow authors who give so generously of their time to get the word out about books, books, books!

Jayne Parker who was instrumental in returning a widow's penny to the family of James Sutton who died when the HMS *Good Hope* was sunk on 1 November 1914.

To the fishermen and wives who have shared their stories over the years – John Meadows, Alfreda Evans, John Evans (Canada), Jim Evans and Janet Evans.

To my mum, dad and nanny Lettie for giving me stories, written and spoken.

This year, I have been without the marvellous support and encouragement of Ray Evans, who sadly passed away in December 2022. He was always the first person I turned to for help with details and fact checking regarding scenes on ship. I miss his smiling face and quiet support. He has been in my thoughts the whole time I have been writing.

Thank you to you, the readers, who support me throughout the year.

And as always, last but not least, to my family. My everything.

ABOUT THE AUTHOR

Tracy Baines is the bestselling saga writer of *The Variety Girls* series, originally published by Ebury, which Boldwood will continue with. She was born and brought up in Cleethorpes and spent her early years in the theatre world which inspired her writing. Her new saga series for Boldwood is set amongst the fisherfolk of Grimsby.

Sign up to Tracy Baines's mailing list here for news, competitions and updates on future books.

Follow Tracy on social media:

twitter.com/tracyfbaines
facebook.com/tracybainesauthor
instagram.com/tracyfbaines

ALSO BY TRACY BAINES

Fishers Wharf

The Women of Fishers Wharf

Trouble at Fishers Wharf

The Seaside Girls

The Seaside Girls

Hopes and Dreams for The Seaside Girls

A New Year for the Seaside Girls

Milton Keynes UK
Ingram Content Group UK Ltd.
UKHW040009130224
437735UK00004B/209

9 781804 265390